The Book of *Caddyshack*

The Book of Caddyshack

Scott Martin

Everything You Always Wanted to Know about the Greatest Movie Ever Made

Taylor Trade Publishing

Lanham • New York • Boulder • Toronto • Plymouth,UK

Published by Taylor Trade Publishing
An imprint of The Rowman & Littlefield Publishing Group, Inc.
4501 Forbes Boulevard, Suite 200, Lanham, Maryland 20706

Distributed by NATIONAL BOOK NETWORK

Library of Congress Cataloging-in-Publication Data

Martin, Scott, 1965-
  The book of Caddyshack : everything you always wanted to know about the greatest movie ever made / Scott Martin. — 1st Taylor Trade Publishing ed.
      p. cm.
  Includes bibliographical references.
  ISBN-13: 978-1-58979-358-3 (pbk. : alk. paper)
  ISBN-10: 1-58979-358-7 (pbk. : alk. paper)
  1. Caddyshack (Motion picture) I. Title.
PN1997.C196M37 2007
791.43'72—dc22   2006026458

∞™ The paper used in this publication meets the minimum requirements of American National Standard for Information Sciences—Permanence of Paper for Printed Library Materials, ANSI/NISO Z39.48-1992.

Manufactured in the United States of America.

Contents

Acknowledgments

THANKS to Peter Burford, Michael O'Keefe, Cindy Morgan, Sandra Grabman, Lizanne Scherer, Debbie Doniger, Nick Price, David Abell, Dennis Cone, Bill Jerome, Jim McLean, Jason Birnbaum, Ken Campbell, Robert Kraut, Dana Rader, Julie Cole, Chip King, Ted Swanson, Marian Polan, Rachel Igel, Stan Jolley, and Jennifer Rothacker.

I am totally certain that I have forgotten to thank someone somewhere for their help; if you are one of these people and you are currently seething because I have not thanked you in person, please contact me and I will send you a bottle of decent red wine. I promise.

Notes about the Text

T HE "early script" to which I refer is a copy of the third draft dated, May 18, 1979.

A person who carries golf bags can be a *caddy* or *caddie*, although the plural is always *caddies* and the third-person singular and plural of the verb "to caddy" are both *caddies*. I have used *caddy* instead of *caddie* because the competition that Danny Noonan wins is the Thirty-Fifth Annual *Caddy* Tournament. He wins the Bushwood *Caddy* Scholarship.

Caddyshack succeeds, in part, because some of the greatest comedians produced their best work for the movie.
(Warner/Orion/The Kobal Collection)

Introduction

EVERY year since 1986, without fail, a group of self-confessed hack golfers has ventured out into the pounding heat of the Australian summer to parrot lines from *Caddyshack*, down some undrinkable (but cold) lager, and participate in a mostly manic tournament they started in Melbourne to honor Ted Knight and his perfect portrayal of Judge Elihu Smails. After golf, they have a few more "tinnies," berate and embarrass the winner, then retire to a restaurant for more ribald conversation and *Caddyshack* banter.

In the expansive and supertrendy bar at the Cheesecake Factory in Palm Springs, California, Stan Jolley, the art director, seventy-nine with the energy of a twenty-eight year old, drops that he was involved with *Caddyshack* to a couple of co-eds who are quietly sipping Manhattans while enduring the inevitable two-hour wait for a table.

A few minutes later, bar staff, wait staff, and various bar attendees are demanding Jolley's autograph. The bartender, who was three when the movie emerged, gloriously admits that he and others in the Palm Springs Cheesecake Factory family use *Caddyshack* lines every day to help them deal with the partial drudgery of working in the food service industry.

The world's number one golfer, who apparently has more than a modicum of control over the creative content of the ads that bear his name, convinces the austere conglomerate that is American Express to organize a commercial based on a *Caddyshack* theme with Woods imitating Carl Spackler. American Express says yes. It's *Caddyshack*, and even Bill Murray comes out of hibernation for the gig.

In the vicinity of Palm Beach, Nick Price, a former world number one, heads out to his boat, a fifty-foot sport fisherman he christened *Caddyshack*. On their trips to various points in the Caribbean, Price and family slip *Caddyshack* into the DVD player and enjoy an evening with the cast and crew.

At a New York City–area golf charity outing, a foursome of eager golfers pays thousands of dollars for the privilege of playing golf with Michael O'Keefe, a.k.a. Danny Noonan. And at a golf tournament near Greenville, South Carolina, Jack Nicklaus calls Michael by his first name and seems somewhat in awe.

In the later afternoon in a golf shop at a swank Pinehurst-area resort, a group of forlorn golfers mills around looking at shirts and logoed shot glasses. It's chucking down outside with no letup in sight. Someone says: "I don't think the heavy stuff is coming down for quite a while," and everyone, including the boys behind the desk, smiles knowingly and retires to the bar for the remainder of the day.

In among one of those palatial, opulent, iridescent, monied, ornate, lavish, abundant, profuse, wantless, and superprivate coastal Florida golf enclaves, a charming real estate specialist is showing the homes to an interested party from the comfort of a Germanic speed machine. The specialist is initially all power realtor: bold yet polite, polite yet firm, firm yet pretty, pretty yet professional. As they pass some homes, they come to a green that's immediately adjacent to a road. The two golfers on that green are a couple in their eighties. The interested party instinctively and even reflexively says:

"Oh dolly. I'm hot today."

All the requisite veneer and polish that the real estate professional has created vanishes, and she cracks up. She knows every line and every word. She knows her *Caddyshack*.

Somewhere in deepest Nebraska, a farmer and his farming buddy are playing for a few denarii while their crops grow. One of them hits a shot into a pond and, after a few seconds of windy introspection, turns and says: "That's a peach, hon." A few holes later, after making a shocking putt that squares the game going into the final hole, the golfer who made the putt says, purely to annoy the other farmer: "Thank you very little."

In northern Iraq, the people who assign call signs to F-15 pilots discover that Dan Rooney, a member of the Oklahoma Air Force Reserve, is a scratch golfer, and thus he gets the call sign "Noonan." No surprise there.

A radio talk show host in Charlotte, North Carolina, Keith Larson, uses the word "Lama" from the Dalai Lama scene as an amusing way to introduce callers and other interested parties. The official bumper sticker for his show says simply: LAMA!

As soon as *Caddyshack* hit movie theaters in the summer of 1980, golfers around the country were repeating the lines and discussing key scenes. Now, more than a quarter of a century later, their children are repeating the lines and discussing the scenes.

What *is* it about this rather simplistic and mostly plotless movie that continues to amuse? How has it so easily beaten off every single serious and comic attempt (including its own remake) to knock it off its perch as the undisputed number one golf movie? Why have millions of sane and totally successful people watched *Caddyshack* over and over, probing for new nuances and discoveries. What makes it so completely watchable time and time again when so many supposedly funny movies are totally unwatchable and totally nonfunny? It's not a belly-buster, but it's funnier than any other sports comedy and funnier and more entertaining than any of the other comedies that made all the top comedy lists that popped up at the dawn of the new millennium. *Caddyshack* made some "best comedy" lists, but it failed to make any impact on any of the "best movies of all time" lists, yet *Caddyshack* endures and grows and becomes more popular every year, while it's only the effete film critics and their assorted cronies who get excited about the motion pictures that made the lists. Quick, my movie critic buddies, give me a line or two from *Citizen Kane*—a line that will make us all laugh even though we've all heard it a billion times. *Caddyshack* lives on and gets bigger while *Citizen Kane* is primarily a film for film students— at least to golfers.

All but a very few golfers love *Caddyshack*, yet plenty of nongolfers love the movie and can pound out the lines at will. *Caddyshack* is part of a quartet of epic comedies that appeared around the same time, three of them in the same year. First there was *Animal House* in 1978. Then, in 1980, came *Airplane*, *The Blues Brothers*, and *Cad-dyshack* in a vintage year for comedies that has yet to be surpassed. Instantly successful when they first appeared, all four movies continue to thrive. Yet it's *Caddyshack* that seems to thrive the most, even though a hard-core movie critic, if forced to choose between the four, would likely rank *Caddyshack* at the bottom. *Animal House* is more graphic, *Blues Brothers* is more polished, and *Airplane* is sillier, yet *Caddyshack* seems to get the most attention—especially among golfers.

The goal of this book is to augment your *Caddyshack* enjoyment. I have to admit, however, to a touch of ironic and perhaps hypocritical behavior: I enjoy the music of certain rock bands and I enjoy the novels of certain British novelists. The bands and novelists are successful and famous, and there are any number of books, articles, and TV shows in the marketplace about said bands and writers. I purposefully avoid them all: I like the music for the music and have absolutely no interest in the interband punch-ups, roadie revelry, and backstage orgies. It's the same with my authors: what they read and what sort of car they drive is of zero interest. So why am I delving into the behind-the-scenes punch-ups, orgies, and revelry that were, and are, part of *Caddyshack*? The answer is simple curiosity. But before I took the first steps on the road to *Caddyshack* discovery, I promised myself that if I started to think less of the movie and not enjoy it any more, then I would stop and go back to my routine work. I'm a golfer, not a film buff, and thus *The Book of Caddyshack* is a golf book and not a film tome—as any reader of film writing will quickly discover. I have little interest in movie reviewing. In delving into everything anyone could ever want to know about *Caddyshack*, I have watched the film forwards, backwards, sideways, and upside down. I have watched it in English with French subtitles and in French with Spanish subtitles. I have interviewed, at length, members of the cast and crew. I have even tried to contact, through a medium, *Caddyshack* participants who are now deceased; it was a waste of time and money. And yet my *Caddyshack* enjoyment ratchets up a few notches the more I write about it and the more I learn about it. And there's plenty about *Caddyshack* that wasn't funny and wasn't comedic:

it was a party but sometimes too much of a good thing; there were ego issues; one of the creators died just weeks after the premier; and so on.

Even though I have spent almost three years, on and off, looking into *Caddyshack* and trying to find out why it continues to be successful, I have only just scratched the surface. Thus *The Book of Caddyshack* is organic and just emerging from the dark earth; I have interviewed numerous cast and crew members in addition to several golfers and nongolfers who are simply admirers. I still have a list of cast and crew members I want to interview so that subsequent versions of this book are even better and even more detailed. If you were part of *Caddyshack* in any way or if you want to have a chat about the movie and you were not involved or know someone who was involved, then please e-mail me at scottmartingolf @mindspring.com. If you are one of the famous members of the *Caddyshack* experience and you're wondering why I never called, please rest assured that I wrote to your agent, called him or her, and sent a flood of e-mails. By the deadline, I had not heard back.

I'll tell you that one of my (golf) friends calls me "The Lama," as in "Big Hitter, the Lama. *Long*." Why? Because it's a line from *Caddyshack*. He started using the moniker after I had the longest drive on the longest drive hole at a charity/corporate outing that approximately seven people attended, none of whom could hold a golf club and none of whom were sober. I think I won a free bowl of soup. The Lama is an amusing nickname because raw length off the tee is not part of my golf arsenal, nor is it ever likely to be. Still, it's a *Caddyshack* nickname, and a *Caddyshack* nickname is a lot better than a *Freddie* nickname or a *Shining* nickname or a *Carrie* nickname or a *Finding Nemo* nickname or an *Apocalypse Now* nickname.

Caddyshack shooting took place in 1979 and 1980, a full two-and-a-half decades before this book was published. Although working on *Caddyshack* was a memorable time for most everyone who worked on the project, memories fade and facts get lost in the haze of ego and addled recall.

I have worked extremely hard to get the facts correct, but it's hard when one cast member says one thing and another says another. And, to boot, much of what's out there about *Caddyshack* is myth. For example, one view has it that much of the movie is pure improvisation; nothing could be further from the truth, as you'll soon discover. In attempting to chase down as many of the major and bit players as possible, I have been mostly successful, although most of the major players have "people" who make it difficult, if not impossible, to reach the stars. I guess my people just aren't powerful enough; I'm changing that right now!

So I welcome feedback and contact, especially if your first name is Chevy, Brian, Bill, or John. Let's have a chat, and I'll even buy the Frescas. As long as I'm around, I'll be honing and refining *The Book of Caddyshack* so that current and future fanatics have a modest tome that will seriously augment their enjoyment of The Greatest Movie Ever Made.

Are You Caddyshack?

You are if:

- After a poor shot on the golf course, you say "That's a peach, hon."
- You have a gopher head cover or anything gopher in your household.
- You have a pet gopher.
- You have the *Caddyshack* video/DVD and watch it regularly.
- You know every line in the movie and recite lines frequently—not just on the golf course.
- Whenever someone says "President Bush" you add, "wood." When you meet President Bush (either one will do), you accidentally say, "It's an honor to meet you, President Bushwood."
- You named your dog Betty or Danny.

- You have looked at *Caddyshack* stuff on eBay.
- You have bid on *Caddyshack* stuff on eBay.
- When someone is about to putt, you yell "Noonan!"
- When someone asks you who your favorite golfer is, you say, without hesitation, "Danny Noonan."
- When you see a photo of His Holiness, the Dalai Lama, you say, "Gunga, galunga. Gunga gungala gungala" or "Big hitter, the Lama."
- You don't hit the ball very far, so everyone calls you "The Lama. Big hitter, the Lama."
- You recite lines from the movie, almost every day, in almost any situation. For example, someone offers you a bet and you say, "Gambling is illegal at Bushwood." Or someone parks illegally and you say, "Porterhouse, there's a brown Audi parked in my space; have it towed immediately."
- You thought that *Caddyshack* should have topped all those "best movies of the twentieth century" lists.
- You think that any movie critic who thinks that *Caddyshack* is bunk, is bunk.
- You routinely imitate Judge Smails's facial expressions.
- You argue passionately that *Caddyshack* is the greatest movie ever made, and your friends agree.
- You see a movie or TV show and see a *Caddyshack* actor, and you loudly tell everyone in the living room or theater, "He/she was in *Caddyshack*."
- The other day, you saw *Jim Thorpe: All-American*, starring Burt Lancaster, and you noticed that Ted Knight, or at least someone who looked a lot like Ted Knight, was in it.
- While watching *Caddyshack*, you recite every line before it's delivered.
- You have (like Nick Price, PGA and British Open champion) a boat named *Caddyshack*.
- You would gladly buy a book about the movie because *Caddyshack* is life and *The Book of Caddyshack* is about life itself.

1

The Gopher Also Rises

Gopher emerges
Reticulated and bent
On easy chaos
—poet/philosopher Basho (son of)

The stars. The sun. A sprinkler. A mechanical gopher that burrows and dances. Roman Catholic large family teenage angst. Training bra lost. Training bra found.

IN midsummer 1980, what must those lucky first *Caddyshack* viewers have been thinking when the initial frames of the movie appeared? The Orion logo came first, with its spinning nebulan O, and the sun rose over what could be grasslands or veldt or desolate shrubbery just about anywhere in the world. Then a semirusty but fully functioning portable sprinkler appeared, cleverly initiating the first percussive bars of the theme song; then came a brief fairway irrigation scene that the filmmakers could have poached from a golf course superintendents' training video.

Perhaps there were slight sighs of relief in the padded seats as the name of one of the biggest stars in the comedy world at that time, Chevy Chase, appeared for four seconds, closely followed by some other names, including *Mary Tyler Moore Show* costar Ted Knight. Any sense of familiarity must have quickly evaporated as, just forty-five seconds in, the earth started to heave a little, Bill Murray's name appeared, some tunneling took place, and at exactly fifty-four seconds, the star of the movie to date, a slick but mechanical gopher, appeared and, after a brief look at the sylvan fairway, gyrated in perfect synchronization with the main chorus of the title song.

I'm alright with the opening minute, but what about the viewers who had trundled to the cinema hoping to see rising *Saturday Night Live* star Bill Murray or a Chevy Chase comedy about golf or, as the trailer advertised, a comedy with balls? Were they watching a movie about golf course maintenance or a movie about gophers or a movie about malfunctioning sprinklers?

Most everyone who watches *Caddyshack* today views it on the small screen. I can only imagine what it must have been like to see that splendidly reticulated puppet emerging on a proper big screen in a proper old-fashioned cinema. When the movie entered the world and began its epic journey, the multiplexing of the cinematic adventure had begun, but movie theaters had not yet started to wedge patrons into what are, today, pretty much glorified high school science classrooms—only darker. I long to see *Caddyshack* on a big screen, mostly because I want to see what the balletic gopher looks like when it's at least twenty feet tall.

After just a minute of the movie, with the opening credits still running, the gopher tunnels some more, and the initial patrons would have been excused for thinking they'd wasted their money and time: the trailer, promos, and marketing muscle promised Chevy Chase, Ted Knight, golf comedy, and Animal House–style chaos, yet the star to date was a rodent—dancing, albeit impressively, to a very late '70s/early '80s Kenny Loggins tune.

Chase fans hoping for at least a glimpse of their hero would have to burrow further into the popcorn and sink more soda before the great man of comedy (in midsummer 1980) would appear. The gopher is a plot hint that becomes a plot channel; after he burrows further into Bushwood Country Club, the large and ramshackle house that's home to the Noonan clan appears.

Much of the purely caddy in *Caddyshack* originates from the Murray brothers' experiences at the course where most of them looped as boys: Indian Hill Golf Club in Winnetka, Illinois, a Donald Ross course built in 1920 in the northern Chicago suburbs just a few miles from Lake Michigan. Brian Doyle-Murray caddied mostly at North Shore Country Club, but the other brothers were Indian Hill boys. Two of the Murray brothers appear in *Caddyshack*: Bill and Brian. The latter double barreled his name to Brian Doyle-Murray to distinguish himself from another actor named Brian Murray who was in the Screen Actors Guild around the time that Doyle-Murray wrote *Caddyshack*. There are two additional Murray brothers in the credits: Ed and John. The credits list the former for a "special acknowledgement" and the latter as a production assistant.

The Murrays were a Roman Catholic collective with six boys and three girls, and thus the Noonan manifestation of the Murray family is only slightly hyperbolic; I spent almost an hour trying to count the exact number of Noonan children, and I think it's fourteen, although the exact number is a moving target. Doyle-Murray, who cowrote the movie with Doug Kenney and Harold Ramis, based much of the Danny Noonan plot channel on the Winnetka experience. In his golf memoir, *Cinderella Story*, Bill Murray describes *Caddyshack* as: "the gripping tale of the Murray brothers' first experiments with employment. . . . [Brian] wrote the events of his and my brother Ed's caddy life in a way that showed he'd paid attention."

After the credits, the movie shifts to the Noonan manse for a family wake-up/breakfast scrum. After deseating Dennis, the Noonan's nephew, Danny Noonan attempts to eat his Cheerios but quickly gets into a classic teenage argument centered around money, work prospects, college, and potential lumber yard employment. It's the least funny part of the movie: it's extremely challenging to make a joke out of teenage angst and father-son friction, although *Caddyshack* almost succeeds in making the near-certain tragedy at least semi-amusing.

With teenage lankiness and athleticism, Danny negotiates the Noonan's lower fire escape ladder, mounts his ten speed, and cycles through a canyon of Pasadena mansions to Bushwood. Those first-time viewers must have been working things out by this stage, although it's doubtful they noticed the 2711.39 mile shift in location from southern California to south Florida, from what was then named Industry Hills Golf Club in Industry Hills to what was then named Rolling Hills Golf Club in Fort Lauderdale.

"OK," the July 1980 viewer might have thought while hoovering his Skittles. "I've come to see a movie called *Caddyshack*, and it's about a lanky teenage caddy named Danny who is struggling with every classic teenage issue except acne. The gopher was cute and Danny's sister has hot legs, but nothing has particularly amused me thus far. So when does Chevy Chase appear? Where's TED KNIGHT? Where's BILL MURRAY????? Where's the comedy with *balls*?"

Scene time line: 00:00:00–00:04:43.

Vital Notes:

The movie shifts locations in the first scene—from southern California to south Florida. The vegetation provides the most obvious clue that Danny leaves the Pasadena Bushwood for the Fort Lauderdale Bushwood. Just after officially entering Bushwood Country Club, he rides up a road with a couple of magnificent cedar trees. Then just as he rides under the expansive *porte cochère*, the sky is no longer that deep southern California azure, as it becomes that midafternoon south Florida light gray mush—especially once Danny is on the other side of the clubhouse. The trees also become oak trees. So, in the first scene, the switch from California to Florida takes place when Danny cycles past the clubhouse entrance.

Danny's sisters let us know early on that Danny is named "Danny" ("Danny saw me NA-KED!"), but there's no indication that it's the Noonan household. Nobody uses the Noonan name in the first scene.

When Danny moves away from his father at the breakfast table to eat closer to his mother in the kitchen, there's a combination clock/pepper grinder that either reads seven past seven or twenty-five minutes to two.

Just after Danny athletically leaves the second-floor fire escape to get on his bicycle with his feet barely hitting the ground, he whizzes through the stop sign (followed closely by another, slower cyclist) then crosses the railroad tracks—just as his name comes up in the credits. I have to believe there's some symbolism here: Danny Noonan—from the wrong side of the tracks.

Michael O'Keefe hadn't played much golf before Caddyshack but he got his game in excellent shape before shooting in Fort Lauderdale.
(Warner/Orion/The Kobal Collection)

00:03:44. Danny Cycles Past the Mansions.

As Danny cycles smoothly through the mega-mansions of Pasadena near Bushwood, the smile he's sporting derives from an upwardly mobile streak. "Yes, I like this and, yes, I'd like to go to college so that I can get on the road to success so that I can live in one of these palaces."

When Mrs. Noonan mounts the stairs and Mr. Noonan can be seen marching into the dining room along the front hall, there's a small child, in green pajamas, hanging onto him. That's the last time that small child appears. Is that Noonan number fourteen or Noonan number fifteen? The Noonan family is probably still producing children today.

For those interested in product promotion, there are two interesting product promotions. A message on the second Cheerio's box (in the kitchen) offers free Pet Pals. These were likely stickers, not toys. More interestingly, the milk carton on view to the right of the screen when Mr. Noonan is trying to find out Dennis's identity has a promotion for free panties and, perhaps, hose. I have to believe that the makers of The Greatest Movie Ever Made saw the panty promotion and made certain that it appeared on the screen.

Mrs. Noonan has a definite New York accent—it comes out when she asks Danny to give the people at St. Copious a *cwawl* about the scholarship.

Poor old Dennis Noonan has a whopping great cold sore on his lower lip.

Dennis's real name was Dennis—actor Dennis McCormack. Perhaps this made it easier to get his lines correct.
"Who are *you*?"
"Dennis!"

Danny's Bushwood CC hat has a large stain on the top of the bill. In the next scene, where he caddies for Ty Webb, it's still there. That's the definition of cinematic continuity—the script supervisor, Susana Preston, right on her game.

Danny goes without a belt in his jeans here—and throughout the movie. There are loops for the belt but no belt—perhaps indicating his penury.

The young member of the Noonan family sitting in the kitchen is keen to show off his belly and chest.

Bushwood Country Club boasts a very impressive gate that we see only twice during the movie.

00:04:28—Danny Gets to the Bushwood Clubhouse.

Before the 1940s, horses were very much part of the scenery at country clubs. The horses and the equestriennes that Danny greets are the only ones in the movie, although I understand that horses play an important role in *Caddyshack II*. I once saw three minutes of *Caddyshack II* by accident and have never seen more than those three minutes. In three seconds, I could tell it was a movie that I would not want to watch. It's rare to see horses at country clubs today, as most country clubs are no longer in the countryside but slap bang in the middle of suburbia.

Danny dismounts his bicycle just after he takes a glance to the right (after saying hello to the gardener) because he sees the horses and probably thinks that they are members and would be upset that a caddy is riding his bike near the entrance that the members use—thus the obsequious doff of the Bushwood caddy hat to the ladies. As soon as they are out of sight, Danny is back in the saddle.

Industry Hills Golf Club in Industry Hills is no longer just Industry Hills. It's part of Pacific Palms Conference Resort, although it's still located in Industry Hills, which is twenty-three miles east of downtown Los Angeles, just south of Interstate 10. The land used to be landfills; golf course architect William F. Bell designed the two courses at Pacific Palms in 1979 and 1980. The official name of the course is Industry Hills Golf Club at Pacific Palms.

The resort calls the longer of the two the Eisenhower Course after the president and the shorter of the two the Zaharias after the famous lady golfer Babe Didrikson Zaharias. Locals call the former "The Ike" and the latter "The Babe." The *Caddyshack* scenes took place on the Babe course—no surprise there. The Babe has hosted TV commercials for Adidas, Holiday Inn, Dr. Pepper, and Pinnacle. The course today is a par 71 that's 6,821 yards from the tips; the Southern California Golf Association held its centennial championship on the course. John Dykstra, the special effects wizard who created the gopher, believes that he shot many of the gopher scenes at a course in the Encino area. So it's likely that the producers used Industry Hills for fill-in shots. The clubhouse that briefly appears in the first couple of minutes is a matte.

I tried very hard to spot any obvious differences between the bicycle Danny uses in Pasadena and the one he uses in Fort Lauderdale. I can't find any; the props people must have found the same bike or carted the same bike between the two locations. Only people dedicated to making The Greatest Movie Ever Made would have gone to this trouble.

◉

There are five steps leading up to the front door of the chateau Noonan. Note the no parking sign where the yellow car is parked and also the small "love bench" in the lower right hand part of the screen.

Inside, there's a shocking vomit-colored 1970s carpet on the landing and in the hallway. The banisters could use a layer of paint—hence Mrs. Noonan's request for some help painting the house after Little League. The baby-urine-colored walls in the hallway completely fail to complement the vomit-colored 1970s carpet.

There are some small toys just by the front door.

The first guitar in the movie appears—set up against the rail. A few seconds later, it looks like it's morphed into an electric model and is now leaning up against a small amplifier. The second guitar in the movie appears in the caddyshack; the third appears in the Fourth of July dance scene; and the fourth appears in the sloop-christening gig.

Long queues outside bathrooms must be endemic to households with fourteen (give or take a few) children. If you're the eldest child, then you must be able to go to the front of said queue—unless the current occupant sees you NA-KED.

As the bathroom door closes and Danny starts to go down the stairs, I wonder what's getting the attention of the two young urchinettes who are staring down toward the first floor.

I have to admit, not being much of a bra expert, that I had to look up the definition of a training bra. I initially thought that it was a close relative of the sports bra. How wrong I was. A Google search for "training bra" produces some fascinating results—in fact, about 1.7 million results that took 0.62 seconds to assemble. From teenadvice.about.com:

"Better known as training bras, first bras are for young girls who have started to develop breasts but who do not yet fit the standard bra sizes. A young girl who has started to develop should wear a training bra, but there is no harm in letting a girl get one before there is a real need. Remember, training bras are intended for girls of any age who have started to get breasts and who are not yet able to be fitted with a regular bra. If your breast size warrants a full fitting bra you should wear one, even if you are very young."

The elder Noonan girls look like they are on the way to inheriting their mother's mammaries.

⊙

I like the Noonan tyke who hangs onto the back of Mrs. Noonan's nightie.

⊙

Mrs. Noonan goes in certain doors only to come out of other doors; she then enters the door she just entered. It gets a bit dizzying.

⊙

The ironing board is pink. The first pink ironing board I've ever seen and possibly the only pink ironing board in any golf movie.

The expansive and well-appointed clubhouse at Grande Oaks in Davie, near Fort Lauderdale. Before becoming Grande Oaks, it was Rolling Hills and the primary location for *Caddyshack* shooting. Note that the club boasts oaks instead of palm trees.

(Courtesy of the author)

Note that Dennis is the first child out of any room and is the first to breakfast. As a possible newcomer to the Noonan homestead, he is perhaps beginning to learn the basics of getting to the breakfast table quickly in order to ensure that eating actually takes place.

Mr. Noonan's bow tie is the only clue as to his profession. He must be one of the following:

- Ultrapompous newspaper editorial writer
- Ultrapompous lawyer
- Ice cream vendor
- Professional clown
- Real estate appraiser
- Gay weatherman
- Gay realtor

There is some type of quasi-impressionistic Japanese painting on the wall at the top of the staircase.

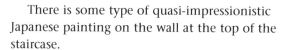

When Mr. Noonan is asking his wife about Dennis, his newspaper almost knocks over the pepper shaker.

For a guy with approximately fourteen children plus an underachieving eldest son, Mr. Noonan has remarkably few gray hairs.

Mr. Noonan has a wedding ring on the third finger of his right hand and another on the third finger of his left hand.

The jar that contains the monies for the college fund is a cookie jar. I sussed this because the word "cookies" is printed in large black block letters on the jar. Thankfully, Danny rotates it so that it's possible to discern the letters clearly.

The first Noonan girl (Deb) has spectacular legs.

Danny Noonan looks at his nubile sister (the one with the training bra issue) and calls her Deb. In the credits, Debi Frank is the actress listed as playing Kathleen Noonan, yet it's not clear which of the approximately fourteen Noonan offspring (if you include Dennis) is Kathleen. However, Danny Noonan calls her Deb—he uses her real name.

Behind Mr. Noonan in the kitchen is a fruit bowl and a *painting* of a fruit bowl.

St. Copious is a completely fictional saint. There is no St. Copious and no St. Copious's Day. St. Copious is not the patron saint of any person, group, garden, school, movie, or entity.

As Danny is about to cross the railroad tracks, check out the very late '70s/early '80s *dude* who is ambling across the crosswalk. He sports a nifty and totally pressed Hawaiian shirt, an organized mop of just below shoulder-length hair, tight jeans, and what might be brown clogs.

The architecture of Bushwood's clubhouse is a cross between mock Tudor, Scandinavian horse barn, about-to-be-obliterated-by-a-category-three beach hut, and Japanese lighthouse. And that's before getting inside.

The first scene also introduces the time line: the party at the clubhouse is a Fourth of July party, so the initial action takes place around late June. Mr. Noonan says that Danny has to have something lined up by September, otherwise he will have to work at the lumber yard/gulag/salt mine. Thus *Caddyshack* takes place within a two-week window—at the most.

Danny takes three spoonfuls of sugar to his Cheerios.

The official US *Caddyshack* release date: July 25, 1980.

The official Australian *Caddyshack* release date: August 21, 1980.

The official Finnish *Caddyshack* release date: March 13, 1981.

Caddyshack had other titles in other countries.

Canada (French): À Miami, faut le faire!
Germany (West): *Caddyshack*—Wahnsinn ohne Handicap (Those Crazy Caddies)
Spain: El Club de los Chalados (The Club of the Crazy People)
Portugal: O Clube dos Malandrecos (The Club of the Crazy People)
Brazil: Clube dos Pilantras

Poland: Golfiarze
Finland: Latvasta Laho
Italy: Palla da Golf
Sweden: Tom I Bollen

Other 1980 movies.

- *Airplane!*
- *Atlantic City*
- *The Big Red One*
- *The Empire Strikes Back*
- *From Mao to Mozart: Isaac Stern In China*
- *Melvin and Howard*
- *Ordinary People*
- *The Stunt Man*
- *Altered States*
- *The Blues Brothers*
- *Breaker Morant*
- *Dressed to Kill*
- *The Elephant Man*
- *Kagemusha*
- *The Ninth Configuration*
- *Raging Bull*

- *Resurrection*
- *9 to 5*
- *Alligator*
- *Carny*
- *Coal Miner's Daughter*
- *The Dogs of War*
- *The Long Good Friday*
- *A Rumor Of War* (TV)
- *The Shining*
- *Superman II*
- *A Town Like Alice*
- *Flash Gordon*
- *The Fog*
- *Humanoids of the Deep*
- *Motel Hell*
- *American Gigolo*
- *Any Which Way You Can*
- *Brubaker*
- *Fame*
- *La cage aux folles II*
- *Modern Romance*
- *My Bodyguard*
- *Popeye*
- *Private Benjamin*

- *Somewhere in Time*
- *Spetters*
- *A Tale of Two Cities*
- *Terror Train*
- *Used Cars*
- *Angel City*
- *Bad Timing: A Sensual Obsession*
- *The Blue Lagoon*
- *Fade to Black*
- *The Final Countdown*
- *Friday the 13th*
- *The Gambler*
- *Grad Night*
- *The Mirror Crack'd*
- *The Monster Club*
- *The Octagon*
- *Oh God! Book 2*
- *Phobia*
- *Prom Night*
- *Scrooge*
- *Cellar Dwellers*
- *The Alien Dead*
- *Battle Beyond the Stars*
- *The Boogey Man*

- *Cheech and Chong's Next Movie*
- *The Exterminator*
- *Foxes*
- *One-Trick Pony*
- *Power*
- *Saturn 3*
- *Schizoid*
- *Smokey and the Bandit II*
- *Urban Cowboy*
- *The Big Stink*
- *Cruising*
- *Hawk the Slayer*
- *Maniac*
- *The Prey*
- *Xanadu*
- *Oblomov*
- *Forbidden Zone*
- *From the Life of the Marionettes*
- *Gideon's Trumpet*
- *Guyana Tragedy*
- *The Last Metro*
- *Loulou*
- *The Naked Civil Servant*
- *Return of the Secaucus Seven*

Clearly a five-star vintage year for comedies, with *Airplane*, *Caddyshack*, and *The Blues Brothers*. *The Shining* isn't exactly a comedy, but it's one of the greatest horror movies, and it only augments the 1980 vintage. I have not yet seen *Return of the Secaucus Seven*, but it's on my must-see list now.

Note, at 02:40, the very brief camera angle change from in front of Danny Noonan to behind Danny Noonan. This shows a crowd at the breakfast table—seven in all, with only Danny and his father in street clothes and the remainder in pajamas. The small girl sitting quietly in her playpen is Violet Ramis. There are what look to be nursery rhyme figurines behind Mr. Noonan, plus a painting of the Last Supper on the wall behind the little girl. When I first studied this scene at full speed, I thought that the dark-haired girl next to the toddler might be Maggie O'Hooligan but, upon closer frame-by-frame inspection, it's clearly not; O'Hooligan turns up during the round that Judge Smails takes with Danny as his looper. Dennis has completely disappeared. From

the behind Danny angle, it looks as though there's a brother right next to him, but from the in-front-of-Danny angle, things are not so tight at the breakfast table.

The golf ball with the *Caddyshack* logo has the type of dimples the golf balls from the 1940s used. On the ball, the word *Caddyshack* appears as *CaddyShack*.

Danny's mother climbs the stairs in her very non-Victoria's Secret nightdress, but Danny's father appears below with his bow tie off to one side. There's also the first appearance of a first child following Danny's father. Danny's mother starts climbing the stairs at 01:22. She climbs fourteen stairs in eight seconds at a rate of 1.75 stairs per second.

Tom Burdick is the proprietor of the lumber yard. Mr. Noonan threatens to talk to Burdick if the college "thing" isn't sorted out.

Notice that the theme song includes the brief refrain: "be the ball, be the ball."

There's at least one set of encyclopedias in the bookcase, plus what look to be reference books or special editions of various classics.

Moving to the second door, there's a carpet sweeper and sewing machine plus the pink ironing board.

In the Noonan conclave, there's a curious mix of blond children with curly hair and dark-haired children with straight hair.

When speaking to his sister (the one with the great legs), Danny does not look directly at her (a brother is punching him, after all); the name of the boy who has the training bra is Pete Scalary. It sounds like Pizza Larry. The adjective *scalar* refers to something that has only magnitude, not direction—like the work of a long-drive contest competitor.

As Danny walks into the bathroom, there's an obvious "Oh God!" as he turns around.

There's a lovely piece of irony as the girl complains about Danny seeing her NA-KED—in a house with a dozen children. The girl delivers her six syllables with superb meter. Then she pops out of the bathroom seminaked. Then we get a superb view of the sister's training bra and training panties as Danny moves down the stairs; Deb actually parts her nightie as she provides this information, although her scowl detracts (only slightly) from the look.

The music continues as Mrs. Noonan starts to mount the stairs—but with just a muted guitar, as if it's on the radio. In fact, she tells one of her children to "turn off that radio."

Elaine Aiken—Mrs. Noonan

Although Elaine Aiken only appeared in three movies in a career that spanned more than two decades, she was an influential and famous New York City acting teacher who fostered the early careers of stars such as Alec Baldwin, Harvey Keitel, and Brooke Shields.

In 1957, she played Ada Marshall in a serious Western, *The Lonely Man*, which starred Jack Palance and Anthony Perkins. Harry Essex directed the movie; he later produced *The Undercover Scandals of Henry VIII* (1970). Aiken periodically makes the lonely man less lonely as Palance ends up on her farm in his quest to find a place to settle down; then she makes Perkins's life less lonely. She is gorgeous in the film—a vixen with a blonde ponytail and slim jeans. Aiken made an appearance in a 1957–1958 TV series called *Harbourmaster* (note the English spelling) about a harbormaster in New England who chases criminals.

It would be sixteen years before she appeared in a movie again, this time playing Mrs. Hennington in *The Spook Who Sat by the Door*. The bizarre affirmative-action-gone-awry plot centers around a black CIA operative who, after grueling training and five years of being berated by whites in the bowels of the agency, resigns, returns to his native Chicago, and uses his training and know-how to start a race war with the help of a street gang.

Next for Aiken came an appearance in a special two-part episode of *Kojak* that first aired in November 1976. Aiken played a Mrs. Foster. Then came the opportunity to play a Mrs. Noonan in *Caddyshack*.

Born in Spain as Elana Arizmendi on July 12, 1927, Elaine Aiken died of cancer on her birthday in 1998 in New York City.

Aiken's parents emigrated to America to flee the Spanish Civil War. A graduate of the Actors Studio, she founded the Actors Conservatory with Lily Lodge in 1984 in New York City. Alec Baldwin had this to say about a woman who was obviously a mentor and crucial influence: "Elaine Aiken had a generosity of spirit that enabled her to probe into each actor's strengths and weaknesses and help them to confront that part of themselves which would open up their acting abilities."

Baldwin fans should thus thank Danny Noonan's mother for helping the actor reach the top of the profession. Without *Caddyshack*, Baldwin perhaps would not have appeared in *The Hunt for Red October*, *Pearl Harbor*, and *Thomas and the Magic Railroad*. While *The Hunt* is one of my absolute favorite movies, Baldwin plays a superb conductor in *Thomas*. When my son was in the four-to-five-year range, *Thomas* movies were *de rigueur*, and Baldwin was a useful addition to the scene, seriously augmenting the animation and not letting the big actor thing get in the way of the story. Ringo Starr and comedian George Carlin have also narrated *Thomas* movies.

Aiken taught acting via sense memory techniques. This encourages the actor to "connect" with the five senses with the aid of several exercises. After getting the hang of sense memory, students move on to emotion memory technique, and then star in submarine movies.

Sharon Angela, who plays Rosalie Aprile in *The Sopranos*, is another former Aiken student.

Albert Salmi—Mr. Noonan

As Danny's father, Albert Salmi plays a massive role in setting up the Danny Noonan plot. Their argument while Danny is trying to eat his Cheerios lets the audience know that *Caddyshack* might not actually be a movie about gophers but a movie about a thin, likable caddy who wants to go to college but can't because his father can't or won't provide the cash. The Noonan patriarch is simply listed in the credits as "Mr. Noonan," and there's no indication in the screenplay or the dialogue that he has a first name. It's just—Mr. Noonan. After the initial father-son angst scene, Salmi fades away and only appears a couple of times during the caddy tournament. He had a much more important role in the early script; much of Salmi's work in *Caddyshack* ended up on the editing room floor, as he discovered when he took his family to see the movie.

Albert Salmi was a prominent, busy, and successful Hollywood character actor; he typically played unusual or even eccentric roles instead of leading roles. Mr. Noonan may not have been eccentric or unusual, but even in the relatively brief role as Mr. Noonan, Salmi puts his acting muscle into it and makes Danny's dad a force, albeit a mildly farcical one. He gets the Danny Noonan plot off to a strong start and adds some quick, dry comedy when he asks Danny, who has just admitted buying four or five Cokes, if he might be a diabetic. A lesser actor might have muffed the part, and the father-son tension would not have been so prominent. And in a movie without a surfeit of volcanic plot lines, the Noonan story is vital.

Caddyshack was Salmi's twenty-ninth movie. After *Caddyshack*, he appeared in ten more. He started his acting career on Broadway and also appeared in over eighty television TV shows, including:

- *Dallas*
- *Gunsmoke*
- *Mission: Impossible*
- *The Alfred Hitchcock Hour*
- *Voyage to the Bottom of the Sea*
- *The Twilight Zone*
- *The Streets of San Francisco*
- *McMillan and Wife*
- *Ironside*
- *Bonanza*

He appeared in episode #30 ("Custom K.I.T.T.") of *Knight Rider* as Buck Rayburn; the episode originally aired on November 13, 1983. There's a touch of nonirony here as Angie D'Annunzio (D'Annunzio's younger brother) sports a Night Riders t-shirt during the Dalai Lama scene (and at other times). This cannot have had any relation to the TV show, as *Knight Rider* (thankfully) only took up valuable prime-time TV slots from 1982 to 1986 and *Caddyshack* first aired in 1980. There's a temptation to think that Angie's t-shirt is from the TV show, but any *Knight Rider* aficionado can supply the full facts.

In all, Salmi made 62 movie and 125 television appearances. His filmography includes:

- *Fatal Vision*
- *Dragonslayer*
- *Viva Knievel*
- *Kung Fu*
- *Escape from the Planet of the Apes*
- *Three Guns for Texas*
- *The Meanest Men in the West*
- *The Unforgiven*

Born in 1928 in Brooklyn of Finnish parents, Salmi spoke Finnish as a tyke, having spent his formative years in the Finnish section of Brooklyn. He changed his name from Alfred to Albert. He spent three years in the military, then used the GI Bill to fund training at the Actor's Studio in New York City in the early 1950s. He also studied at Irwin Piscator's Dramatic Workshop and the American Theater Wing. He starred on Broadway in *Bus Stop*, playing Bo Decker.

Fans of Westerns shot in the 1960s and 1970s will likely recognize Salmi. His work was so popular that, in 1967, the National Cowboy Hall of Fame presented him with the Western Heritage Award—primarily for a role in a *Gunsmoke* episode.

Quiet, with a fun sense of humor, Salmi was primarily a nonglitzy and unpretentious family man who suffered from depression in his later years, which he spent in Spokane, Washington.

Salmi married actress Peggy Ann Garner in 1956. They had a daughter but divorced seven years later. He remarried in 1964 and, with Roberta Pollock, had two daughters. Salmi passed away in 1990.

His daughter Lizanne remembers her father taking the family to see *Caddyshack*. Lizanne was particularly interested as the film starred some stars from *Saturday Night Live*.

"When he first got the role, he told me that he was going to be in a movie that was going to be shot in Florida," says Lizanne. "He said there would be some *SNL* cast members in it, which I thought was very cool. I watched *SNL* though he did not."

After seeing the movie, Salmi was embarrassed—his part was much smaller than he had anticipated.

"He did have a bigger part initially when it was filmed, but they cut the parts with Danny

Noonan and my dad because they wanted to focus on the club more—which makes sense! He was embarrassed, though, when we went to the opening and his part was so small. He was embarrassed because he took the family to the opening and his part was smaller than the one he had actually shot."

If *Caddyshack* had stuck to the early draft of the screenplay, then Albert Salmi would have been much more prominent—after the scene at the Noonan household, he only appears in large group scenes such as the caddy tournament and the finale, and he has no further lines. When it came time to edit the movie, the decision makers decided to ramp up the gopher's importance and highlight the ad-lib performances that Bill Murray, Rodney Dangerfield, and others had produced. This, I suppose, is the lot of the character actor—always playing behind the more famous actors, getting paid well enough, but never becoming the star.

Those wishing to learn more about Albert Salmi can visit http://www.angelfire.com/ok/nambarg/. There's also a biography available written by Sandra Grabman: *Spotlights & Shadows: The Albert Salmi Story*, published by Bear Manor Media.

Caddyshack was the first and only movie for Debi Frank, who played Kathleen Noonan.

In the early script, the movie starts directly with the Noonan household. Ramis and the producers only added the gopher after the conclusion of the filming in south Florida.

The scene in the Noonan household is mostly faithful to the third draft of the script. Bits that failed to make it into the first scene from the script were:

- A barking dog—specifically a collie.
- Mrs. Noonan refers to two Noonan brothers—Andy and Billy.
- Danny has a room that he shared with Andy and Billy. The script refers to the room as "an incredibly messy boy's

bedroom littered with dirty laundry, books, comics, broken toys, and an electric guitar. The walls are covered with KISS posters, framed athletic awards, cheesy trophies on a homemade bookshelf, Little League team pictures, and a poster-sized blow-up of John Belushi.

- The script gives Danny's age: eighteen. The script describes him as a "manly, good-looking, athletic kid with a kind of quick, natural intelligence."
- One of Danny's sisters, Nancy, is in the bathroom trying on her mother's makeup.
- Danny begins the toothbrushing process.
- A much more involved fight occurs over who gets to go into the bathroom next.
- Danny nearly runs into one sibling, age three, who is pooping and says to Danny: "I'm pooping, Danny." Danny replies: "I'm proud."
- Mrs. Noonan is making fried egg sandwiches.
- In addition to the dog barking, a radio is blaring and the telephone is ringing.

- The script describes Danny's father as very ornery—even disaffected after having so many kids and feeling like a "guest in his own house."
- Danny tells his mother that he hasn't heard from St. Copious about the scholarship, and the excuse he uses for not wanting to go there is that there's too much snow and it's in the middle of Nebraska. There's a great line in addition to the "two nuns" dialogue. "This guy had to take a cow to the prom and the cow had to be in early."
- Mrs. Noonan tells daughter Sally not to put egg in her hair.
- It's Pepsi in the script, not Coke.
- Before leaving the house, Danny gets a letter from St. Copious saying that he hasn't gotten a scholarship.

Five Murray brothers were caddies. Today, none are caddies, although Ed Murray, the eldest Murray brother, won a prestigious caddy scholarship—the Chick Evans—and is now an investment banker with Morgan Stanley Dean Witter.

- Brian Doyle-Murray wrote the screenplay and played Lou Loomis in the movie—more on him later.
- Bill Murray plays Carl Spackler—more on him later.
- Andy Murray is a chef, restaurateur, and cofounder and cochairman of Murray Bros. *Caddyshack* restaurants.
- John Murray is described on the *Caddyshack* restaurants Web site as a "Renaissance Man who has starred in a movie, bartended globally and partnered in restaurants."
- Joel Murray, also an actor, was featured on the hit ABC sitcom *Dharma and Greg* and produced the brothers' new television golf show.

The daddy of all caddy scholarships is the Evans, run by the Evans Scholars Foundation and sponsored by the Western Golf Association. Charles "Chick" Evans founded the program in 1930 and, since then, more than eight thousand high school–age caddies have earned college scholarships and graduated and become Evans Scholars Alumni. Most scholars attend one of fourteen universities where there is a special dormitory for the scholars. To date, no Evans scholar has attended St. Copious. However, the scholarship is a particularly big deal in the Chicago area, and it's likely that the caddy scholarship in *Caddyshack* resembles the Evans.

Orion Pictures backed *Caddyshack*. Arthur Krim, Robert Benjamin, and Eric Pleskow formed Orion in 1978 after leaving United Artists, where they had been top-level executives. Movies that emerged from the Orion stable included *Time After Time*, *Sharkey's Machine*, *A Little Romance*, and *Arthur*. Warner Brothers and Orion had a joint operating agreement—primarily for distribution purposes. In 1982, Orion and Filmways, initially mostly a TV production company, merged. The new partnership made further memorable movies—*The Terminator*, *The Silence of the Lambs*, *Platoon*, *Robocop*, and *Dances with Wolves*—but none of these would be as memorable as *Caddyshack*. Ironically, despite numerous box office successes, Orion went bankrupt, before eventually emerging from bankruptcy in 1996. MGM purchased Orion in 1998 but received the rights only to movies produced after 1982. Thus what is now Time Warner received the rights to movies that Orion produced during the time that Orion and Warner partnered. Thus Time Warner currently owns the rights to *Caddyshack*.

Arthur Krim endowed a scholarship at his alma mater, Columbia University—the Arthur Krim Memorial Scholarship in Film. Krim's wife, Mathilde, was an early AIDS activist. Arthur Krim was a big-time Democratic fund-raiser and activist and was part of the Camelot scene, often hosting parties in New York City that the likes of Marilyn Monroe, Maria Callas, and John F. Kennedy attended. Krim's apartment was adjacent to the Car-lyle Hotel and, according to legend, there was (or is) a secret passage between the two buildings, and through that passage, Kennedy was supposedly able to visit various visitees.

"Arthur . . . lived in a world that was infinitely more important than the movie business, and this ultimately made [him] better at making movies," said Orion partner Bob Benjamin. Thus the genius of *Caddyshack* comes perhaps not from the writers, actors, crew, editors, janitors, and others involved with the movie, but from the political and social connections that Krim nurtured.

Eric Pleskow was equally accomplished; he joined United Artists in 1957 and rose to become its chairman and CEO, a position he held from 1973 to 1977, before leaving to form Orion. During the '50s–'70s, UA produced a string of Oscar winners, including *Marty*, *Around the World in Eighty Days*, *The Apartment*, *West Side Story*, *Midnight Cowboy*, *One Flew Over the Cuckoo's Nest*, *Rocky*, and *Annie Hall*. So the boys who ultimately decided that *Caddyshack* would be worth taking from screenplay to finished movie knew a thing or two about great movies, although *Caddyshack* is significantly better than any of the movies listed above. Even though *Caddyshack* is The Greatest Movie Ever Made, it earned zero nominations for any awards. No Oscars. No Golden Globes. This seriously brings into question the legitimacy of Hollywood's awards apparatus. *Annie Hall* was OK if you like that sort of thing, but how many people go around, at any time and for any reason, blurting lines from that movie?

The Orion Nebula is the closest nebula to Earth. A nebula is (loosely) defined as a cloud of gas and dust in outer space. The nebula is part of a much larger cloud that covers most of the Orion constellation. The Orion Nebula (a.k.a. the Great Nebula in Orion) is an emission nebula that's a mere 1,500 light years from Earth, making it the closest to our solar system and thus among the most studied. Nicholas-Claude Fabri de Peiresc discovered Orion in 1610. The Hubble Space Telescope (HST) started capturing better images of the Orion Nebula in the 1990s. Apparently, small bits of the nebula are on the verge of collapsing—which may explain why Orion experienced financial hassles in the 1990s. Recent HST spying on Orion indicates the possibility of interaction between the young hot Trapezium cluster stars and the protoplanetary disks.

2

What Do You Want to Be When You Grow Up?

Caddy seeks wisdom
In grass by blind golfer's web
Spun in Lumber Yard.

—poet/philosopher Basho (son of)

The best golfer at the club. The career advisor. Even a blind pig can hit that shot over water. The missing mower.

NOW comes Chevy Chase, or at least a golfer with a fine swing who looks like Chevy Chase. The swing, even from around two hundred yards, looks like it's completely on plane, with beautiful tempo and balance.

Based on the conditioning on view in this first look at the venerable club, it's a certified dump—a goat farm and dog track. There's mud, sand, scruffy edging around the water, bare spots, and poorly maintained turf grass.

The touching boy-mentor conversation continues the plot theme of Danny Noonan trying to find his way in the world; in Ty Webb, the disconnected playboy, he's asking the wrong person. Michael O'Keefe (who played Danny Noonan) and

Chase improvised some of the scene, including the famous "Do you take drugs, Danny?" question. It's wonderful dialogue that ping-pongs between wedges, lumber yards, aptitude tests, Russia, and college in Nebraska.

With O'Keefe's able help, Chase quickly sets up Ty Webb as the aloof, unwordly, and bamboozling trust-fund baby who also happens to be in the wood business. Any member of a country club knows that most well-heeled clubs have at least one Ty Webb around—the guy who can really play without ever working on his game but can't string three consecutive thoughts together.

The DVD version of the movie places a chapter break just as Danny takes the clubs off his shoulder, but it's clearly one scene and is treated as such here.

What may be Danny Noonan's best facial expression in the movie takes place just after Webb says that he's about to impart some advice—such is the young caddy's thirst for life-changing knowledge.

But the knowledge he receives must disappoint the young Noonan, as it pertains to golf and not college, and not life, and not money. The "be the ball" line is so superb that it almost makes the normally stony-faced Webb laugh.

With the ball suddenly on a *downslope* in some light rough, Chase hits a perfect blind wedge that's beautifully filmed. Danny tries to emulate the blindfolded shot and makes a good-looking swing but dunks the ball in the hazard. Like all golfers after hitting a blind shot well, there's that moment of having to know the result. The "right in the lumber yard" line ends the scene perfectly.

Now almost eight minutes in, the cinemagoers know that Chase is on form, Danny Noonan is still the hero, and golf is actually going to occur during the movie. The golfers are happy. The Chevy Chase fans are happy.

Scene time line: 00:04:43–00:07:48.
Danny Noonan and Ty Webb on the golf course.

I have to believe that the costumier, André Lavery, modeled Ty Webb's look on Tom

Weiskopf. There's a striking similarity between the two—especially with that dimple and the Hogan-style lid.

Webb hands Noonan a driver or fairway wood, but he clearly hits an iron from the tee—based on the trajectory just before landing and the lack of roll.

In 1980, Wilson was one of the top three golf brands. Callaway, Nike, Adams, and others have knocked Wilson off its perch, but the company still produces some of the finest golf equipment. As a scratch golfer, Webb would likely have been playing Wilson's Staff Tour Blades.

Irons that Wilson made in the 1970s included the Staff Dyna-Power, the Fluid Feel, and the FG Series blades. Pepsi owned Wilson at the time the movie was made.

When the cameras were not rolling and the cast and crew were together off screen, the partying was fast and furious. The "Do you take drugs, Danny?/Every day/So what's the problem?" dialogue is among the most oft-repeated and is not in the early script. It's one of the many in-house jokes in the movie, as drug use was rampant during the fall and winter months that the group gathered in south Florida to shoot the movie. This was perhaps an offshoot of the *Saturday Night Live* scene, which during the late 1970s was notorious for abuse of cocaine and other drugs. On the *Caddyshack* set during daylight hours, the cast performed, but once Harold Ramis said "cut" for the final time, the partying started, primarily in the dormitory immediately adjacent to the Rolling Hills clubhouse, where most of the cast lived during the filming. Drug use is a controversial subject best left to those who write at length about such things, but there was an innocence about narcotics in the late 1970s in the United States.

"Nobody even thought that cocaine was even addictive back then," said one cast member.

The true scope of the damage that it could initiate was not fully understood, or perhaps not fully admitted. Once the filming ended, there were casualties among the crew—weeks and months spent in rehab and broken careers. Exactly how Doug Kenney died when he fell to his death in Hawaii soon after the movie hit American cinemas is still a mystery, but there was nothing mysterious about the extent of Kenney's cocaine use; whatever happened to him, the life of the writer who initiated the "sophomoric" school of comedy of which *Animal House* and *Caddyshack* are the best examples ended way too early. Anyone who loves these movies must surely wish that Doug Kenney's answer to Ty Webb's question would have been: "Not any more—I've got too many good movies left in me and I need to continue to help America take itself less seriously."

The TV version of *Caddyshack* differs from that seen at the cinema or on DVD, and the first major difference occurs in this scene. In lieu of the "Every day" answer to Ty Webb's question, Danny Noonan replies: "No." Webb continues: "Good. So, what's the problem?"

The scene is supposed to take place very early in the morning, but Ty Webb hits the blindfolded shot toward the seventeenth green.

The second scene in the movie closely follows the second scene in the early script. It continues the primary plot line of Danny Noonan trying to find his way in life. The script describes Ty Webb as "a handsome, thirty-ish bachelor with clear eyes and an air of relaxed self-control. His outfit is all soft flannel and cashmere. Everything about him tells us that he is the perfect golfer."

Anyone in golf knows that there's no such thing as perfect in this crazy game, but Ty Webb manages, until the climax of the movie, to be closest to perfection (at least in his own mind and in the early version of the script). Danny asks Webb about the problem of deciding what one wants to be, and Webb admits that the choices were challenging for him: going to West Point, sailing his father's ship to the islands, or taking a year off and going to the Alps to ski. Then, in the early version of the script, he says: "I had the same problem at eighteen, at twenty-one, twenty-five, twenty-nine, and thirty-two—and yesterday. I almost blew out my brains with a silver-plated Beretta. So what's your problem?"

The script details the pond in front of the seventeenth green as a "beautiful lake that cuts across the fairway." At Rolling Hills, the pond looks like it contains raw sewage.

Initially, the "Be the ball" line was an extension of a reference to *Star Wars* and the "the Force," but that reference thankfully failed to make it into the final movie version. *Caddyshack* is a lot better than any *Stars Wars* incarnation, and it would have been tragic to find a reference to the latter movie.

00:05:20—Danny Discusses the Cooter Preference Test.

The Cooter Preference Test is a wonderful pun, even though the test to which Ty Webb and Danny Noonan refer is the Kuder Preference Record, Form C, according to Don Zytowski, the director of research at the National Career Assessment Services, Inc. (NCASI), the company that owns the Kuder. It's called the Cooter Preference Test in the early script. The founder of the test, Dr. Frederic "Fritz" Kuder, died in 2000 at ninety-seven.

Widely used from 1947, the Kuder Preference Record became well-known in high school guidance programs and in the process of approving college plans for GI Bill veterans. The test is technically an "interest inventory" presented in series of threes. The person taking the test responded to certain questions with a simple "most preferred" or "least preferred" or "in between most and least." The Kuder candidate punched holes with the help of a pin; the administrator counted the number of holes, using a key in the answer packet.

The Kuder Preference Record, Form C, offered percentile scores on ten different scales, including mechanical, literary, and social service. Test takers then referred to a separate booklet that provided a list of occupations associated with the final results from the form.

Today's Kuder is the more modern Kuder Career Search; the candidate takes the test on-line through the NCASI web site (NCASI.com). Items from the former test made it to today's test, which a computer scores. The punched card and associated booklet are gone; the result is instant.

Dr. Kuder was well aware of the mention in *Caddyshack.*

"Dr. Kuder was quietly delighted with the appearance of his work in a movie," says Zytowski. Although not mentioned by name, the Kuder appears in Phillip Roth's short story, "You Can Tell a Man by the Song He Sings," from the short story collection, *Goodbye Columbus.*

The current owners of the Kuder estimate that over 100 million people have taken a version of the test. There's a Web site, kuder.com, where those interested in Kuder can learn more about the test. There's also a Web site called cooter.com that's a little different.

I took the Kuder test that, today, comprises sixty questions grouped in threes. The test asks you which of the three options you enjoy the most (or least). Here is one of the sets of choices.

1. Take a several-day hike in a national forest.
2. Help a friend shop for clothes for a job interview.
3. Analyze different pizzas for their fat content.

Candidates rank the three choices, from the one you like the most to the one you like the least. After twelve pages, it's over, and the results come in. In lieu of a great big flashing banner saying "You Should Be an Underachiever!" it provides a sort of quasi-aptitude rating based on clusters; the two clusters to which I am most suited are sales/management and arts/communication. The results page then provides six examples of suitable jobs within each cluster. The first one that popped up was *grocery store manager.* I would rather have razor wire spun through my nose than work as a grocery store manager; thankfully, the other options under sales/management were slightly more appealing. These included marketing director, utility writer, contract administrator, hotel sales manager, marketing representative, and not-for-profit store manager. However, under the arts/communication segment, the test was right on, recommending that I seriously consider editorial consulting or freelance writing—or fiction writing or being a librarian.

A cooter is a North American river turtle with a dull brown shell and (usually) yellow stripes on the head. But I think that Brian Doyle-Murray, Harold Ramis, and Doug Kenney had another type of cooter in mind.

The early script refers to Webb's ball being close to a "beautiful lake" that's close to a "lovely green." However, "be the ball" is in the screenplay, as is the rest of the scene, with a few minor changes: at the end of the scene, Webb, after telling Danny that his shot went into the lumberyard, says, "We'll work on it—honestly. Just figure out what you really want. Once you know, everything else takes care of itself."

The subtitles say that Ty Webb lent Danny Noonan $2.50, but surely it was more like $250.

Both Noonan and Webb are beltless, as was the trend in 1980. Just look at Jack Nicklaus and his attire at the time. Thankfully for belt manufacturers around the world, Sansabelt trousers are no longer popular—at least in golf clubs around the globe.

Ty Webb carries a driver, three wood, and four wood in his bag.

The French for "Be the Ball" is "sois la balle." The French subtitles also have Webb hitting an eight iron, "Le 8," and not the wedge.

Just after Webb hits the shot across the pond, the clubs that he has sprayed all over the fairways are magically back in that big tour bag.

In the early script, the scene ends with Webb and Noonan seeing what the script describes as a "huge tractor mower." In the TV version of *Caddyshack*, the producers augmented this with Bill Murray on an industrial-strength lawn mower. The scene also appears, with commentary from Chevy Chase and Harold Ramis, in the documentary, the *19th Hole*, a bonus in the twentieth-anniversary DVD version of *Caddyshack*. The mower is yellow and has a big smiley face on the front. Murray jumps off and starts to provide the best golfer in the club with swing advice. Chevy Chase then jumps on to the tractor to get the ball that Murray has just hit; Murray takes a hard left and almost spills Webb into the mowing units. They almost run over Danny Noonan, and it looks as though his role in the movie will end right there, until he jumps out of the way.

Chevy Chase has the type of slightly lanky yet athletic physique that's perfect for golf. The writers made Ty Webb the best golfer at the club, so a stunt double was inserted for the first swings in the movie—a stunt double who was obviously a good golfer. Chip King, the head golf professional at Pine Needles and Mid Pines in Southern Pines, North Carolina, analyzed the two swings that Chevy Chase made—the first two swings in the movie:

"Even though the golfer who is playing Chevy Chase is a long way from the camera, it's clear that he's a very good player. He has great set up, maybe just a hair open at address, which means that he's probably going to hit a slight fade. He has an excellent one piece takeaway, and the swing is completely on plane. He has an excellent position at the top of the backswing. There's good drive with the legs, and the hips have opened up very quickly, which also means that he's going to hit a fade. He has a perfect finish, with a bit of pose, obviously demonstrating that he's hit a good shot. It looks like he was hitting an iron off that tee.

"The swing that Chevy Chase makes over the water would not have produced the excellent result—with the ball ending up just a few feet from the hole. In the set up, his right side is way underneath and his posture is poor. He is basically setting himself up to be really handsy. Chase has a good waggle, though. There's a lot of up and down motion in the swing—I'd like to see a much better turn. He dips down in the backswing and therefore he must lift up going through. The club was also shut on the backswing. But his position at impact is actually pretty decent. That swing probably produced a low pull."

Chevy Chase is 6'4". Michael O'Keefe is 6'1".

Ty Webb's golf shirt isn't much of a golf shirt—until Webb is tying the handkerchief around his eyes and reveals a touch of sweat underneath the armpits.

The early script has this as the first hole but it's the seventeenth. Let's give them all a bit of a break here! Webb could have started on the seventeenth or played that hole backwards or sideways. Plenty of golfers have eschewed the normal routing to have a bit of creative fun on the golf course—why not Ty Webb? If there's a golfer who would not conform to normal standards, surely it is Webb.

Stan Jolley—Production Designer

Today's movie world calls the production designer the art director. As Jolley explains it:

"I've been a voting member of the Academy of Motion Picture Arts and Sciences for over forty-six years. They announce one of the awards by saying 'And this year's Oscar for art direction goes to ———.' " And Stan Jolley should know: he was nominated for an Oscar for *Witness*. Also, Stan's art direction on Walt Disney's Oscar-winning icon *Donald in Mathmagic Land* is still popular in schools fifty-two years later.

Whether you call him or her art director or production designer, it's this person's responsibility to give the movie its look. Ironically, if the production designer and his team complete their work competently, or even brilliantly, the audience will completely fail to recognize the work: the sets and the feel of the movie will seem completely natural; the illusion will be completely and totally effective and easy. Needless to say, it's difficult and complicated: the producers or director hand the script to the production designer, and he or she must then, as Jolley puts it, "create the ambiance of the film, first finding the right locations, designing new structures, exteriors, or interiors that are designed to accommodate the actions of the written word, be it actors, animals, machinery, exploding golf courses or whatever. If the script says that Bushwood is a 'crummy snobatorium' then the production designer must create a 'crummy snobatorium' that not only augments the script but meets all the time schedules, budgets, and related studio constraints—often with script changes at a second's notice."

Just after Orion had given *Caddyshack* the green light, Stan Jolley received a call from production manager Ted Swanson, who asked Jolley to meet with a first-time director named Harold Ramis and a first-time producer named Doug Kenney who were going to produce a movie titled *Caddyshack*: "They had just finished writing *Animal House*, which was a huge success," says Jolley. "They asked me what I had done, so I told them about the various movies and TV shows, and I also mentioned that I had played a big part in designing Disneyland, and Walt had asked me to stay on at Disney and not go back to 20th Century-Fox, where I had been out on loan."

This part of Jolley's portfolio particularly impressed Kenney and Ramis, who started to tell Jolley about the look they wanted for the clubhouse. They showed Jolley a photo of the current "facility" at Rolling Hills, and Jolley, who has an architectural degree from the University of Southern California, asked for some tracing paper and started, on top of the photo, to outline his vision of the three-story Bushwood Country Club clubhouse. Kenney and Ramis liked the look and, on the spot, hired Jolley for the *Caddyshack* gig.

"I had stayed with Walt Disney for eight years after Disneyland, and I've been forever grateful because Walt made me the youngest art director in the history of Hollywood."

It wasn't the first time that Jolley had worked with a first-time director; he had helped Howie Morris in a collaboration that generated one of the most artistically and commercially successful television shows of all time: *Get Smart*. Jolley created the titles with various slamming doors and gates, plus all the hilarious sight gags, such as the cone of silence.

Swanson and Jolley soon got to work on the preproduction phase of *Caddyshack*, with Jolley moving to Fort Lauderdale from Beverly Hills: "The really fun part of any motion picture for the production designer comes in the formative stages," says Jolley. "With *Caddyshack*, I really enjoyed taking the existing clubhouse, which was really just a very small golf complex, and turning it into rarified Bushwood Country Club."

Ramis, Kenney, and others involved with *Caddyshack* who were relatively fresh to motion pictures were fortunate to be working with Ted Swanson and Stan Jolley. Both had extensive experience in the motion picture industry, and both were very strict, very organized, and very talented. Swanson had a Fort Lauderdale–based crew he trusted, and Jolley had five key associates he brought from Hollywood: a set designer, a construction coordinator, a carpentry foreman,

a painter, and a special-effects man. Swanson helped Jolley and his "gang of five" find additional help. Perhaps most importantly, Swanson and Jolley had the experience necessary to deal with big egos and, in the case of *Caddyshack*, a group of mostly crazed youngsters who had received a ton of adoration and gratification for *Animal House* and/or *Saturday Night Live*. This group of mostly crazed youngsters badly needed industry veterans to keep production nonchaotic.

Stan Jolley, who is also a director and a producer and who had an impressive directorial portfolio long before The Greatest Movie Ever Made, liaised with Ramis well in advance of shooting and would go through storyboards and other details. Jolley would simply provide some basic suggestions in a nonthreatening fashion: "I'd say—look, you can do it any way you want, but here's a suggestion," Jolley says. "I wanted him to feel that he had every rein in his hands. The most important thing for him, a first-time director, was to make sure that he was ready and prepared for each day's shooting for *there are no tomorrows when you are shooting*."

Another key crew member was cinematographer Steven Larner: "The cameraman is extremely important," says Jolley. "You can have everything ready to shoot and the best sets in the world, but it will never work without a cameraman being in synch with the production designer."

Jolley got a kick out of designing the Bushwood Country Club logo, which Jolley modeled somewhat after the logo from Lakeside Golf Club in Toluca Lake, California, where Jolley grew up. Lakeside was the golf club of the stars—the likes of Bing Crosby, Bob Hope, John Wayne, Doug Fairbanks, Harold Lloyd, Ronald Reagan, Howard Hughes, Jack Carson, and Forrest Tucker.

There was some irony here, as Lakeside for many years had a restrictive membership policy—so restrictive that a certain and prominent Warner Brothers executive could not become a member, even though the studio that bore his name was just a block from the club. Frustrated studio executives and other Jewish golfers formed Hillcrest Golf Club, which for many years accepted only Jewish members (and Wang: see chapter 5). For many, many years, the most restrictive enclave was the Los Angeles Country Club; none of the members were in the motion picture business, and the club was right in the midst of all the studios.

"Also," Jolley added laughing, "to this day I have many friends at by far and away the most restrictive and exclusive golf enclave in the heart of Beverly Hills, the Los Angeles Country Club. They have an unwritten rule that no one in the "picture business" can become a member. They laugh around the club to this day; the only exception was actor Randolph Scott, who married a very wealthy socialite, and he would shrug it off with: 'I'm such a lousy actor, I don't count.'"

The original Bushwood coat of arms from the picture hangs in Stan Jolley's wet bar in one of his two guest homes he owns in the Rancho Mirage Racquet Club in the heart of Palm Springs—which has its fair share of golf courses and enclaves. Jolley, due to his fondness for tennis, slightly altered the logo so that it had a couple of tennis racquets in lieu of golf clubs and there are tennis balls in lieu of golf balls.

After each day's shooting, the crew would retire to a screening room to look at the "dailies" or, in nonmovie parlance, the raw film from the previous day. Jolley attended the first couple of the sessions but soon stopped going, as the screening room was one big bong hit. This may have been amusing for those in the room, but it led to problems when it came time to get ready for the next day and still leave time to scout an important location—like Judge Smails's home.

Jolley scoured the Fort Lauderdale area looking for a house that was stately without being too opulent. It had to look quasi-aristocratic yet appropriate for someone as pompous as Judge Smails; but most importantly, the home had to have some owners who would be at least acquiescent to filming. Jolley and Swanson found the right house and had organized for the owners to stay around for a site visit from Ramis, Kenney, and Mark Canton. The owners told Jolley and Swanson that they had a half-hour window because they were leaving for a party. Jolley gave Ramis, Kenney, and Canton the directions and the time to be there, but the threesome spent too much time in the screening room stoned and turned up ninety minutes late, according to accounts from both Jolley and Swanson, who had been making small talk trying to keep the increasingly irritated homeowners from leaving. The house was at 4531 NE 25th Avenue in Fort Lauderdale, next to Coral Ridge Country Club.

"When the bleary-eyed Ramis, Kenney, and Canton arrived and stood at the front door with their stoned, sheepish grins," says Jolley, "I threw open the front door and in front of the owners put my finger in Kenney's nose and said: 'I don't know who the hell you think you are keeping these good people waiting all this time!'"

Then, with their charm blasters on full, the assembled *Caddyshack* brain trust managed to persuade the homeowners to let them use the house. From that time, Kenney would, throughout the filming, salute Jolley and call him "the admiral." Jolley and Kenney became the best of friends and played a lot of tennis together—Kenney's father was a tennis professional and Kenney himself was a fine tennis player.

Jolley's dedication to getting the locations just right led him to persuade the producers to film the Noonan house scene before going to Florida: "I didn't feel like we were going to find a large, Chicago-style working-class Catholic family home in south Florida," says Jolley, who found such a house in Eagle Rock, California. The interior and exterior, with the fire escape, were perfect. Part of the result was that none of Danny Noonan's brothers and sisters made it past the first scenes.

Before the bulk of the cast arrived, Jolley and his crew, including his long-time construction coordinator Wally Graham, stayed in the now-famous motel immediately behind what are now the 12th green and 13th tee at Grande Oaks; the low and ugly structure is still clearly visible. Jolley, Swanson, and the crew had already been working long hours, and they were about to work harder once shooting started. After the day's work, the construction crew would make it an early night before getting up at around five in the morning. Once the hellions arrived and began partying until all hours of the night, Jolley moved the crew out of the motel. The bigger-name stars such as Ted Knight were already booked into rented homes and had drivers to take them back and forth to the sets every day.

Jolley's most significant visual achievement was the new Bushwood Country Club. In addition to the three stories that Jolley and his crew built, the work included the leaded windows, the coordinated awnings, the *porte cochère*, the mock-tudor look, and the massive deck. Today, Jolley is happiest with the way his country club looked in the night shots before and after the Fourth of July dinner dance.

There was no swimming pool at Rolling Hills. Jolley and Swanson found an abandoned swimming pool at a golf club then called the Plantation. This became the Bushwood swimming pool.

"It was a true dump, with all sorts of sludge and slime and other stuff," says Jolley. "And there were plenty of really dumpy, run-down houses around it as well."

To make it look like the elite Bushwood's swank swimming pool, Jolley's team had to clean out the pool and the surrounding area and make it fully functional; they also hid the aforementioned buildings with a surfeit of foliage, most of which is visible at the far end of the pool near its entrance.

"A big part of being a production designer revolves around being a problem solver," says Jolley. "You take situations that are not ideal and you have to make them work. And you have to do it with imagination and creativity to get it somehow up there on the screen."

Today, approaching his eightieth birthday, Stan Jolley has the energy of a twenty-something, and the only reason that he lacks the bounce is a pair of soon-to-be-replaced knees. A self-confessed workaholic, Jolley has put together a unique production company with a group of Academy Award–winning talents—in the same vein as the formation of United Artists. They have several movies, television shows, and international destination parks in the works. And there's nothing small scale about any of the plans.

Jolley and his wife, Beverley, split their time between a home and office in Los Angeles, a large triplex in Newport Beach, plus the two aforementioned guest homes in the Rancho Mirage Racquet Club in the Palm Springs area: "Someone has to do it," he laughs. "Besides, it's for our six kids and seven grandkids that are the love of our lives."

Jolley had the most influence on almost all the Florida *Caddyshack* locations and sets; he was completely responsible for finding the southern Californian locations. After Danny Noonan leaves his overcrowded family digs, he crosses the train tracks on his bicycle. This is South Pasadena; the houses he rides by are in Hancock Park. The gated official main entrance to Bushwood Country Club is actually the entrance to Bel-Air Country Club, directly off Sunset Boulevard. Jolley created the Bushwood entrance and blocked off the famous road for the shots—one of Danny Noonan cycling in and one of Judge Smails rolling the Rolls Royce through the entrance.

While a chunk of the rock-solid golf authenticity in *Caddyshack* comes from coscreenwriter Brian Doyle-Murray, a significant chunk also comes from Stan Jolley, an athlete and golfer who has played at most of the better golf courses in southern California. Jolley used a room at Rolling Hills to create the locker room, the men's bar, the judge's office, and other interiors. Jolley built "wild walls," grills, and fake windows, and brought in all the requisite accoutrements to make it look authentic and still meet the script requirements. Rolling Hills had a golf shop, but Jolley expanded it and organized it so that it looked much larger and more like the golf shop at an upscale club. Golf had played an important role in Jolley's early education. In New Jersey, before the family moved to Hollywood in 1935, Jolley's father had put an eighteen-hole miniature golf course on the top floor of an office building. It had a bar at either end, a balcony with tables, and dance floor over the golf course.

"My sister and I grew up with a putter in our hands, so I've always been able to putt pretty well," says Jolley.

Jolley also found the location for, and designed the interior of, Ty Webb's shag pad, a house they scouted in Key Biscayne, near Virginia Key, scene of the yacht club christening.

Shooting at Virginia Key took four days, but preparation was longer. Jolley found a restaurant that could serve as an exclusive yacht club; he then had to build the walkway from the restaurant/yacht club to the dock and rig it so that it could sway as if in a mild tsunami. Jolley also designed and organized the party platform into which Al Czervik's boat smashes. This was more of a technological achievement than the dock: the party pontoon had hydraulics to lift it at one end so that the partiers (and their band) could be tipped into the azure waters of Biscayne Bay. And so the partiers (and their band) would not get hurt in the process, Jolley built the guard rails out of balsa wood. It was a one-time shot with several cameras from different angles. Several takes would require that the partiers (and their band) dry off between shots. Jolley would have had to rebuild the deck as well, which would have taken a couple of days.

Another major set and location that needed to be tied down was the elegant Bushwood dining room. Ted Swanson found the ideal location at the Key Biscayne Hotel. It was later torn down in 1997.

"The toughest problem I had to design and solve on *Caddyshack* was where to build the final fairways and green for the final explosion scene," says Jolley. "One requirement for letting us use the golf course was we had to keep at least nine holes open at all times, whether during shooting or construction time, for the Rolling Hills golfing faithful. After walking the course several times, I saw only one solution. If I built the phony raised green between the first and 18th fairways on one end and I brought in the trees that were going to be rigged to blow up and fall down on the diagonal, it would look exactly like it was the 18th fairway heading to the Bushwood clubhouse. And we didn't impede the golfers hardly at all except to bring in construction trucks and materials once in a while.

"Rolling Hills is practically underneath the flight path for Fort Lauderdale International,"

says Jolley. "When the wind was coming from the sea, the planes would be landing almost right on top of us."

Just after the *Caddyshack* explosions, a pilot who was flying into the airport called the control tower to say it looked as though a plane had crashed at Rolling Hills.

One key member of Jolley's team was Wally Graham, a construction coordinator who had worked with Jolley since 1969.

"Wally was my right arm and leg, and I took him everywhere with me," says Jolley. "Somehow the brain trusts forgot him, and he should have received a credit."

Every member of *Caddyshack*'s cast and crew played a role in the immediate and subsequent success of The Greatest Movie Ever Made. In every industry and every business, there's a tendency for the rank and file and their immediate leaders to feel as though they are the ones who made something important happen and to feel that the "suits" or bureaucrats got all the love, money, and slaps on the back. The factory worker who toils on the shop floor for weeks, months, and years attaching bolts to great assemblies will almost always resent the CEO and his executive team, with their corporate jets, helicopters, big pay packets, and secretaries with huge mammaries (no other way to describe them). A lengthy discussion about the how much work those at the top of the production tree actually did is not necessary; however, those who really want to know who really made *Caddyshack* happen should watch the "19th Hole" documentary, which comes with the DVD. Listen carefully to what Jon Peters and Mark Canton say, and remember that *Caddyshack* helped to put them on the map as producers and eventually studio chiefs.

Note: Almost all of Jolley's quotes he graciously shared from the book he's working on: *Hollywood: Just a State of Mind*. After seventy years in the business, nobody could be more qualified to write such a book. He also comes from a multi-generation show business family. Jolley's grandfather owned a small traveling circus in the late nineteenth century and was one of the early people in the radio business. Stan Jolley's father, I. Stanford Jolley, was on Broadway and later became an important early Hollywood actor.

3

The Rodent (Burrowing). Attention Marmotte!

Watching ladies tee off
Morning beams of light glisten
Total death gophers.

—**poet/philosopher Basho (son of)**

The judge arrives. The superintendent and his associate staff. Carl plays with his ball washer. The ladies tee off. The death sentence.

THE gopher discovery scene introduces the two characters who are perhaps the most important to the various plot lines: Judge Elihu Smails and the gopher. It's another scene that spans California and Florida; the exact split comes just after the 14th flag comes down and Smails gets out of the car. One minute, he's in California moving toward the fairway; the next he's in the fairway, only he's in Fort Lauderdale looking for Sandy McFiddish, the sweaty, red-faced Scottish greenskeeper who is dressed like he's in Scotland in late January.

We also meet Carl Spackler, the assistant greenskeeper. We "meet" him as he's mock-masturbating and ogling a group of lady golfers who are not exactly in the first flush of youth, despite the classic "girls gone wild in the late '70s/early '80s" apparel.

After watching the ladies tee off, Carl gets the plum job of killing all the gophers, a plot theme that keeps going through the movie and even keeps the movie going. What would *Caddyshack* be without Carl and the gopher?

Once Carl gets through the English/Scottish language barrier, the death to gopher plot line is off and running.

The scene begins with the second and final shot of the entrance to Bushwood Country Club—California campus. It's the entrance to the famous Bel-Air Country Club in Los Angeles.

Scene time line: 00:07:49–00:09:58.
Judge Elihu Smails arrives. We meet Carl.

In the French subtitles, the gopher is called *Une Marmotte*. This is not necessarily an indica-tion that the gopher is female. A male *marmotte* is still *la marmotte*. A marmotte d'Amérique has several translations, including groundhog and woodchuck, but a marmotte is a marmot, the hardy mountain beast. There is no direct translation for gopher. In the Spanish subtitles, the gopher is a *topo*. There's a more direct translation for gopher—*ardilla terrestre*. A *topo* is a mole, which is the animal originally cast in the movie. However, the Spanish phrase *más ciego que un topo* translates to "as blind as a bat."

In the French version, Sandy McFiddish has a solid, run-of-the-mill, workaday French accent.

Carl talks about Mrs. Crane. It sounds a little like "Mrs. Craig." The type of ball washer that Carl uses costs around $350, and that's without the stand, which is another $150. Then there's that special cleaning goop that costs $100 for a case of four large bottles. Those wishing to save money on the goop element can choose a box of lemon-scented ball-washer detergent tablets. The ball washer that Carl is using is a version of the Par Aide King Ball Washer that retails for $368.

The amusing thing about Sandy is that "gopher" is how a Scotsman would actually say "golfer."

The second-best-dressed male golfer appears in the scene, just having teed off in the background as Sandy McFiddish berates Carl. The gentleman is wearing a yellow cardigan, black shirt, and red trousers. In fact, the Bushwood golfers are a nattily dressed lot, specializing in plaid and garish trousers and skirts.

John Dykstra—The Man behind the Gopher

The most decorated yet least famous member of the *Caddyshack* team is John Dykstra, a special effects specialist. The credits list him as the special effects supervisor. His team created the entire world of the gopher, including explosions, fire and floods in the tunnels, plus the tunneling. Dykstra has won two Oscars: one in 2005 for *Spider-Man 2*, the other in 1978 for *Star Wars*. He earned three additional nominations, including one in 1980 for *Star Trek: The Motion Picture*, and he received an Oscar for the visual effects on *Spiderman 2*. His resume includes numerous additional prizes and awards, although none, surprisingly, for his work in The Greatest Movie Ever Made. Other movies in which Dykstra has been involved include:

- *Silent Running*
- *Firefox*
- *Batman Forever*
- *Batman and Robin*
- *Avalanche Express*
- *Stuart Little*
- *Spider-Man*

With George Lucas and Gary Kurtz, Dykstra formed the famous Industrial Light and Magic company. He also produced all the special effects for the TV series *Battlestar Galactica* in 1978. By the time he worked on *Caddyshack*, he was working for the newly formed special effects company Apogee. Today, he is in development on a project that he will direct for Walden Media. This interview took place in mid-January 2006.

BOOK OF CADDYSHACK: You were the mind behind the gopher. . . .

JOHN DYKSTRA: I came into the film, as was the custom in those days, after the producers and director had shot most of the principal photography. They were really getting into the editing of the film and were making decisions about what the movie needed to finish the film off, so to speak, and give them the entire package they wanted.

They worked on a very tight schedule in Florida. I believe they worked at a country club that had been decommissioned. They were going to turn that property into condos or something of value. During the editing process, they discovered that there was a huge amount of effort put into each of the facets of the movie, but that things

weren't all going in the same direction at the same time. So they created a new character to tie all this great stuff together. The gopher was that character.

When they filmed the movie originally, they had a hand puppet gopher and the hand puppet gopher is still in the film. I'm trying to remember where he was. There's one shot of the hand puppet gopher coming out of a hole, but I may be wrong about that. It's only been twenty-six years! I know at one point I saw a cut which the hand puppet gopher was still in. In fact, I think the gopher that shows up in the advertising campaign is the hand puppet gopher.

At any rate, they discovered there was an opportunity to expand the role, so they came to us as we were going to do the visual effects for the film. There were some additional things they wanted to do with the explosions and various and sundry things. But the focus was in fact the gopher. So we started by working with head of the model shop at Apogee, Grant McCune, and a model maker/puppeteer named Joe Garlington; we set out to design and build this gopher. Everyone who was involved with this really put on their creative shoes. We worked on this character from a traditional puppeting point of view, with a head separate from the shoulders and a body that was semirigid so we could make his little chest move in and up and create motion for his arms. Joe was really seminal in the design of the puppet; he was the one who really got it to perform.

Because the golf course was no longer, we built a piece of golf course, basically a flat top trailer that we covered with dirt, contoured, and then planted with sod. Then we had to grow it out in the parking lot so the sod would all come together and look contiguous, and that trailer was the one we used when we worked at the golf course where we shot most of the gopher material—but I don't think it was Industry Hills. The course where we worked when we did the gopher work was actually in Encino—there's a country club there. We made a deal with them to access certain parts of the course. So we brought our trailer in, parked it in the foreground, and used their country club as the background.

BOC: So it's not Industry Hills.

JD: I can't guarantee that Industry Hills wasn't used for some pickup work, but Industry Hills was not the name of the country club where we worked. We shot the gopher material at a private club in Encino. In fact, we not only used that club for backgrounds for our trailer, we also set up some guys on the golf course itself. Where you see the gopher tunneling into the ground using what we call runnels—that was all dressed into golf course elements at that country club. We also created a flag that wiggles and goes down into the ground. All of those kinds of things were gags we worked out either using the golf course trailer or a small area at the golf club. We used a practice green a couple of times or a second green on a hole where they had two greens.

And then we built the tunnel—for all the bits with the water and the fire and all of that. In one instance, we had a huge dump tank that dumped what could have been ten thousand gallons of water, something like that, to create the shot where the hose comes down the hole and the gopher runs through the tunnel.

The tunnel had only three walls so that the camera could follow the gopher. Then we used natural gas canisters to create the scene where fire comes raging through the tunnel.

One of the things that was a great deal of fun for us was getting the gopher to dance—and dance with great personality. Grant and I and a couple of other guys sat down, and we had a piano and guitars at the job and we made up some basic music tracks so that Joe and the other puppeteers could get the gopher to dance. Working up some of the dance steps and getting him to perform with some personality was great fun. Getting him to dance is one of the things that makes the character endearing.

BOC: Did you give it a name?
JD: Gopher.

BOC: Just Gopher?
JD: I'm sure Joe had other names, some of which were potentially unprintable. He was Gopher for the most part.

BOC: How did you get the assignment?
JD: I tried to remember who it was I spoke with initially. John Peters was the executive producer, and I spoke with him over the course of the production a couple of times. I talked with Harold Ramis early on. Don MacDonald [associate producer] was the one who spent the most time with us while we were doing the work with the gopher. He was often in the editing room; Doug Kenney and John Peters were doing other movies. So we didn't see too much of them, except when we were at a stage when it was OK to show them something. But Don MacDonald was around a lot.

BOC: Harold Ramis wasn't there a huge amount?
JD: He was, but here's the trick. It takes time to bring a character or an effect to a level at which you're ready to show it. You can make the director anxious if you show him something that's not ready or still in a kind of rough draft form. So you work out a routine, and you polish the performance as best you can in order to give them several different versions so that they

have options—but you want them selecting from something that is polished as opposed to something in raw form.

Harold would give us input in regard to what he wanted to do, and he would see videotapes and give us feedback, so we were working with him closely, but not physically on site that much.

BOC: What was your initial reaction when these well-known producers came to you and asked you to make a dancing gopher?
JD: You know, it's funny. Responding to some of the requests can put you in a bit of a quandary. Invariably in a script, someone would write "unlike anything you've ever seen before," and it isn't unusual for someone to come to you and say "we don't know what it is we're looking for but we'd like you to make something nobody has ever seen before." So a request as simple as "can you make us a puppet that's a gopher" was actually kind of refreshing. As a result, we knew pretty much what we needed to do, and we knew that we needed to create a design that had a persona. It needed to look enough like a gopher and

not be a cartoon character. But it had to have personality.

BOC: It has great character.
JD: That really is kudos to the puppeteers and the people who created the puppet initially. It initially had quite a bit of stuff in terms of facial features that could be conformed. Most rodents are monocular, which means they have eyes on opposite sides of the head, so we had to bring the two eyes together on the front of the head without making it look too human—that was a good trick, too. Designers contributed to its anti-symmetric feel. And Joe and other puppeteers did a terrific job of giving it the physical traits. It really comes down to not so much a broad range of performance, but specific personality types in the body language of the character.

If you'll notice, he rolls his shoulders when he walks and he rolls his shoulders when he dances. And that comes from a synchronization of the movement of the device which is holding the puppet at the bottom in conjunction with the movement of the arms.

BOC: Are you a golfer?
JD: I played at golf once, but I'm not a golfer.

BOC: When did you first see *Caddyshack*?
JD: I saw it several times over the course of the job as we were putting the gopher elements together. It was perfect, it's so funny; it was terrific to be working on a film as contemporary as it was. This was *Saturday Night Live*; this was all of the comedy that was current at the time. The quality and the presentation and the deliveries were all signature pieces for the people who were in the movie. It was fun to be in a movie that was so hip.

BOC: Did people ask you about the gopher?
JD: People don't necessarily know that I did *Caddyshack*. And if I'm talking to someone about *Caddyshack*, if they see it on my credit list, they ask: "What did you do?" I go: "We did the gopher." They say: "The gopher—that was my favorite part." I'm sure it would be for each of the individuals on the movie if someone spoke with them that whatever they did was their favorite part. But I do get that, and it's sort of fun. It's generally based on performance; it isn't so much the creation of an illusion, it's the creation of a character. It was a lot more creative than a lot of stuff we were doing at that time—which was more of an issue of engineering.

BOC: How long did it take you to build Gopher? Was there just one?
JD: There was more than one. I don't believe we ever finished two complete gophers, meaning two versions of the same gopher to do the exact same stuff. For running sequences, we used the one that had less performance characteristics in his head because the head was so fragile. For the dancing sequences and the close-ups, we had the super trick version of the gopher, with all his bells and whistles. There were several gophers; they were not all the same, but designed and built for specific purposes.

There wasn't a huge amount of money involved in this production, so the idea of building a second gopher if you didn't need it didn't make much sense. We were also in a production situation, shooting various exteriors with a very small crew, so if we had a gopher failure, it wasn't a big deal for us to shut down long enough to get him repaired. It wasn't like going on a set where you're working in $100,000 or $200,000 days and every split second is burning money at an outrageous rate. So it was more leisurely, and I believe that contributed to how much fun we had with the gopher.

If you watch a film, the personality of the production usually comes through. Doesn't matter whether the film is drama or comedy. The energy level of the performances on screen and all the things that contributed to the making of the movie sort of reflect how the crew felt about what they were doing. And we were having a great time doing *Caddyshack*, and I think that came through in the work itself.

BOC: Looks like it was fun to do the gopher scenes.
JD: Oh yeah, it was a kick.

BOC: Is it true the sounds are dolphin sounds?
JD: I can't prove or disprove that, because there were a variety of sounds used. I don't know about the dolphin sounds.

BOC: How did you actually get the gopher burrowing through greens and bits of golf courses?
JD: It's very straightforward. We would dig a trench, determine the path we wanted the gopher to follow, and then we would lay a piece of vinyl tube—about three inches in diameter—in the trench all collapsed. And then we had a piece of strong fishing line that went through the tube, and then into the tube where the burrowing was to start; we attached this to a compressor or tank of compressed air.

The line, which went through the tube, was attached to a tennis ball. So when we wanted the runnel to go across the green or across wherever it went, we rolled the camera, then we triggered the air and had somebody yank on the string. So the ball would come through the tube, lifting the dirt, which had been dressed back in on top of the flat tube, thus lifting the dirt; then the air would follow behind the ball, keeping the tube inflated so that the dirt didn't fall back in. If you made the curves too sharp, the trench tended to want to make it a straight line. Our crew members overcame those problems.

BOC: Did you get to meet any of the cast members?
JD: Yeah, briefly, but it was just by passing one another in the editing room or in the production offices. We didn't do anything with any of the live actors. The live actors were all onto other projects by the time we were busy shooting the gopher.

BOC: Did you study gophers?
JD: Oh yes. We had pictures of gophers, chipmunks, you name it. The trick was to find the cutest and most charming attributes. There was a lot of effort put into the fur—I believe it was rabbit fur. We went through a whole series of tests to get the right hair color with the dark roots and the light tops—we did all of this stuff to give him the real contrast that a real wild animal has.

BOC: What was the time line?
JD: I tend to believe it was about six months from the very beginning to completion. But it might have been four. It took us about a month to create the character and probably another month to do the photography. And then another month beyond that to do some of the other stuff that had to be done. So it was about three or four months, but gee whiz, it's such a long time ago!

BOC: What is *Caddyshack* about?
JD: (Laughs) What is *Caddyshack* about? You know, it's funny. I'm sure if you come from a golf culture, it has significantly greater ramifications. My feeling was that *Caddyshack* was about the whole class structure that country clubs exemplify. And I think to a great extent it was saying the more tight-assed you are, the less fun you have. It seems to me that the people who were the most rigid were the ones with the most problems. So much went on in that film. So many disparate groups were working on it at the same time—it's pretty miraculous how well it fit together in the end.

BOC: Does it surprise you that *Caddyshack*, which is chaos on film really, endured and is attracting a new generation of fans?

JD: It's a fun movie; it's improv on film, and I think that sets it apart. Other films I've worked on have improv as such a small component; this movie to me seemed almost all improvisation. If you ask somebody who hasn't made a movie that they have a choice between making a film totally scripted and designed and story boarded or a film where each day you'd have to come up with new relationships for the characters because the people who were performing those characters were making them up as they work, everybody would choose the structure, because you'd have to be a genius to make the other sort work. I guess that makes Harold Ramis a genius.

All of the people who were in the film did a terrific job of not eating the scenery, so to speak. Each of the people made their performance appropriate to the character, but made it exceptional. Often what you find in a movie like this is each guy is trying to outperform the other guy. There was a certain kind of consistency thanks to

Harold, but also thanks to the people that were performers in the movie.

The real issue is it was a lark for the people making the movie in the sense that it was done with a real sense of enjoyment. As a result, that showed up on the screen.

Additional artists listed under special effects:

- Rocco Gioffre, matte painter
- Robert Shepherd, effects production supervisor
- Michael Douglas Middleton, visual effects still photographer
- Denise Shurtleff, Apogee crew member

As Smails rolls up the road in the Rolls, a man with a white shirt and red pants darts behind a tree.

"Do you know what gophers can do to a golf course?"

Sandy McFiddish, the greenskeeper, fudges the answer by saying that the gophers are tunneling in from the construction site "over yonder," and thus the Czervik/Smails battle begins. In a lovely moment of dramatic irony, the judge tells McFiddish to eradicate all the gophers. Careful what you ask for, judge, you might just get it—and it might cost you a few pennies.

In the early script, Sandy McFiddish chases a mole—just briefly. There is absolutely no mention of a gopher.

In the gopher world, the "real" gopher is the pocket gopher—about the scale of a rat, as short as five inches and as long as fourteen inches. Pocket gophers spend most of the time underground, munching on roots. Gophers let the world know where the burrow lies because they leave holes in the ground and mounds of dirt—a superintendent on a golf course only has to connect the dots to find the line of the burrow. It's less complicated, apparently, than reading a putt. Those intent on ridding the golf course of the pest need not resort to dynamite or plastic explosives fashioned into various animal shapes. Today's gopher eradication expert places commercial-grade gopher baits in the burrows with the help of a tube or rod that, of course, penetrates into the burrow. If the baits fail to work, then gopher traps may work.

In the computer world, a gopher is a special system that sorts and displays files on servers. Students at the University of Minnesota, who developed the code, or program, or whatever it's actually called, named it "gopher" because the Golden Gopher is the official mascot of the university. If you're inclined to search global indexes of resources stored in gopher systems, you can use two additional systems—Jughead and Veronica.

Putting the hat aside, Sandy McFiddish is not necessarily dressed like a Scottish greenskeeper, but he's close. He looks much more like a Scottish farmer going down to the pub for a quick pint after a hard day digging for turnips in late February.

It may initially seem as though there are two Rolls Royces in the movie, but there are actually three, according to Rolls Royce expert Malcolm Bobbitt, author of *Rolls-Royce Silver Shadow and Bentley T-Series*, *Rolls-Royce Silver Shadow Bentley T-Series Camargue & Corniche*, and numerous other car-related books. Judge Smails drives two different brown cars. The RR that appears initially is a "first series" Silver Shadow. Bobbitt says that "bumpers with the overriders are the giveaway."

Al Czervik's car is a coach-built Silver Cloud III drophead coupe. It was a Mulliner Park Ward design. The clue: the slanting twin headlamps.

"All other Silver Cloud IIIs and Bentley S3s have straight twin lamps," adds Bobbitt.

The other brown Rolls Royce looks like the first one that Judge Smails drives, but it's a long-wheelbase Silver Shadow from the first series, the second series being known as Silver Wraith IIs.

"The bumpers are again the clue here," Bobbitt concludes.

Rolls Royce produced the Silver Shadow from 1965 to 1977, building just over twenty thousand. Depending on condition and other factors, a Silver Shadow averages around $15,000.

The fourth golf swing in *Caddyshack* belongs to the lady who might be Mrs. Crane—at least she's the woman in Mrs. Crane's group. Dave Vandeventer, head PGA golf professional at Piney Point in Norwood, North Carolina, describes the swing thus.

"In the set up, it looks like she's sitting on a stool with her knees so bent. But she straightens up her posture. Her shoulders are open at address.

She takes her swing back to a fairly good position at the top, although her shoulders stop moving and her arms get a bit 'lifty' as she tries to get a bit more power. She has also taken the club a little bit inside. Her move from the top is the infamous 'chopping wood' move—this probably comes from those shoulders being open at address. She 'casts' the club early in the downswing, which means her wrists unhinge early, so she loses power even though she thinks that she's getting more power from the wood chopping motion. There is little or no extension going through the ball, but she ends up in a solid finish with great balance. But the swing probably leads to a low slice."

Note that the golfer initially forgets her tee.

Mrs. Crane may well be the lady with the green skirt who is just leaving the tee when we first meet Carl; she's the one with the gray hair, green skirt, and large mammary glands (no other way to describe them). She must have hit a great shot, as she's got a whopping smile on her face.

Sandy calls Carl a "great git," which is exactly something a Scotsman might say, periodically.

I like the various golfers who meander in and out of the background behind Carl, then Carl and Sandy. That's the type of background action that adds to the authenticity of the movie.

Why would Carl have a scythe stuck in an oak tree? That's a good question, but every assistant greenskeeper has a scythe or two at all times—right?

Note the weather vane on top of the clubhouse.

It's here that the movie departs from the early script—not just syntactically. Scene three in the original screenplay features about six caddies getting off a bus and coming to work at Bushwood; the caddies are spirited and rambunctious. Latin and black maids and others arrive with the caddies. The scene in the script introduces Tony D'Annunzio and his brothers, Angie and Joey. The script describes Tony as "nineteen, a tough-looking, inner-city kid with disco haircut and a cigarette dangling negligently from his lips."

Tony gives one of the maids, Maria, a hard time about a sexual encounter, saying, "You know, there's a law if you screw an Italian, you're an automatic citizen." Two additional caddies get in the action: Motormouth, a "fast-talking, eighteen-year-old class clown," and Goofy, a "gawky, bespectacled sixteen year old." Only Motormouth made the cut. Slightly later in the scene, the caddies play a trick on Dr. Beeper; a version of this scene made it into the television version. The caddies, led by Tony D'Annunzio, fake being hit by Dr. Beeper's "black Porsche Turbo Carrera." In the script, we learn Dr. Beeper's first name: Blaine. The early script describes him

as a "rich, conceited, big-city surgeon." There's a pretty good crack at this point in the script. Joey D'Annunzio fakes being hit by the car; Dr. Beeper rushes out to see if the boy is alive, but by the time the doctor is out of the car with his kit, all the caddies have vanished. Dr. Beeper smashes his bag against the car and "hears a $6,000 tinkle of broken glass and instruments."

How exactly a filmmaker gets across a "$6,000 tinkle" is a bit of mystery, but the effort would have been interesting.

Would *Caddyshack* have been an "OK" movie without Ted Knight? Possibly. But would *Caddyshack* have been so massively successful and memorable without the great man? Would *Caddyshack* have been The Greatest Movie Ever Made without Ted Knight? There's no way. Every actor in *Caddyshack* contributes, but Ted Knight is *the man*. His portrayal of the uptight judge is immortal, rock solid, perfectly consistent, and beautifully comic. Every plot channel revolves around the judge: gopher, ambitious caddy, and "snobs versus slobs." All three story lines merge at the final scene, and that scene would not work without Ted Knight, who provides perhaps the most memorable moment with his "Billy Barroo" and lucky putt. Even his final scene, running away from Moose and Rocco, is perfect: the uptight closet deadbeat running away from Rodney's goons.

The writers gave Knight some great lines, and he delivers them flawlessly. Of all the actors and characters, Knight sticks the most closely to the script; there's little improvisation. But which *Caddyshack* fan cannot pass the Frescas in the supermarket and at least think: "How 'bout a Fresca?" But it's Ted Knight's ever-changing facial expressions that make his performance so superb. The portfolio of said judicial visages:

1. Preround serenity
2. Pure shock
3. Sour indignation
4. Petulant indignation
5. Open-mouthed aghastness
6. Military bombast

Ted Knight played Judge Elihu Smails. Off screen, he and Rodney Dangerfield were not the best of mates.

(Warner/Orion/The Kobal Collection)

7. Judicial rage
8. Spanish Inquisition
9. Here comes a lawsuit (from me)
10. Thunderstorm approaching
11. Two-foot-putt-missed horror
12. Two-foot-putt-missed angst
13. Two-foot-putt-missed shock
14. Mild irritation
15. Serious irritation
16. Moderate irritation
17. Hemorrhoidal irritation
18. Instructional bombast
19. Bossy annoyance
20. Happy curiosity
21. Jocular sincerity
22. Pure snobbery
23. Haberdasher-induced coyness
24. Standard irritation
25. Normal annoyance
26. Testicular bull's-eye
27. Joyous welcome
28. Familiar rage
29. Golfish concentration
30. Golfish indignation
31. Constipated clownishness

32. Self-congratulatory bonhomie
33. Wide-eyed semishock
34. Contrived jocularity
35. Muted shock
36. Pure rage-fueled embarrassment
37. Pure embarrassment-fueled rage
38. Fear/shock/horror
39. Fibbing indignation
40. Quasi-apoplectic apology
41. Get out of jail free card
42. I want to help young people
43. Big tip coming
44. Meat-carving concentration
45. Full-bore bore
46. Irritated recognition
47. Pre-eruption
48. Eruption
49. Posteruption
50. Puffed chest irritation
51. Old-timers dance-floor disco love
52. Pure aghastness
53. Snobby rage
54. Congratulatory bonhomie
55. Touchdown
56. Invitational bonhomie
57. Yacht club gaiety
58. Scatological shock
59. Nautical bonhomie
60. Metered happiness
61. Poetic grace
62. Waspish joke-telling
63. Lear-like tragedy
64. Jack Nicholson
65. Confidential man-to-man
66. Sacred pomposity
67. Pure pomposity
68. Juicy relief
69. Know-it-all mentoring
70. Hollow reminiscing
71. Corn-cob-up-the-xxxx insincerity
72. Country-club back slapping
73. Puzzled amazement
74. Blood pressure up
75. Seconds out—round one
76. Just heard a silly statement
77. Leering
78. Snobbish insincerity
79. Boorish ambivalence

80. Cheat on the run
81. Inglorious winner
82. Orbiting space trooper
83. Legal harrumphing
84. Clownish repetition
85. Illicit joy
86. Veiled angst
87. Thin reverence
88. Prayerful reverence
89. Happy bombast
90. Dead air
91. Giddy insouciance
92. Structural vanity
93. Stressful vindication
94. Boyish brief uncertainty
95. Gilded sarcasm
96. Fierce resistance
97. Lawyer looking at lawsuit

To boot, Knight even developed a special Judge Smails "seven iron up the keister" gait/waddle that he maintains throughout the movie. Knight moves from expression to expression effortlessly; the best example comes in the "How 'bout a Fresca?" scene, where Knight seamlessly moves through the bulk of his facial repertoire. It's award-winning stuff, yet the five actors who got the nod for best actor Oscar for 1980 movies were Robert De Niro (*Raging Bull*), Robert Duvall (*The Great Santini*), John Hurt (*The Elephant Man*), Jack Lemmon (*Tribute*), and Peter O'Toole (*The Stunt Man*). Boxing fans might like *Raging Bull*, but golfers like *Caddyshack* and Ted Knight more than any of the above. De Niro got the nod for the Oscar. Best picture that year was *Ordinary People*, and best costume design was for *Tess*. Made for around $6 million, *Ordinary People* grossed a respectable $56 million, but it's a late '70s chick flick. The tag line: "Some films you watch, others you feel." Compare that with the *Caddyshack* tag lines, and it's easy to understand why nobody cares about *Ordinary People* (except director Robert Redford) and everyone (or every golfer) cares deeply about The Greatest Movie Ever Made.

- At last, a comedy that bites!
- Some people just don't belong.

- The snobs against the slobs!
- Playing a round of golf at the Bushwood Club isn't just confined to the golf course!
- At last, a comedy with balls!

Ted Knight failed to receive the nomination he so richly deserved. *Caddyshack* received zero nominations for anything that year, although Michael O'Keefe was in the mix for best supporting actor for his pre-*Caddyshack* work in *The Great Santini*. Timothy Hutton won best supporter for his surely sizzling work in *Ordinary People*. *Caddyshack* never won any awards, yet it's The Greatest Movie Ever Made, which tells us something about awards and the people who award the awards.

When *Caddyshack* first hit the big screen, Knight was best known for his role in the *Mary Tyler Moore Show*. He played the news anchor Ted Baxter in a series that lasted eight seasons, from 1970 to 1977, and 168 episodes. The show won numerous awards. Knight won two Emmys, in 1973 and 1976, for his Ted Baxter role. He earned two Golden Globe nominations for the same work.

In the series, one of Knight's idiosyncrasies was mispronouncing the names of certain countries. The newscast that Baxter anchored was consistently ranked at the bottom of the ratings. Initially, Knight's character was serious and self-absorbed, but Knight persuaded the writers to open Ted Baxter up and give him more latitude—and comedic opportunities.

After the *MTM Show*, Knight kept his mojo going, primarily with TV projects, including appearances in *The Love Boat, Japan Cruise, Pride of the Pacific, Too Close for Comfort*, and his very own *The Ted Knight Show*—about Roger Dennis (Ted Knight), who runs Dennis Escorts in New York City. The show lasted just six weeks. *Too Close for Comfort*, about a couple of parents who live right next door to their grown daughters, was more successful and ran for six seasons. Knight also hosted an episode of *Saturday Night Live* in 1979. Desmond Child was the musical guest, and Andy Kaufman appeared as well. The *SNL* cast at the time included Dan Aykroyd, John Belushi, Jane Curtin, Bill Murray, and Brian Doyle-Murray. The episode aired on December 22.

Caddyshack would be Ted Knight's final movie. Prior to the *MTM Show*, Knight appeared in several movies, including *MASH*, *Anatomy of a Crime*, *Young Dillinger*, *The Candidate*, *The Pigeon That Took Rome*, *Cry for Happy*, *Key Witness*, and *Psycho*. Ironically, Knight also appeared in *Hitler*, a 1962 treatment of the dictator's story. In 1944–1945, Knight played a part in Hitler's downfall; Knight was a soldier, earned five bronze stars, and was one of the first troops to enter Berlin. But Knight never wanted to talk about war, says Bill Jerome, creator of the Ted Knight Web site (billjerome.com/tedknight). Jerome grew up in the same Connecticut town (Terryville) as Knight, and Jerome's grandmother grew up next to Knight. Jerome's interest in Knight originated from Terryville links. But the spark became something more when Jerome started to work for the same ABC Albany affiliate where Knight started his career, and in the WTEN basement Jerome found numerous photos and artifacts. At the station, Knight played several roles, including "Windy Knight," a bearded Western type who introduced cowboy movies. In the early 1970s, Knight returned to the Albany station to host charity telethons with Gavin MacLeod; during those appearances, Knight would read the news in the Ted Baxter style.

Knight even produced an LP titled *Hi Guys* (1975; Ranwood Records). It features a photo of the *MTM* Knight adjusting his tie. Songs (in order):

- "Those Oldies But Goodies Remind Me of You"
- "The Mermaid"
- "Chick-A-Boom"
- "Itsy Bitsy Teenie Weenie Yellow Polka Dot Bikini"
- "May the Bird of Paradise Fly Up Your Nose"
- "Male Chauvinist Pig"
- "Mr. Custer"
- "Who Put the Bomp?"
- "The Cover of the (Rolling Stone)"
- "A Man Who Used to Be"
- "Hi Guys"
- "I'm In Love with Barbara Walters"
- "Blueberry Hill"

The well-produced album has its amusing moments, especially in the title song. Knight's singing voice is such an acquired taste that the work is best described as Judge Smails's Criminal Record. When he simply uses his regular voice, or a version of it, it's much better. The liner notes, from KIIS radio's Charlie Tuna, are worth the price of admission. From said liner notes:

"Living an affluent Southern California lifestyle, Ted Knight finds time between TV and recordings to walk his pet rock 'Hudson,' who Ted has successfully attack-trained to answer his fan mail whenever the opportunity presents itself. When you finally decide to stop paper training your pet with the album cover and play the record, 'Hi Guys' has thirteen heavy hits featuring everything from ballads to bomp. Ted cautioned the music industry after hearing the first playback of the enclosed LP, 'Look out, Sinatra! Watch it Springsteen!' So go ahead, live dangerously, and put the album on the turntable. At least after hearing both sides, you'll be able to accept the fact that life does exist elsewhere in the Universe because Ted Knight can't be all that much a Superior Being."

In the bottom right-hand corner of the back of the album cover, there's an address for the Ted Knight Fan Club: 18107 Sherman Way, Reseda, California, 91335.

"My grandmother always said that Knight was a really nice guy," says Jerome. "He was always making jokes and being funny—and that was before going into acting. In the winter, he would happily shovel snow for people and open frozen car door locks with a lighter."

When he came back from Europe after the war, Knight started his acting career at the Randall School of Dramatic Arts in Hartford. He then had a variety of jobs, including disk jockey, announcer, and singer, and he eventually created his own television show for a station in Providence, Rhode Island. He also studied at the American Theater Wing in New York.

Terryville was home to numerous Polish immigrants. Knight's given name was Tedeus Wladyslaw Konopka. On June 12, 1976, the town recognized Knight with a five-hundred-person dinner. Knight was the grand marshal of the town's bicentennial parade. The feelings of many townspeople about Knight were summarized at the testimonial dinner Saturday night by Helen Grabowski, chairwoman of the event, who said, "Hearts swell with pride . . . to welcome back our home-town boy made good." Three times Knight was given a standing ovation by the crowd of more than five hundred who dressed in their finery to honor him. At one point, he curtailed his comments because he was simply overcome with emotion.

The Hartford Courant put the number of attendees at fifty thousand. It wasn't a free lunch for Knight, who had a very important duty at the event: "After the parade, Knight helped judge 27 contestants in the beard-growing contest. Hundreds of onlookers gathered around the reviewing stand in Baldwin Park as the celebrity presented certificates to the winners. . . . Dr. Joseph Rich won the best beard and mustache prize, while Gerald Doty was judged to have the best Lincoln-type beard. Other winners were Andrew DellaVechia, best mustache; Edward Kamens, Van Dyke; Armand Scoville, best bushy beard; and Gerald Williams, best connected sideburns and moustache."

In the January 3, 1981, edition of *TV Guide*, fellow actor and *MTM* star Ed Asner said: "Ted is refreshing, capricious, amazingly honest and an occasional pain in the behind. He is one of the biggest talents—bright, witty and he can charm the pants off you. We had violent arguments and he can be an s.o.b., but he was always awfully easy to forgive. He taught me so much about humor and I still find myself imitating him. I don't know how many dinners we had together and I remember two things about all of them. He was tons of fun and I always got the check."

Ted Knight was born on December 7, 1923. He died in 1986 from cancer at age sixty-two, after battling the disease for several years.

Knight was raised at 18 Allen Street in Terryville. His father was a Polish immigrant who became a bartender but died when Knight was young. Knight graduated from Terryville High

School in 1943 and entered service. A local resident who knew Knight told *The Bristol Press* that even though Knight's brothers caddied, Knight hated golf. At Knight's funeral, close to two hundred friends and family attended the memorial mass that took place at St. Casimir Church on 19 Allen Street; Knight had been baptized in the same church. The week before, a mass for Knight had taken place in California. Telegrams arrived from Ronald and Nancy Reagan and Walter Cronkite. During the 1960s, when Knight was busy with films, appearing mostly as a bit player, he was equally busy with television work. He appeared in *Gunsmoke*, *Gomer Pyle*, *Alfred Hitchcock Presents*, *Get Smart*, and numerous other shows.

Soon after Knight's death, his hometown named a bridge after him. Originally opened as the Canal Street Bridge, it is now named the Ted Knight Memorial Bridge, and it spans the Pequabuck River. Knight also lives on in Australia, where a group of golfers have gathered each year since 1986 in Melbourne in the Australian summer for the Ted Knight Memorial Gof Invitational.

"We are a bunch of hack golfers who are never short of an excuse to get together, drink beer, and parrot *Caddyshack* lines to each other," says organizer Val Pope. From the tournament's Web site (geocities.com/tedknightmemorial): "Established way back in 1986, after Bob Sandford had watched the movie *Caddyshack* 99 times . . . yes, that's right, 99 times! Ted Knight was, of course, cranky old Judge Smails in that ripper of a Golf movie, and when he died on Tuesday, August 26, 1986 . . . a Golf game was arranged, but not any old tournament . . . our very own tournament . . . The Ted Knight Memorial Invitational!!! Co-founder Val Pope, who has only watched the film a pathetic 40 times, has hosted all 19? tournaments with Bobby . . . we look forward to the next one . . . join us if you dare. . . ."

The "Gof" in lieu of "Golf" is intentional—that's how Judge Smails, in yet another pique of total ignorance and snob-induced stupidity, describes how the Scots call the game they invented: "They invented the game there [Scotland], you know, except they call it GOF without the 'L' as we do."

This shows deep, deep appreciation for *Caddyshack*. It's also taking the piss out of the Scots, as Australians never need an invitation to have a go at anyone who isn't Australian. Further from the Ted Knight Memorial Web site: "Co-founders Bob Sandford and Val Pope have hosted 19 consecutive annual tournaments, and in that time we have had 68 different golfers turn up to play 324 rounds of Gof. As well as lots and lots of golf, we have drunk so much beer that we have lost count! (that's why we have to start over again, every year!!!)."

The event currently takes place at Elsternwick Public Golf Course in Melbourne. The organizers call the event "Gof's most prestigious tournament," yet it's clear that the tournament comprises some of the worst golf played in Australia—quite an achievement. For a full list of winners and contestants, see the appendix. On the championship's Web site, Val Pope analyzes the golf swings of the various contestants: "From his swing I can state that Barry is a chain-smoking closet commy who wears women's undies and constantly breaks wind." And:

"Bobby Tatts, Golfer, Babysitter, Assassin, you name it, this man can do it all . . . hey what are you doing Sunday? How'd you like to mow my lawn?"

Ted Knight rests in peace in Forest Lawn Cemetery, Glendale, California.

Ron Green Sr. is a golf writer who has spent more than fifty years covering the game, primarily for the *Charlotte News* and the *Charlotte Observer*. He is the author of several books, including *Shouting at Amen Corner*, which is a compilation of more than forty-five years of coverage of the Augusta Masters. He clearly remembers what it was like when *Caddyshack* first came out in 1980.

"Everyone was talking about it at the golf course," he says. "And a lot of people started using the lines right away. The person who wrote it clearly knew the game, and so it just struck a chord with golfers."

To Green and friends at Cedarwood Country Club in Charlotte, North Carolina, *Caddyshack*

90

presented any number of recognizable figures. But, more importantly, the movie helped (and helps) everyone take themselves a little less seriously.

"So many golf movies take themselves so seriously," adds Green. "*Caddyshack* was just plain silly."

Thomas Carlin, who plays Sandy McFiddish, was an accomplished character actor, often appearing on Broadway. Like Albert Salmi, Carlin appeared frequently in numerous shows in the nascent stages of American television. He died at age sixty-two from heart failure.

Films in which Carlin appeared include:

- *One Good Cop*
- *Family Business*
- *The Pope of Greenwich Village*
- *Fort Apache the Bronx*

Caddyshack was Carlin's most successful movie commercially. Carlin also appeared in several TV shows and movies, including *Law and Order*, *Route 66*, *The Nurses*, and *The Alcoa Hour*. There's a significant gap in Carlin's career from 1964 to 1980. Carlin and his wife, accomplished actress Frances Sternhagen, had six children. Sternhagen and Carlin married in 1956. She has enjoyed a very successful career in film and TV and has appeared in *Law and Order* and *Sex and the City*.

If the movie had more closely followed the third draft of the script, Carlin would have had a larger role. There's no Carl Spackler in that script. McFiddish's contrived Scottish hat is most likely made of the tartan of the Wallace clan. Note McFiddish's long gait. The minibattle between McFiddish and Smails is somewhat typical of the battle that exists between the greenskeeper and, if not the president of the club, then the greens committee. At times, members may praise the condition of the golf course but never call or write the superintendent, but once an influential member of the club starts missing putts, then it's time to fire the entire staff and bring in a golf course architect for a total renovation of the greens and entire course!

So, what can a gopher do to a golf course? According to Jeff Bollig, director of communications for the twenty-one-thousand-strong Golf Course Superintendents Association of America (GCSAA), the most prevalent gopher-related problems are holes in the fairways and tearing up turf grass. Golfers tend to turn ankles (and worse) in gopher holes. Thus gophers are, indeed, a menace, if not to society, then certainly to certain members of the GCSAA.

The very mention of the movie generates a mild cringe from Bollig, as the portrayal of the two superintendents in the movie, Sandy McFiddish and Carl Spackler, isn't exactly flattering, and it's *not* the image of the members that the director of communications would like to portray. But Bollig admits that *Caddyshack* fans are generally intelligent enough to know the difference between the fictional and the real. He also admits that, among GCSAA members, *Caddyshack* is the most admired movie—this based on an official GCSAA survey.

Jon Jennings, the golf course superintendent at the wonderful Chicago Golf Club, has seen a few gophers in his time.

"You find gophers on the periphery of golf courses," he says. "They mostly stick to the rough and the boundaries of the golf course. They are private and shy, and so they tend to avoid places like the middle of the fairway."

Thus, to Jennings, the gopher presents a comic exaggeration. Of course, in the early script the problem-causer was a mole.

"Now moles can be a real problem," adds Jennings. "They can burrow under the snow and even get into the greens."

Because gophers stay to the sides of golf courses, superintendents tend to leave them alone. However, to rid the course of moles, the superintendent and his crew will lob the occasional smoke bomb replete with noxious gasses. In England and Scotland, particularly on courses on sandy soil, rabbits are the issue. At Ganton Golf Club in North Yorkshire, locals get to roam the golf course twice a year—purely to blow up bunnies.

4

So He Jumped Ship. The Big Punch Up. Pick Up That Blood!

Lou losing at track
Noonan, D'Annunzio fight
Where Lou loses shirts.

—poet/philosopher Basho (son of)

The first view of the caddyshack. The Dalai Lama himself. I'm hot today. Denial of Coke. Gumball machine annihilation. Complaints. Poor old Carl Lipbaum who swallowed his pizza twice!

CADDIES have appeared in *Caddyshack* to this point, but these next scenes (five, six, and seven in the DVD) are all about the caddies—just as in the original script. It's the first view of Bushwood's star caddy, Tony D'Annunzio, and his brothers, Angie and Joey. The acerbic caddy master, Lou Loomis, brilliantly starts and ends these scenes. All the caddies are present and incorrect. The Havercamps are a doddering old couple still intent on hacking it around, played superbly by a couple who had never appeared in a movie before; Mr. Havercamp supplies two of the most famous and oft-repeated lines from the film. But before this comes Carl Spackler and his adventures in Hong Kong and environs. Every golfer thinks that he or she knows this speech verbatim, but every golfer butchers the lines. But who cares? It's *Caddyshack*.

Scene time line: 00:09:58.

In the very first shot of the caddyshack, there are eighteen caddies and one golfer. The building the producers used for the caddyshack was a maintenance barn that is no longer on the property.

Eddie Cochran's "Summertime Blues" is the first "imported" music. It's a great choice: a rambunctious tune with the two lines:

Well I'm gonna raise a fuss
And I'm gonna raise a holler

It's exactly what these caddies are going to do. Sadly, we get but two lines of the song and

almost a full minute of a vastly inferior song from *Journey* (more on that a bit later). "Summertime Blues" dates to 1958; the following bands and artists are among the myriad who have covered the song:

- Alan Jackson
- Brian Setzer
- The Who
- The Rolling Stones
- T-Rex
- Cheech Marin
- Guitar Wolf
- Joan Jett
- The Flaming Lips
- Rush
- The Stray Cats (no surprise there)
- The Beach Boys
- Motorhead (*quite* a surprise there)
- Van Halen

The best cover of the lot might be the very spare T-Rex version, but the most famous belongs to the original Who lineup; there's a lot of critical acclaim for the Rush version. The original is available on the album *Eddie Cochran: Greatest Hits*. The single reached number eight on the U.S. charts and number eighteen on the British charts. The first two lines of the song blare through; the rest is pretty much muted.

The brilliance of production designer Stan Jolley and his crew shines through in this scene. As the production designer, it's was Jolley's job to organize all the scenery, props, and other items that help to create the illusion that this part of the shed is not a shed but a caddyshack and caddy master's office. There are five telephones, indicating that Lou is a busy man; there seems to be an outside line for "sport" and a line that's probably from the pro shop. There's a decrepit desk, a taped-up window, a tired lamp, plus some filing cabinets that might harbor any variety of stuff. There are golf clubs plus an old canvas golf bag hanging on the wall. It's the office of a gambling, smoking, whoring member of the golf club underbelly; there's nothing about it that says

Years of Clean Living. Tony D'Annunzio (Scott Colomby), Danny Noonan (Michael O'Keefe), and Motormouth (Hamilton Mitchell) at work. All three actors are still active in film and television. In the early script, the caddies had a more prominent role.

(Warner/Orion/The Kobal Collection)

"clean living," and Lou only contributes to the notion with the hustler hat and big island shirt.

You'll notice that the only caddy wearing a bandana around his neck is Danny Noonan.

00:14:59—Lou Lectures the Caddies.

While addressing the caddies after the non-fight, Lou Loomis levels the turgid threat, "if you want to be replaced by golf carts. . . ."

At 99.99 percent of golf courses in the United States, golf carts have replaced caddies or caddies were never even part of the picture. Organizing and running a caddy program is never easy and takes a lot of time and money, but it's a minor tragedy for American golf that the golf cart is the way that people get around today's golf courses. The addiction to the golf cart has:

- Made golf more expensive
- Turned the club professional into a part-time golf cart mechanic and leasing agent

- Taken away the pure joy of walking a great (or really awful) golf course
- Provided golf course architects with the latitude to build silly golf holes (even though the American Society of Golf Course Architects once pledged, when golf carts started to take off, to make golf courses walkable)
- Made golf dangerous—there are several golf cart–related injuries every year
- Made golf take longer than it should
- Negated the opportunity for young people to get into the game as caddies

But, most importantly, the golf cart has taken the caddy out of the game; caddies, as *Caddyshack* proves, bring tremendous character to the game.

Outside the office, the illusion of the shed as caddyshack continues with the Bushwood garbage can and the decrepit lockers for the caddies. The only time we hear the word *caddyshack* in the movie is when Lou answers the phone.

Just after Lou leaves his office, he calls for two caddies: Joe and Feeb. In the early script, both characters had speaking roles. The script describes Joe as Injun Joe, a "big silent Indian of indeterminate age," and Feeb as a "twitching adult caddy with just a hint of mental deficiency." The original script gives the Dalai Lama speech to two caddies, Ray and Goofy, who never even made it to the Injun Joe and Feeb stage. Goofy was going to be a "gawky, bespectacled sixteen year old," and Ray was going to be "an old professional caddy wearing a dirty golf cap from the 1946 Buick Open." Goofy should not be confused with Motormouth, the caddy who gets the line "And kiss his ass . . ." a little bit later in the scene.

Here's how an original version of the Dalai Lama speech went.

RAY
I jumped ship in Hong Kong and made my way to Tibet, where I got on as a looper at this golf club up there in the Himalayan Mountains.

GOOFY
A looper?

RAY
A caddy—a jock! So I tell 'em I'm a pro, so who do they give me? The Dalai Lama himself—flowin' white robes and everything. So I give him his driver and he tees off—right into this glacier and his ball goes down this 10,000 foot crevice. And you know what the Dalai Lama says?

GOOFY
No.

RAY
"Shit." Yeah—"Shit!" And you know what else? "I'm full of shit." Yeah.
[Goofy stares at him with his mouth full of doughnut.]

It's been said that the Dalai Lama speech was improvisation, but it's clear from the early script that it was part of the plan. However, the producers had booked a local actor to recite the speech, and the results were so awful that director Harold Ramis had Bill Murray have a try. While the speech is one of the most perfect pieces of comedy ever produced, I still like the more scatologically oriented ending from the script, even though it's tough to think of the Dalai Lama thinking that anyone could be a shit. However, since that speech, it's impossible for any golfer to see a photo of the Dalai Lama and not think of "striking" or "big hitter, the lama" or "So I got that going for me" or "total consciousness."

Jesse Ventura, the former governor of Minnesota, is rumored to have asked the Dalai Lama if His Holiness had ever seen *Caddyshack*. The Dalai Lama replied that he had not. However, at the end of the meeting, the Dalai Lama apparently leaned over to Ventura and said the magic words: "Gunga galunga. Gunga gungala gungala."

For the purpose of digging up as much totally nonvital information as possible, I decided to contact His Holiness the Fourteenth Dalai Lama to ask if *Caddyshack* had played any role in his life. I thought about sending an e-mail or even calling the number on His Holiness the Fourteenth Dalai Lama's Web site (bighitter.com), but I opted for a letter. Sending an e-mail seemed a hair rude.

February 27, 2006
His Holiness the 14th Dalai Lama
The Office of His Holiness the Dalai Lama
Thekchen Choeling
P.O. McLeod Ganj
Dharamsala H.P. 176219
INDIA

Your Holiness:
I trust that you are well and that the struggle for a free Tibet continues with success and optimism. I am a writer based in Charlotte, North Carolina, in the United States; I am writing a book about *Caddyshack*, the 1980 comedic golf movie that features John Barmon, Jr. as Spaulding Smails III, first son of the Smails (II). Your Holiness may be aware that you are a star of the movie: Bill Murray, the well-known actor, mentions your name at 10:56 in the famous "Dalai Lama" speech that is very, very popular among millions of golfers around the universe.

My research for the book would not be complete if I failed to ask these questions.

1. Are you a golfer and/or do you enjoy the game?
2. Are you aware that your name is part of *Caddyshack*, The Greatest Movie Ever Made?
3. Does *Gunga galunga. Gunga gungala gungala* actually mean anything in your language?
4. If you are a golfer, are you a "big hitter?"

I very much appreciate your assistance with my tome. If you have any questions, please contact me at any time.

Sincerely,
Scott Martin

I received a polite reply via e-mail.

31 March 2006
Scott Martin

Dear Scott,

I have been directed to reply to your letter addressed to His Holiness the Dalai Lama dated 27 February 2006.

We weren't aware of the comments about His Holiness the Dalai Lama in the movie *Caddyshack*. His Holiness does not play golf, he spends his exercise time walking and doing prostrations. I can't make any real sense out of the words Gunga. . . . It might be just a name, but if you want to be sure, you can try and find a Tibetan living in your area that might be able to help you. You can contact the Office of Tibet in New York, our official representatives for North America, and maybe they can help you to locate someone who could assist you. Their address is:

The Office of Tibet
241 East 32nd Street
New York, NY 10016
U.S.A.

The distance from Hong Kong to Tibet is approximately the same, as the crow flies, as from Charlotte, North Carolina, to Denver, Colorado. But it would not have been an easy journey in 1980—the entire way would have been through very remote parts of China.

In the French subtitles, "Big hitter, the lama" becomes "Il est tres fort, le lama." *Gunga galunga. Gunga gungala gungala* becomes "Gunga galunga. Gunga gunga da gunga." "Total consciousness" translates to "la conscience absolue." And "which is nice" becomes "et c'est bien."

"The Havercamps had never been in a movie," said Marian Polan, now in her early nineties and the Fort Lauderdale casting agent who organized most of the actors and extras in *Caddyshack*. The "Tony's Tough Day" scene introduces Tony D'Annunzio, played by Scott Colomby. The Havercamps were a couple in real life—Kenneth and Rebecca Burritt. *Caddyshack* would be their only contribution to American cinematic excellence but, despite having only a few lines in the movie, they rock. Mr. Havercamp gets the immortal "Oh Dolly, I'm hot today!" and "That's a peach, hon." While Mrs. Havercamp gets the equally excellent "That must be the tea!" later in the movie, after the yacht club scene. It's my favorite line in the movie. Neither Havercamp was a spring chicken at the time of filming. Mr. Burritt was eighty-one and Mrs. Burritt was eighty. The former died in 1984, but the latter out-lived many of the younger stars and died aged ninety-eight on February 24, 1996.

"We had a lot of retired people come and register with the agency," said Polan. "Initially, the original casting person didn't want them, but she left and they stayed, and I think they worked out really, really well."

In the early script, the Havercamps appeared in more scenes.

Caddyshack includes a number of lesser-known moments of instant irony that add to the color and help make it The Greatest Movie Ever Made. The first comes in this scene, when Tony D'Annunzio is chasing after Mrs. Havercamp to give her a club.

TONY
[Handing her the club]
You might need that.

MRS. HAVERCAMP
[Looking at the club (slightly annoyed).]
Oh—I might need that.

In the early script, Danny Noonan caddies for the Havercamps.

Just before I interviewed Marian Polan, she and her husband had decided to hang up the golf spikes and clubs. They played golf until their early nineties, and most of the golfer "extras" in the movie were Polan golfing buddies.

The first Havercamp scene takes place in one of the many small but attractive oak groves on the Rolling Hills property. The "Forest of Haver-camp" was likely around what is now the 10th green.

Matching, but not quite totally matching, the Havercamps are perfectly clothed and kitted out. Their lids are particularly stylish. And both have rings on the third finger of their respective left hands. The sound people inserted a tropical bird of paradise sound just as Tony is getting to Mr. Havercamp's ball. Odd, because the producers went out of their way to use Rolling Hills because it had no palm trees: they wanted the course to look like a Chicago-area enclave. While Tony is organizing Mr. Havercamp, Mrs. Havercamp takes a few practice swings.

Tony's walk into the caddyshack and the subsequent denouement with Danny Noonan expose more of the interior of the caddyshack. There's a poster with the tag line: "Are You a Nerd?" There's a pile of junk on the table, including some type of broom, a softball, and a pair of large white golf shoes. There's a sign under the barricaded doors that reads: "YOU <u>MUST</u> HAVE YOUR TICKET TO BE PAID." There's also a discarded can of Coke on the first-aid box. The radio is still playing, but it's impossible to determine the song. Tony sports the black golf glove he wore while caddying for the Havercamps.

Just before the big fight, Danny Noonan hands the Coke to Grace, the blonde caddy. After the nonfight, when Lou has broken things up, those in search of the men's room will be delighted to see that it's right next to Lou's office. Behind Lou, there's a dart board and a "demerits" board. Halfway through the scene, someone turns the dart board around or replaces it.

At this stage in the early script, after the Dr. Beeper incident, the caddies are prominent, but there are significant differences.

- Tony is originally taking over for Lou in the caddy master's office.
- Angie D'Annunzio, described as "Tony's rat-like brother," is trying to flog clock radios . . . wink, wink.
- There's a lot of horseplay between Angie and Joey D'Annunzio and Danny Noonan—this results in the broken gumball machine, which leads to Lou's tirade.

Lou's tirade, which begins with him pushing Angie up against the "NO FIGHTING" sign, made it from the script to the movie mostly intact. Goofy, not Motormouth, gets the "I heard he swallowed his vomit during a test" line, but Motormouth gets the "And kiss his ass" line.

Peter Berkrot played Angie D'Annunzio, the middle D'Annunzio brother and the one with the Night Riders t-shirt. He's also the one who has to listen to the Dalai Lama speech—during which Bill Murray almost punctures his neck with a pitchfork. Recently, on eBay, a person representing Berkrot had his original Bushwood CC baseball hat on sale for a mere $7,000 (starting bid). The hat failed to garner any bids. I attempted to contact Mr. Berkrot through the seller but never received a reply. After *Caddyshack*, Berkrot appeared in two short movies, *Sticks and Stones* and *The Observer*; he provided additional casting help for *Missing in America*. According to the eBay listing for the baseball hat, Berkrot plans to auction off the Night Riders t-shirt and the swim suit that gets "lost" during the swimming pool scene.

From the twentieth-anniversary DVD version of *Caddyshack*, which features the enlightening "19th Hole," it's clear that quite a bit of Scott

Colomby's work ended up on the cutting room floor; he's barely even seen in the trailer. Certainly, in the script he has a much larger role, a role that's almost as important as Danny Noonan's. During his "19th Hole" interviews, Colomby, who still looks just like Tony D'Annunzio, gets almost emotional when he talks about how the caddies really made Caddyshack: "Myself, Hamilton Mitchell, Michael O'Keefe, we were the stars of that film . . . and we got lost in the shuffle."

Colomby then says that the movie was never intended to be a comedy, a statement that's easier to understand upon seeing the early script, which includes a number of dramatic scenes featuring Tony D'Annunzio and various caddies. Unfortunately, Colomby appears only sparingly in the "19th Hole"; there's a sense that he either revealed, or was about to reveal, all sorts of useful secrets. The "19th Hole" is a semi-microcosm of the movie: it would have been much more interesting, probably, to see more of Scott Colomby and Hamilton Mitchell and Cindy Morgan but, even in the "19th Hole," they have to cede to the bigger names.

Caddyshack was Colomby's first big-screen movie. To that point, he had appeared in various TV shows and TV movies, including *Can Ellen Be Saved?*, *Sons and Daughters*, *Senior Year*, *Quincy*, *Charlie's Angels*, and *One Day at a Time*. Colomby's role in *Caddyshack* provided him with the perfect platform to win roles in comedies from the same sophomoric/teen/just-plain-silly-but-wonderful genre. He subsequently appeared in all three *Porky's* films as Brian Schwartz. The first *Porky's*, made for $4 million, grossed $106 million. Kim Cattrall went on to the most successful post-*Porky's* career. After *Caddyshack* and *Porky's*, Colomby continued to work, appearing in or completing voice-over work for successful films and television shows including:

- *Saving Private Ryan*
- *Jack Frost*
- *Fight Club*
- *Die Hard: With a Vengeance*
- *Walker, Texas Ranger*
- *Robocop*
- *Midnight Caller*

- *The Knife and Gun Club*
- *Dirty Dancing*
- *The A-Team*
- *St. Elsewhere*
- *Lois and Clark*

Colomby was in his late twenties when he appeared in *Caddyshack*. Both parents were in show business in the New York City area at the time of Colomby's birth. The family moved to southern California, and Colomby graduated from Beverly Hills High School before taking acting lessons and appearing in numerous TV shows and films. Outside "routine" acting, Colomby has taught acting, played in a band, and performed Shakespeare live—then invited the audience to participate, which sounds rather fun.

Ted Swanson, the Miami-based production manager who also played Bushwood Country Club's PGA head golf professional, says that Brian Doyle-Murray probably had the most influence on the *Caddyshack* script—at least the final, *final*

version around which Swanson organized shooting. Part of *Caddyshack* lore is that the producers, actors, and directors essentially threw out the script fairly soon after shooting began and just winged it, improvising almost everything. While there was some improvisation, Swanson says that shooting was much more structured and organized, and that the script provided most of the day-to-day structure.

The "golf authenticity" in *Caddyshack* comes from Doyle-Murray, the golfer and former caddy. Harold Ramis wasn't a golfer; nor was Doug Kenney. Of the producers, cast members, crew, and others involved in the film, Doyle-Murray, Bill Murray, and Michael O'Keefe had been around golf extensively. Golf, like bowling, yachting, chess, curling, skiing, dogsledding, and other pursuits, has its own language; it's clear, within microseconds, when someone writing about golf or talking about golf is a nongolfer. For example, a nongolfing copy editor at a newspaper might write a headline like: "Tiger Wins Golf Match at Masters." It sounds acceptable but, to a golfer, the syntax is clunky, and it's clear to the golfing reader that the writer is not a golfer. Martha Burke, the university professor and feminist who challenged Augusta National's membership policies, provided another excellent example of what it sounds like when a nongolfer pretends to know a lot about a golf. In her numerous TV appearances on shows such as *Hardball*, it was instantly clear that she knew nothing about golf. In fact, in a letter she sent during the whole fracas to Tim Finchem, commissioner of the PGA Tour, she addressed it to Pratte Vedra, Florida. Well, any prat with an ounce of golf knowledge knows that the PGA Tour's is headquartered in *Ponte* Vedra, Florida. One of the many reasons that golfers love *Caddyshack* above all other golf movies is that the golf is pitch-perfect, even though only a few of the people involved in the movie played the game. But the few who were golfers had key roles. Ted Swanson played a lot of golf and could hit the ball three hundred yards off the tee; he "built" the movie so that it had golf authenticity. He wrote to all the major golf manufacturers at the time to request equipment; all

but one said yes and sent their latest and brightest stuff. Marian Polan, the local casting agent, played golf and chose extras who looked like, or could act like, caddies or golfers. Michael O'Keefe had been a caddy for a summer at Westchester near New York City. The nongolfing actors, armed with Doyle-Murray's characterizations, acted like people we all know from our golf experiences. Every club has a Judge Smails. Every club has a Dr. Beeper. Every club has an uppity dinner dance. Every club has a Ty Webb. Every club has the Havercamps. Every club has a Lacey Underall or Bishop Pickering, and occasionally, at every club the Al Czervik shows up, much to the consternation of the Judge Smails types. Caddies may be dying out in the United States, but the caddies in *Caddyshack* are just like the caddies at the places with caddy programs— even the exclusive resorts.

Other golf movies, whether comedies or dramas and whether consciously trying to capture *Caddyshack*'s magic or not, fail in large part because the "golf authenticity" is lacking. *Tin Cup* fails because Don Johnson fails as the flashy professional and the movie is part chick flick. *Happy Gilmore* is pleasant enough, and there are good bits (the woman in her underwear holding two pitchers of beer), but the basic plot line of a hockey player smacking the ball outrageous distances is contrived. *Follow the Sun*, *The Legend of Bagger Vance*, and *Bobby Jones: Stroke of Genius* all take themselves way too seriously. Yes, there are people who take golf way too seriously, and these people run the United States Golf Association, but for 99.8 percent of the roughly 25 million golfers in the United States, golf is fun—a diversion from the grind of real life and writing books about The Greatest Movie Ever Made. And producers of numerous golf movies feel the necessity to introduce contrived female plot lines simply to give their films a chick-flick component. With their unashamed scatology, pure raciness, pedal-to-the metal disorderliness, rude plots, lovely vulgarity, and luscious uproariousness, movies such as *Animal House*, *Airplane*, and *Caddyshack* not only created a brand new genre but also totally blew up the notion that a

film had to be a chick flick or have a chick-flick element in order to be successful. *Animal House*, *Airplane*, and *Caddyshack* have their gaudy female stereotypes, large mammaries (no other way to describe them), and overt misogyny, but there are plenty of women (golfers and non-golfers) who love *Caddyshack*, *Animal House*, and *Airplane*.

Brian Doyle-Murray came to *Caddyshack* from *Saturday Night Live*. He was a cast member and writer from 1978 to 1982. Before that, he was with Chicago's *Second City TV*, where he worked with Harold Ramis. Doyle-Murray has been busy in television and film as an actor and writer. His projects have included:

- *Getting Hal*
- *Bedazzled* (Harold Ramis version)
- *Snow Dogs*
- *Stuart Little*
- *The Jungle Book*
- *Doctor Doolittle*
- *Waiting for Guffman*

- *Groundhog Day*
- *Wayne's World*
- *Christmas Vacation*
- *Ghostbusters II*
- *Scrooged*
- *Sixteen Candles*
- *Yes, Dear*
- *Justice League*
- *Lucky*
- *Buzz Lightyear of Star Command*
- *King of the Hill*
- *SpongeBob SquarePants*
- *Ellen*
- *Seinfeld*
- *Lois and Clark*
- *Married with Children*
- *Wings*
- *Get a Life*

He also played Jack Ruby in *JFK*, and part of his work today is voice work for cartoons. One of the many reasons that *Caddyshack II* failed so completely was that Doyle-Murray was not involved.

Lou Loomis appears frequently throughout the rest of the movie. The next major shot takes place at the caddy tournament—he sports the same hat but has changed into a light blue shirt. He's also in the scene where Danny Noonan sinks the putt to win the caddy tournament. Loomis consoles Danny after the argument with Maggie over her ovarian tardiness. The outfit this time, early in the morning, is a nifty cardigan and flat cap—plus cigarette and Styrofoam coffee cap. Finally, Doyle-Murray referees the crazed match at the end of the movie, providing the classic line "Your honor, your honor." Loomis has reverted to the semi-Panama.

5

Shoe Shine. Now Comes the Real Estate Tycoon. Any Way You Want Your Noise Statutes.

Journey starts the dance
Of fairway bag carriers
Smails spins around
—poet/philosopher Basho (son of)

Testing (the Beeper). "Do you have any . . . eights?" Porterhouse. The Joke. Hat/Free Soup Promotion. Madonna. Meat Balls. A Thousand Bucks. Fairway Dancing. Noise Statutes. Ditch Diggers of the World.

FROM the arena of the caddy, *Caddyshack* now moves to the world of the club member, starting with a wonderful locker room scene that introduces Drew Scott, Gatsby, Smails III, Dr. Beeper, Smoke Porterhouse, and a host of toga-clad middle-aged members swanning around the place. And Judge Smails, who has only had a bit part thus far, establishes himself as the club's boss man and main fart. Rodney Dangerfield also enters the fray, introducing the smiling Dr. Wang, who in real life may have been a professor of philosophy at the University of Miami—sorry, "The U." Judge Smails meets Al Czervik, and the hate is mutual and instant. The vixen, Lacey Underall, also appears, initially trying on shoes (why not?) but then accompanying her uncle around the golf course in her Fila top, tennis skirt, and not much else. Thus, at just twenty minutes into the movie, those first-time *Caddyshack* viewers in the summer of 1980 have met the major players and know that all the stars that the publicity and the reviews and the trailer promised are present and suitably and predictably incorrect. There's even some movement in two plot channels, as the tension between Ted Knight and Rodney Dangerfield gets going. A few minutes later Danny Noonan begins to massage Judge Smails for that caddy scholarship. You have to hand it to Danny Noonan—he's not about to give up, despite Judge Smails demoting him from the lumber yard to the ditch.

Scene time line: 00:09:58–00:23:15.

Four old boys in togas saunter in front of Dr. Beeper while he's calling the office, golf club at

the ready in his left trouser pocket. Perhaps the togas are a Doug Kenney–inspired nod to *Animal House* and the famous toga party—although these boys were not likely in a fraternity at any time in the twentieth century.

The two younger club members are Drew Scott and Gatsby. Drew Scott (Brian McConnachie) is the one with the hair, in the blue shirt. Gatsby is just Gatsby in the script; Scott Powell is the actor. These two have relatively small speaking parts in the movie but are often in the background and part of the large cadre of extras and bit players who help to make *Caddyshack* The Greatest Movie Ever Made. I love these two; they turn in epic performances, even though their playing time is limited. They are playing the card game Go Fish.

Those were the days, when doctors had secretaries call the hospital to reschedule surgery because the doctor had a tee time.

"Mrs. Moore?"

"Yes."

"Everything is fine but we're going to have to change your surgery time a bit. The doctor is only just teeing off now."

"Oh good!"

"And here's the tube that we're going to snake down your nose. This won't hurt too much!"

You'll notice that Gatsby is sockless. Gatsby and Drew Scott are indulging in what looks to be a quick Bloody Mary before they are due on the first tee. Every time I hear or read or see the number eight, I ask: "Do you have any . . . eights?" These two are the members who dare to laugh at Judge Smails in his presence.

My father, around the late '70s, had a brown Audi 100. In 1980 in the United States, an Audi could have been an Audi 4000 with four doors, a five-cylinder engine, and about one hundred horsepower. It probably was not the newly introduced Qauttro, a car with remarkable performance for its day: the Quattro was not available in brown. However, the car slated for towing could have been the Audi 5000—larger than the 4000 and plagued with significant technical difficulties. Note the mild panic on the face of the Audi owner as he leaps from the massage table.

The Audi driver who has his massage cut short must seriously fear Judge Smails—he bolts for the door in only his towel. At today's Bushwood, a fleet of hyperkeen valets sort out any parking hassles.

The early script describes the locker room in great detail.

INT. MEN'S LOCKER ROOM

A cloud of steam billows from the steam room as the door opens. Several portly members can be seen through the mist. They look like ancient Roman senators wrapped in their sheets and towels. Several other members stand or sit around the locker room, playing cards or changing in and out of golf and tennis togs.

The action in the early script goes straight to Judge Smails complaining about the wax buildup on his shoes. The action cuts to Doctor Beeper, then Ty Webb and Smails get into a Jewish joke-telling session. The scene ends with the classic sight of Porterhouse wrecking the judge's shoes and *really* dealing with the wax buildup.

SMOKE
He frowns and presses the Judge's golf shoe against the buffering wheel until the shoe begins to smoke and sparks shoot out. Then he looks at the shoe and smiles at the big burned patch on the toe.

As Judge Smails instructs Porterhouse how to clean shoes, note that Porterhouse nods vigorously in mock understanding; for a moment, there's a lot of nodding and head bobbing going on. Just behind these two, the judge's nephew is watching, wearing perhaps the ugliest jacket ever made. He has a cigarette in his hand, and he tries to flick it into his mouth; instead, he inelegantly launches it over his head onto the top of the lockers. Then the young Smails (later referred to as Smails III, but given the perfect name, Spaulding) tries to use the asthma excuse for not playing golf. "What about my asthma?" It's the first time the moviegoers see Smails III. Lou Loomis calls him "Smails III" when doling out caddy assignments just a few moments later.

Measuring Ted Knight versus Chevy Chase by height. Five-nine vs. six-four. Perhaps this is why the "by height" barb goes right over Judge Smails's head.

The Muzak in the background is "Raindrops Keep Falling on My Head."

Notice that Gatsby (bald, seated) and Dr. Beeper sport the same clothes—or at least the same color combo.

The movie has already introduced Judge Smails, but the script only introduces him now—as "a rich old fart and presiding head of Bushwood."

There's no listing in the credits for the man with the brown Audi, the one who has to leave his massage. There are two listings for an "Old Crony," and there's an "Old Crony" in this portion of the script. The two actors listed for "Old Crony" are James Hotchkiss and Bruce McLaughlin. *Caddyshack* was the only movie for Hotchkiss; McLaughlin appeared in several other films and TV series, including *Lenny* and *Cocoon: The Return.*

At the end of the row of lockers behind Judge Smails, there's a toga-clad member on a scale plus a member on what looks like a weight-lifting bench.

00:17:30—The Judge Tells the Bishop a Joke.

The Bishop refers to Judge Smails's joke as a "doozy." The dictionary defines "doozy" as "something outstanding or unique of its kind."

In the early script, there's no mention of Porterhouse. He's simply called "Smoke" or "Westinghouse" and described as the black locker-room attendant.

Wouldn't we all like to know what type of competition the plaque on the locker celebrates?

The bigoted Bishop appears in the original script, initially as an "old crony" who, reacting to a joke says, "You have to hand it to the Jews—they know how funny they are." Another member chimes in with, "You're not suggesting we change our membership policy?" Here, the crony puts on his Bishop's collar, then delivers the punch line: "Oh, no. They have many fine clubs of their own." So the Bishop's sight gag was quite well planned, only it's anti-Semitic and not racist.

Jackie Davis, who played Porterhouse, was a local area musician, according to Marian Polan, the Fort Lauderdale casting agent. He made several notable film and TV appearances, including:

- *The Truman Show*
- *Cape Fear*
- *Smokey and the Bandit Part 3*
- *Only Fools and Horses*
- *Till We Meet Again*
- *Extralarge* (several episodes)

In *Caddyshack*, Davis is yet another actor who has only a small part yet produces a superb performance. In jazz and popular music, Jackie Davis was an important figure, one of the first keyboardists to use the Hammond organ, now a staple in "jam" bands such as Galactic and Modeski, Martin, and Wood. In the 1950s, Davis recorded numerous albums for the famous Capitol label; it was a time when few black musicians made it to the cover of an album. Born in Jacksonville, Florida, in 1920, Davis was performing on the piano before he was ten years old, playing in a dance band. Of that time, he said that he had "eighteen godfathers who kept their pedal extremities in sensitive areas of my anatomy." Davis spent the money he earned on his own piano. He later earned a music degree from Florida A & M, graduating in 1943. After service in the army, Davis was an accompanist for some of the early postwar jazz singers, including Sarah Vaughan. However, in 1951, he purchased a Hammond organ, loved the sound, and made it his trademark. He started out at a club in Philadelphia, where his gig lasted five months. The work led to two singles with RCA, and he joined the Louis Jordan band, a move that helped Davis's performance skills. As a recording artist, Davis's big break came when he signed with Capitol Records. Davis would record nine albums in five years with Capitol; the first was *Hi-Fi Hammond*. Most of the work featured Davis with a simple combo of drums, rhythm guitar, and bass guitar. The lime-tinged cover of *Hi-Fi Hammond* features Davis happily seated at the Hammond, which incidentally has bass pedals. It's Porterhouse, only younger.

Davis signed with Warner Brothers Records (Orion's distribution partner—what goes around comes around) in 1961. He made two records with Warner, and that was almost it for records. Davis continued working as a musician, pounding away all over the United States, even working on Ella Fitzgerald's album, *Lady Time*. In the 1980s, after *Caddyshack* started his part-time film career, Davis played in the Hilton Head area for twenty-six weeks at a time; during the day, he played golf. How Davis got the *Caddyshack* gig is unclear but, like so many actors, artists, and musicians, he likely registered with talent agencies then got the call when production manager Ted Swanson asked Marian Polan to find a black locker room attendant.

Davis made his home in south Florida. Hurricane Andrew destroyed his home in 1992, and a period of poor health ensued; he tried to keep playing after a brief period of recovery, but he eventually died in a Jacksonville nursing home on November 2, 1999.

The Jackie Davis discography:

- *The Jackie Davis Trio*, Trend LP 1010
- *Hi-Fi Hammond*, Capitol Records T-686
- *Chasing Shadows*, Capitol Records T-815
- *Jumpin' Jackie*, Capitol Records T-974
- *Most Happy Hammond*, Capitol Records T-1046
- *Jackie Davis Meets the Trombones*, Capitol Records ST-1180
- *Hammond Gone Cha-Cha*, Capitol Records ST-1338
- *Tiger on the Hammond*, Capitol Records ST-1419
- *Hi-Fi Hammond Volume 2*, Capitol Records ST-1517
- *Big Beat Hammond*, Capitol Records ST-1686

- *Easy Does It*, Warner Brothers WS1492
- *Jackie Davis Plus Voices!* Warner Brothers WS1515
- *Organistics*, Kapp KL1030
- *Ambiance*, EMI (France) 2C04850704

I purchased a "Jazz Masters" collection of Davis's work. The sound that the Hammond that Davis uses differs from the version that several jam bands use today; the sound, however, is recognizable and must have been something of a novelty in the 1950s. Fans of easy listening will love Jackie Davis; the tunes simply roll along effortlessly, guided along by a fine musician who is putting his heart and soul into his music. The challenge for the sound engineer at the time must have been dealing with Davis's pumping of the hair-trigger volume pedal. The early Hammond could go from zero to eleven extremely quickly, and the boys in the booth must have worried about their ear drums a couple of times. Later in *Caddyshack*, when Lacey Underall invades Ty Webb's house and he's playing the organ, the organ that Webb plays makes a sound

that's relatively close to the sound that an older Hammond organ makes. Davis recorded one final album for EMI in 1980—the year of *Caddyshack*.

Moments of Lovely Irony

Irony, intended or otherwise, is the heart and soul of *Caddyshack*.

- Spaulding says that he forgot about his language, then two seconds later, uses foul language again.
- At the yacht club, Spaulding complains that Danny Noonan isn't a member and that he's just a caddy, but in the final scene in the movie, Spaulding is, guess what? A caddy!
- Al Czervik beeping his horn to get attention even though he's driving the most "look at me" Rolls Royce ever.
- Judge Smails telling Lacey Underall that she might be interested in knowing that the captain of the "Links of St. Andrews gave this to me." Lacey could not be more disinterested.

- Just as Al Czervik is heading for the first tee, he says, "So where do we tee off?"
- Maggie O'Hooligan asks Danny Noonan to go inside with her and sort out the holy cards, yet there's nothing holy about the act that's just about to happen.
- In the locker room, Judge Smails tells Ty Webb that Webb should play with Smails and Dr. Beeper. Careful what you ask for judge! It might cost you $80,000!
- Just after Smails parks his ball in the woods, he yells "Damn," yet has been telling his grandson to mind his language.
- The judge is a cheat.
- Maggie O'Hooligan accuses Lacey Underall of being loose.
- Danny Noonan tells Bishop Pickering: "I've often thought of entering the priesthood." Michael O'Keefe, who played Noonan, became a Zen priest in 1996.
- Dr. Beeper wants to smoke marijuana with the assembled young people at the yacht club. He's a doctor.
- If the judge had not cheated in the woods, Al Czervik would not have hit the judge in the testicles with the orange ball. And if the judge had not turned around to acknowledge the adulation of nobody in particular, he would not have had to deal with the testicular pain. In the script, the ball hits Smails in the chest, not the toilet area, and after it happens, Czervik "waves apologetically."
- On the set—snobs versus slobs—the guys who did the work versus Jon Peters and others.

The locker room scene also introduces another accomplished musical entertainer—Scott Powell, who was a member of Sha Na Na, the rockabilly band. The band is still performing, although not with Powell, who is an orthopedic surgeon in Los Angeles. Sha Na Na had their own television show that ran from 1977 to 1981. Sha Na Na fans would certainly have recognized Powell. In *Caddyshack*, Powell plays Gatsby; there's no mention of "Gatsby" or a first name in the movie—the only clues lie in the credits and the early script, in which Gatsby is part of the "FUN COUPLES: SCOTT, GATSBY, and their foxy, tipsy wives, SUKI and WALLY." When first introduced, the Fun Couples are: "Hosting a new face at Bushwood, AL CZERNAK, a stocky, balding, cement block in a flaming leisure suit. His voice is loud, his manner is deliberately offensive, and he seems to really enjoy the company of these rich, young marrieds."

Czernak became Czervik (an improvement). Powell's performance in *Caddyshack* was one of the finest in the movie, and it's worth focusing solely on Gatsby in the scenes in which he appears:

- The locker room
- Golf with Al Czervik
- Fourth of July dance
- On Al Czervik's boat (in sun hat)
- Drinks in the men's bar
- The final game

Powell puts his Sha Na Na skills to particularly good use in the fairway scene, where Al Czervik reveals the radio in his golf bag, and his four-some (with the exception of Tony D'Annunzio) starts dancing to the Journey tune *Any Way You Want It*. Powell is easily the best dancer.

There's barely a moment in the movie when Gatsby is without a beverage. He starts with a Bloody Mary in the locker room, moves on to a martini just before teeing off, enjoys a midround beer from Al's golf bag, has a martini and glass of red wine at dinner, drinks another martini postdinner, has a beer on Al Czervik's boat (out of a plastic mug—to stave off global warming), sips cognac or brandy in the men's bar, and finally has a pitcher of martinis at the finale (where he's dressed for tennis). Even though Rodney Dangerfield is a guest of the Scotts, his best friend at the club seems to be Gatsby, who has much more dialogue with Al than any of the "Fun Couples." Gatsby also seems to be slightly in awe of Czervik throughout the movie.

Caddyshack was Powell's only theater movie; however, he appeared in the TV concert *Alice Cooper & Friends* (1977) as part of Sha Na Na. Nazareth and the Tubes also supported Cooper in that show. Cooper is a keen golfer and makes frequent appearances in celebrity golf events. Vince Welnick was the keyboardist for the Tubes; he eventually joined the Grateful Dead in the early 1990s. Thus the obvious connection between the Grateful Dead and The Greatest Movie Ever Made.

According to the thousands of shoe-shine experts contacted for this book, wax buildup on fine leather keeps the fine leather from breathing. This means that the foot perspires more and perspiration can break down the leather; and, of course, the foot that perspires more tends to smell more, and it's important for a lawyer not to smell more than is absolutely necessary, especially when the lawyer-turned-judge's name is Smails. On superfine Cordovan leather, wax buildup creates the following hassles: a coarse texture in certain spots, destruction of the natural beauty, and dust attraction.

Those looking to remove wax buildup need only use a shoe cleaner, such as Saddle-Soap, Ivory Soap, or Murphy's Oil Soap. Put the cleaner on with a damp cloth, wipe it off, then let the shoes dry. Buffing the shoes to the point where the shoes are shooting flames out is another method of wax buildup mitigation.

One has to laugh when Porterhouse attempts to destroy the judge's shoes as reparation for the "colored boy" comment. It certainly amuses Porterhouse.

One has to laugh when Porterhouse attempts to destroy the judge's shoes as reparation for the "colored boy" comment. It certainly amuses Porterhouse.

There are seventeen pairs of shoes visible at Porterhouse's shoe-shine station.

In the French audio, the Bishop is "Monseigneur Pickering."

Brian McConnachie played Drew Scott, part of the "Fun Couples" gang. We first meet him next to Gatsby as they play a preround game of cards in the locker room. McConnachie is the tall, thin man with the curly hair and blue shirt. His wife Ann, listed in the credits as Ann Crilly but with her name spelled "Crilley" elsewhere, played his on-screen wife, Suki. *Caddyshack* was Ann's only movie appearance. Ann and Brian McConnachie live in the Hudson Valley outside New York City. Brian is a writer and actor; Ann heads Governor George Pataki's New York City office. McConnachie's key achievement in *Caddyshack*, as Scott, is inviting Al Czervik to Rolling Hills.

McConnachie was thirty-five in 1980. He was a *Saturday Night Live* writer from 1978 to 1979 and was occasionally a guest writer in the 1980s and 1990s. McConnachie came to *SNL* from National Lampoon, where he was a cartoonist and writer and a friend of Doug Kenney, *Caddyshack* producer, writer, and the founder of *National Lampoon*. McConnachie had also worked with Bill Murray and Brian Doyle-Murray on projects outside *SNL*. In addition to writing, McConnachie has appeared in numerous movies, including *Sleepless in Seattle*, *The Curse of the Jade Scorpion*, *Deconstructing Harry*, *Bullets over Broadway*, *Six Degrees of Separation*, and *The Adventures of Bob and Doug McKenzie: Strange Brew*.

Caddyshack brings back a number of excellent memories for Brian and Ann McConnachie. They took their baby daughter to Fort Lauderdale, and the cast and crew organized the daughter's first birthday celebration. There wasn't a baby in *Caddyshack*, but if there had been, the McConnachie baby would have gotten the gig: she had already appeared in a *Saturday Night Live* skit as a clone of Maurice Ravel. The level of pampering on and off the set, modest by Hollywood standards, sticks with Ann McConnachie.

"I have never been treated so well in my whole life," she says. "I flew first class, there were baby sitters, if the rental car broke down someone came to get you. It was a different way of life. It was very nice, and nobody will ever be able to take that away from me. I take a lot of pride from it; I watch it from time to time, and it was one of the highlights of my life—plus I have more lines than Brian." Her *Caddyshack* experience comes in useful in her work for Governor Pataki's office.

"The work involves some acting," she says. Like most members of the cast and the crew, Ann McConnachie never thought that *Caddyshack* would be as popular as it has become.

Approximately four times a year, Brian McConnachie plays golf. The subject of his appearance in *Caddyshack* rarely comes up. During the filming, McConnachie stayed in the dormitory that was immediately adjacent to the clubhouse and tennis court. McConnachie remembers the partying, but also recalls numerous bridge games with members of the cast and crew. He remembers a conversation about philosophy with Dr. Dow, who played Wang. And although it's not in one of the early versions of the script, McConnachie remembers a "Fun Couples" scene that never made it to the filming stage; in the scene, the "Fun Couples" are going to go swimming in the water hazards on the golf course—until a crew member mentions that the water is infested with snakes. There may have been other McConnachie scenes that never made it to the final print.

"People were always lobbying and coming up with ideas," says McConnachie.

McConnachie first saw the movie at the New York premier. He had some interesting initial thoughts.

"It was pretty broad," he says. "It was this big, sprawling thing. It wasn't shooting fish in the barrel, it was blowing up the entire barrel. But the movie had a tempo. It was basically a collection of scenes with a tempo."

Around 1980, there was internal *SNL* competition: a portion of the team (Belushi/Aykroyd) was organizing *The Blues Brothers* while another portion of the team (Doyle-Murray, Murray, Ramis) was organizing *Caddyshack*. And the two teams were looking over each other's shoulders, according to McConnachie. There was also a split of the *Animal House* team, with director John Landis working on *Blues Brothers* and Doug Kenney joining team *Caddyshack*.

A comparison between the movies is tricky, even though both were, and continue to be, extremely successful. But they are very different movies with completely different parameters. The *Blues Brothers* is longer (even after being cut from its original three hours), had a much bigger budget ($27 million versus *Caddyshack*'s $6 million) and grossed more ($55 million versus $40 million). But to McConnachie, *Caddyshack* ended up being slightly better.

"*Blues Brothers* was brilliant, but it made some fundamental mistakes," he says. "The Aretha Franklin scene stops the movie. How can you leave after a performance like that? So it sort of ran out of gas for me after that. There weren't any mistakes in *Caddyshack* like that."

Caddyshack received poor reviews in part due to the poor behavior of Doug Kenney and Chevy Chase when promoting the movie. Even after the New York premier, which took place at the Rockefeller Center, there was a party afterward in a nearby hotel, and after the party Doug Kenney was running around begging to suckle his mother's breast just one more time.

However, during a break in filming, Kenney took the time to go for a long walk on the beach with McConnachie—in part, to make up not being able to spend time together during shooting.

"He wanted to spend some time with me," says McConnachie. "I really liked that."

McConnachie received about $1,500 a week plus all expenses. There was a free car, and numerous cast members would purposefully run the car out of gas, tell the crew it was broken, then demand a new one. This was part of the "routine" quasicomic friction between cast and crew. In the mid-'80s, when the McConnachies were living in a New York City brownstone, they received a letter from Warner Brothers saying that they had been overpaid by about $10,000.

Even though the scene in and around the movie was sometimes a touch chaotic, according to McConnachie, the movie brought together a number of very pleasant people—especially some of the older actors such as Lois Kibbee (Mrs. Smails) and Henry Wilcoxon (Bishop Pickering). McConnachie went out to dinner often with

Wilcoxon, who enjoyed his refreshment and, once refreshed, would tell numerous stories about the Hollywood of old. Wilcoxon had been Cecil B. DeMille's son-in-law. McConnachie gets a kick out of watching *Caddyshack*.

"Golfers are fortunate because no other game or entity has anything like *Caddyshack*," he adds.

In addition to his film and TV work, McConnachie has written several books, including:

- *Blowing Smoke: The Wild and Whimsical World of Cigars*
- *Flying Boy RLB*
- *The Job of Sex (A Workingman's Guide to Productive Lovemaking Illustrated with Pictures)*
- *Elmer and the Chickens vs. the Big League*
- *National Lampoon Presents: The Naked and The Nude*

With *SNL* currently obsessed with political jokes and skits that are never funny, one can only hope that talents such as Brian and Ann McConnachie get the call from *Saturday Night Live* that they so richly deserve.

Dan Resin—Dr. Beeper

"Everyone was pretty much like they were in the movie," says Brian McConnachie. This applied to Dan Resin, who spent quite a bit of time on the telephone organizing acting deals—primarily TV commercials. Resin compiled a decent portfolio of movie and TV credits.

- *That's Adequate*
- *Wise Guys*
- *The Man with One Red Shoe*
- *Soggy Bottom*
- *The Private Files of J. Edgar Hoover*
- *The Happy Hooker* (as the senator)
- *Deadhead Miles*
- *Till We Meet Again*
- *Remember WENN*

The early script provides Resin with a bit more latitude, a bit more conceit, and, get this, a wife.

The *porte cochère* up to which Rodney Dangerfield drives is in roughly the same position as the *porte cochère* at Grande Oaks. The aspect remains the same.

If you have some time one evening, have a few beverages and watch the DVD with the French or Spanish voice-over or subtitles, especially if you have seen the movie more than twenty times. You will not be able to stop laughing. If you watch *Citizen Kane* the same way, will you be laughing similarly?

There is no listing in the credits for the bag boy who gets the whopping tip from Al Czervik.

After Czervik's Sino-phobic comments toward Wang, one has to love the line, "I think this place is restricted, Wang, so don't tell them you're Jewish. OK. Fine."

Just after Czervik enters the pro shop, the audience gets its first view of the movie's vixen, Lacey Underall, played by Cindy Morgan. The early script introduces her as "a very beautiful girl, walking toward him [Danny Noonan] in a short, very alluring tennis skirt. She has slim, shapely legs, long, golden hair, a great tan, and a cover-girl complexion."

By movie and TV standards of today, when movies like *Austin Powers* make millions from product placements and then make jokes (and funny ones) out of the standard practice, *Caddyshack* was mild and even charmingly spiritually innocent. Production manager Ted Swanson, who ironically plays the pro in the pro shop, simply wrote to all the major golf manufacturers of the time and requested the requisite kit. He backed up his promise to provide some exposure, and the pro shop scene provided some results.

The assistant professional, helping Lacey Underall with her shoes, finds himself in an

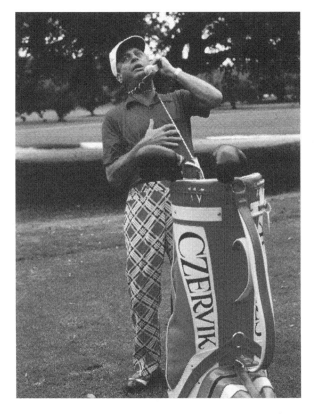

The exact whereabouts of Al Czervik's bag is a mystery; replicas can be found.
(Warner/Orion/The Kobal Collection)

excellent position as Underall finds herself wedged between two Wilson staff bags. To the right of Lacey, you'll notice a very odd-looking and rather tall trophy—sort of ballet dancers falling on the Ryder Cup.

The shop is selling several golf bags. There's a green-and-white MacGregor bag that soon reappears. It has a big green "M" on it.

The pro shop in the movie was the pro shop at Rolling Hills, only dressed up to look a little more upmarket. The only indication of the golf pro's name—Sam Riviera—comes in the script.

Al asks the pro for half a dozen "of those Vulcan D-10s" before asking the pro to set Wang up with the requisite kit. The scene in the pro shop comes much later in the script—well after the Fourth of July dance. The scene begins with the pro waiting on the judge and Spaulding. Judge

Smails is asking about the price of the Vulcan
D-10s. The scene from the early script:

SMAILS
Sam, Spaulding needs some balls. [He looks in
the display case.] How much is that new Vulcan
D-10 with the high compression center?
[Sam reaches into the display case and takes
out a ball that comes in its own velvet pouch.]

SAM
Three dollars each, your honor.

JUDGE
[Hiding his surprise]
Uh-huh. And how much are these?
[He reaches into a goldfish bowl full of used
balls.]

SAM
They're forty cents each, sir.

JUDGE SMAILS
[selecting some balls]
That's more like it.

SAM
Ah, Judge, that's a Queen Royal.

JUDGE
So?

SPAULDING
It's a ladies (sic) ball!
[Judge Smails drops it quickly and selects
another.]

JUDGE
This Ram-2 looks all right.

All this happens before Rodney shows up with
Wang, who is "Yamamoto" in the script. And
surely taking it out of the club pro in general,
the script has Sam Riviera gravitating to the big
spender, suddenly ingoring the very powerful
and influential (but cheap) Judge Smails to suffer
through the arrival of Al Czervik: "His [Sam Riviera's] eyes light up when he hears Czernak's order, and he practically runs over to Czernak, leaving the judge alone."

The hat gag is in the original script, although the superb "free bowl of soup" line came later, either in a later draft of the script or as extemporaneous Dangerfield. The "free bowl of soup" line is a quiet classic that makes the rounds at thousands of mostly upscale golf shops around the world. When one *Caddyshack* fan sees a really awful hat, the other will invariably ask: "So, do you get a free bowl of soup with that hat?" Ironically, it's just the type of crazy offer that a golf club pro shop might make. However, it's unlikely that the offer would ever take place as, at most golf clubs, there's at least a Berlin wall between the golf shop operations and the food and beverage operations. Thus, for the pro at most clubs to get permission to offer a special "soup for hat" promotion, he would first have to contact the club manager. Then the club manager would have to contact the director of food and beverage. Then the director of food and beverage would have to evaluate what he (or she!) would have to get in return from the pro shop. The director of food and beverage would then walk over to the pro shop (with the permission of the club manager under section 5.6.9 (b) of the club by-laws) and request a spot on the agenda of the next meeting of the club's general issues committee. Once the general issues committee approves the promotion, it would submit the proposal to the general purposes committee, which would suggest several changes, then send it back to the general issues committee. In this committee, the discussion would center around whether the bowl of soup that the person who purchases the hat would receive would be a large bowl of soup or a small bowl of soup. After a three-month cost-benefit analysis, the committee would recommend a small bowl for hats purchased on Friday, Saturday, and Monday and a large bowl of for hats purchased on other days of the week. Once the program receives final approval from all committees, all the hats are gone and the pro has left to go into movie production.

There is no evidence of a golf ball manufacturing company called Vulcan existing at the time of

Caddyshack's release. There is, however, a company called Vulcan Golf, based in St. Charles, Illinois, that produces an epic-looking driver—one of those Fisher-Price–sized jobs with all the adjustable weights. The Vulcan portfolio includes a number of attractive clubs but no balls. Company president Gary Hansberger states that he has been in the industry for twenty-five years, meaning that he got into golf in 1981, so there's no chance that he could have produced a golf ball for *Caddyshack*.

Vulcan D-10s are not available on eBay and other auction sites. However, naked lady tees are readily available and often packaged with an exploding golf ball. Five tees cost approximately $10, including shipping. Orange balls were available in 1980.

The judge has trained his grandson superbly—Spaulding has the snob leer perfected.

When Czervik looks at Smails, wearing the hat, and says: "Oh it looks good on you." the mannequin seems to be smiling in appreciation.

Note that, during the scene, Lacey Underall has managed to sneak away, and just as the judge places the hat back on the clubs and walks out with his perfect "corn cob up the keester" walk, Lacey is cruising outside.

There are fifteen caddies in the brief caddy assignment scene; not all are dressed in Bushwood kit. There's also a telephone, the seventh one to appear to this point.

As the movie quickly moves to the bag rack, there are nine bags, including the green MacGregor bag that was in the pro shop just seconds ago. The superlative Al Czervik golf bag is there as well. And the caddy who tries to carry it is Joey D'Annunzio, the diminutive brother of Tony and Angie. Angie is a boy with a girl's name, and Joey is a girl with a boy's name. The actress who played Joey was Minerva Scelza; her maternal grandfather was Hank Scelza, the transportation captain for *Caddyshack* and numerous other movies filmed in south Florida, including *Absence of Malice, Black Sunday*, and *Hot Stuff.*

Minerva Scelza was just twelve at the time she auditioned for Harold Ramis.

"It was supposed to be a role for a boy," says Scelza. "But my grandfather went to Harold Ramis and asked if they would like to see me; he told them I was a real tomboy." Minerva Scelza got the role and performs extremely well with her speaking and nonspeaking scenes. She's certainly a brat. Her first words come just before the Noonan/D'Annunzio nonbout: "Kick his ass, Tony!" The Czervik golf bag gag was Minerva's idea—at least the spinning around part.

"Everyone clapped after that," she remembers. "I remember that it was really, really heavy."

Scelza missed an entire quarter of school, as she was on the set for most of the day for the better part of two months; there was, however, a tutor. She rode to the set early each morning with her grandfather. She remembers filming being mostly organized, Harold Ramis as a fun leader, Rodney Dangerfield as a nervous wreck, and Bill Murray as a friend.

"I used to push notes under his door, and he would send them back," she says of Murray. "He was the most fun and the most ready to play."

Brian Doyle-Murray and Sarah Holcomb also took Scelza under their respective wings.

"They would take me on golf cart rides."

Scelza also played tennis with Doug Kenney and remembers the wrap party with Chevy Chase spinning the tunes. Anne Ryerson (Grace) was also a buddy on the set.

Several years later, Scelza called Harold Ramis to see if she could get into *Caddyshack II*. She continued acting, studied theater at New York University, and continues to act today, primarily in independent movies. At the Trenton Film Festival, she received a nomination for best supporting actress in *Home*, by Matt Zoller Seitz.

Even though she remembers her *Caddyshack* work as being tremendous fun, the best part was spending time with her grandfather, who as transportation captain was responsible for all the vehicles in the movie plus helping find certain crew members. He also organized the honey wagons—the trailers that the producers provide for the stars.

"He was really well-loved among everyone there," says Scelza. She saw the movie with her grandfather in Miami. However, she has only recently purchased a copy of the DVD, although she used to have a reel of outtakes. Her daughter, eight, like so many young children, loves *Caddyshack*—in part because her mother is in the movie.

"*Caddyshack* is about parodying the ridiculousness of the haves from the perspective of the have-nots," says Scelza.

With Rodney Dangerfield around, the subject of money must come up. *Caddyshack*'s budget was $6 million—roughly $25 million in 2006 money—much more than an independent movie budget but less than blockbuster cash. *Caddyshack* has

grossed almost $40 million in the United States. *Caddyshack* continues to make money by running on television and through DVD sales. Financially, even though there were no merchandising spin-offs and no Burger King tie-ins, *Caddyshack* has performed tremendously well.

Now comes Lacey Underall, bra-less, and wearing a very sporty Fila tennis shirt. She is about to embark on the most boring activity any sane individual can undertake—following a foursome of hackers for eighteen holes. Initially, she's carrying a tennis racket, but when she stops so that the D'Annunzio brothers can ogle her, she's carrying a golf glove.

"Madonna with meatballs" is a huge line, totally original, highly Catholic, and not in the early script. Tony's admiration was heartfelt: Scott Colomby and Cindy Morgan dated for two years after shooting. You'll notice that Grace, the tall, blond caddy, isn't quite so enthralled with Lacey.

Notice the same configuration of woods (one, three, four) as Ty Webb's bag, only the head covers are white, not red.

Lacey Underall moves to the next group of caddies, a group that includes Danny Noonan, who is every bit as impressed as Tony D'Annunzio. Note the variety of caddy wear. Danny Noonan is true to his normal kit, with beltless jeans, Bushwood t-shirt, and Bushwood caddy hat. Motormouth has plaid shorts, Bushwood t-shirt, and additional shirt. The unnamed caddy behind them has a red hat with a non-Bushwood logo.

The "Fun Couples" are lying in wait behind Judge Smails's head, the males about to get rid of the wives as there is golf to be played. They are hoovering martinis. A couple of fat, older women saunter by as well; they look as though they have never played golf yet are part of a never-ending army of people who populate just about every scene in the movie.

Manhattan can never be just Manhattan again. It will always be *dreary old* Manhattan.

Lacey has donned her golf glove, even though she's not going to play golf. Spaulding has donned a hat and has a large red something tucked into his back pocket. Note the cross on the Bishop's golf shirt.

Wang has done well in the pro shop, but must have been in a hurry—he is still wearing all the tags. When Wang walks, it's clear that he's getting accustomed to walking in golf spikes—especially down that steep slope. In the script, he comes up a little hill "talking at the top of his lungs," whereas in the movie, he goes down a little hill. In the script, Czervik refers to Smails as Smells.

CZERNAK
So where do we tee off?
[sees Scott and Gatsby and waves]
Fellahs!
[sees the Smails's party]
We waiting for these guys? Hey, Smells! Nice hat!

As Czervik says "Let's go. While we're young," we get close enough to Wang to see the tags clearly and, most importantly, that he is sporting a Nikon. His hat is off to the side—he must have been a rapper in his spare time.

When the judge says that gambling is illegal at Bushwood, it's one of the rare moments in *Caddyshack* when he's telling the truth. Of course, the fact that it's illegal means absolutely nothing later in the movie. Before his tee shot, Smails says that he never slices, yet the ball sails into the woods on the right side of the fairway. Once again, he is telling the truth: Smails's swing could not have produced a slice, but would produce a block or duck hook, according to Ken Campbell, the head golf professional at Machrihanish Golf Club in Scotland. Campbell describes the swing thus:

"In his set up, his left leg is straight and his right leg is bent. His legs are basically in a very awkward and nonathletic position. His shoulders are very open and he's too far from the ball. His feet are also too far apart, which explains why his knees are so close together. He's also hunched over. His backswing is way too shallow and to the inside; it's also a short backswing—too short. At impact, the weight is on the back foot. So based on that swing, he's either going to hit a push to the right or a nasty hook. He's absolutely right, though, when he says that he never slices—with that swing, he can't."

The shot of the Smails ball flying into the woods was likely shot in postproduction, as the trees at Rolling Hills, while dense in places, are not that tall.

Czervik, the "fun boys," and Wang are laughing at the judge, and Lacey is joining them. The others in the group are not laughing. In the script, the caddies are rolling around on the ground.

Note Lacey Underall's curious way of putting her hair up.

The "No, he's not my type" gag probably went straight over the head of young Minerva Scelza. But then again, based on her character, maybe she got it. Dangerfield changed the joke slightly (see below) to add some much-needed homophobia.

In the script, there's a brief scene of interaction between Grace and Wang.

THE FIRST TEE
[Grace, the six-foot girl caddy, walks up to Yamamoto with his bag. All his equipment still has price tags on it, too. She looks down at him, he looks up at her towering pulchritude and they both giggle amicably. JOEY crosses to the tee, hobbling under the weight of Czernak's incredible bag as the caddies cheer and jeer at him.]

JOEY
[to Czernak]
You want your driver?

CZERNAK
No, tell him to pick me up later. Hah! No, yeah, gimme it.

Wang (a.k.a. Yamamoto) has a brief line in the script while Al Czervik is organizing the game. The original bet is ten cents a hole with Scott and Gatsby. However, it's a $10,000 Nassau with an optional press and "one hundred Bingo-Bango."

As soon as Judge Smails finds his ball in the rough in the woods, he gets the foot wedge out and blatantly cheats, claiming that he was interfered with. Not surprisingly, there is nothing in the rules about being interfered with directly. Under rule 22.2, "Ball Interfering with Play:" "Except when a ball is in motion, if a player considers that the ball of another player might interfere with his play, he may have it lifted." The penalty for breaching the rule is loss of hole in match play and two strokes in stroke play. Rule 18 covers moving a ball that's not moving ("Ball at Rest Moved"). The judge would have incurred a one-shot penalty for moving the ball and another one-shot penalty for not putting it back in its original spot. There is, however, provision in the rules of golf for interference from what's defined as an outside agency—defined as "any agency not part of the match, or in stroke play, not part of the competitor's side, and includes a referee, a marker, an observer and a forecaddie. Neither wind nor water is an outside agency."

There is wiggle room in the rules should an outside agency move the ball, but there is nothing in the rules about a person interfering with the swing. So, if Rodney Dangerfield had smacked Ted Knight in the middle of the backswing and Ted Knight had missed the ball, then it would have counted as a shot.

Although *Caddyshack* filming took place in the early winter, the setting is July. Thus it seems unlikely that the judge would be playing under winter rules. First, if winter rules were in effect, then he would have to drop the ball away from the hole, not toward it.

In most instances, the USGA prefers that golf courses mark areas that are not playable as ground under repair. However, there is a provision for winter rules: "Adverse conditions, such as heavy snows, spring thaws, prolonged rains or extreme heat can make fairways unsatisfactory and sometimes prevent use of heavy mowing equipment. When these conditions are so general throughout a course that the committee believes 'preferred lies' or 'winter rules' would promote fair play or help protect the course, the following Local Rule is recommended."

What follows this quote is the lift, clean, and place rule, which we see come into play on waterlogged PGA Tour events. Thus, as Judge Smails is likely the committee, it's possible that he could have instituted preferred lies, which is the same as winter rules. However, if he is playing winter rules, then he may not move his ball from the rough, as it's not "closely mown," plus he has completely muffed the drop.

The foot wedge scene would have provided a good opportunity to see whether the wax buildup is no longer an issue for the judge. Unfortunately, he's not wearing the shoes he handed to Porterhouse.

Spaulding's language:

- turds
- double turds
- shit
- damnit
- shit
- damnit
- shit
- asshole
- double farts

In the French, "turds" becomes "merde," but seeing as there is obviously no reliable translation for "double turds," the translator went for "merde et merde." When it comes to "I never slice," the translation uses the verb rater, which translates to "muff." *Je ne rate jamais la balle.* And Spaulding is "Maurice" in the French version.

Notice the absence of tee markers, although there is what looks like a tee marker placed in the semirough behind the tee near the hedge. Anyway, the boys must think that they are players, as they are right at the tips.

00:22:03—The Judge Takes It in the Private Area.

The producers shot the "shot in the balls" scene along the 12th hole at Rolling Hills, although they used the 10th tee as the first tee.

Those of you, like me, who thought it rather odd that Lacey Underall should sport a golf glove need not be so befuddled. While Spaulding is hacking away and Judge Smails is working out the finer points of winter rules, Lacey is trying her hand at the game.

Spaulding takes nine shots in the fairway. In slow motion, the shaft looks like it's going to break with the torque. And when he makes contact, the descending blow descends so sharply that he generates tremendous backspin. He leaves his trolley in the fairway. Watch the Smails foot wedge moment focusing purely on Spaulding. You will keel over.

By the time that Czervik and his foursome have teed off, the tee markers are back.

There would have been no penalty for Al Czervik for hitting into the group ahead, and he would have had to play the ball as it lies, even after Judge Smails kicked it away.

Further proof that the golf knowledge is near perfect in *Caddyshack* comes in the "Smails hit in the balls" moment. Al Czervik has obviously annoyed Judge Smails on the tee, but the *number one* way to annoy people in the group ahead is to hit into them; behavior like this has started fights—even on the PGA Tour.

Every sophomoric comedy needs a fart joke, a getting-hit-in-the-nuts sight gag, plus a shot of bare large mammaries (no other way to describe them). *Caddyshack* has all of the below:

- Fart Joke . . . check
- Large breasts (bared) . . . check
- Someone getting hit in the nuts . . . check

Pretty much everything that can go wrong in a golf swing goes wrong in Al Czervik's swing, according to Jason Birnbaum, who teaches golf at the Manhattan Athletic Club. Birnbaum is associated with Mitchell Spearman, a *Golf Magazine* Top 100 teacher who has taught Nick Faldo, Greg Norman, and numerous other golf luminaries.

The script describes Czernak's golf thus: "He drives off the first tee with no technique but with amazing power."

Birnbaum describes the swing slightly differently.

"He's bow-legged," Birnbaum starts. "He spins out. He never gets off his right side. He 'one arms' the shot and is totally out of balance. In real life, he would have hit a low push-slice with a swing that bad. There's no way that he could have hit Judge Smails with such 'pinpoint' accuracy."

In the script, Angie D'Annunzio continues to carry the Czervik bag. A few hundred yards later, when Czervik is marching down the fairway, Tony D'Annunzio is on Czervik's bag, which is a good move from a child-labor standpoint and a great move for the movie, as the instant tension between Czervik and Tony D'Annunzio is superb.

Judge Smails (Ted Knight) disputes a decision with Czervik (Rodney Dangerfield). Ted Knight wasn't a golfer but he played one beautifully.
(Warner/Orion/The Kobal Collection)

Joey D'Annunzio remains in the scene, struggling to carry Drew Scott's MacGregor staff bag.

Certain golf bags have bells such as cell-phone pockets and whistles such as cigar holders, but there isn't a functioning golf bag on the market that includes a radio. There's a radio shaped like a mini–golf bag. There's a SpongeBob shower radio. But, after scouring the PGA Merchandise Show for hours in search of a golf bag that incorporates a radio, I failed to find one.

In 1980, Journey was one of the biggest acts of the completely forgettable "big hair" era of pop music. The lyrics and the band ooze banality, poor writing, and really bad styling. Approximately 216 Web sites list the full "Any Way You Want It" lyrics. Here is a burst:

I was alone
I never knew
What good love could do
Ooh, then we touched
Then we sang
About the lovin' things.

Inspiring stuff.

"Any Way You Want It" appears on the Journey albums *Greatest Hits Live* (1998), *Greatest Hits* (1988), *Captured* (1981), and *Departure* (1980). For those who list the song among their favorites, there's even an "Any Way You Want It" cellphone ring tone.

Two Journey songs appear in the 1982 movie *Tron*, which starred Cindy Morgan. Those who feel that Journey was not the worst band of all time can visit any one of several Journey fan club sites, including JourneyMusic.com. "Any Way You Want It" may be a really bad song by a really bad band, but it worked as a song that:

1. really annoyed Judge Smails
2. got the Drew Scott foursome dancing

Mission accomplished: a great result from a really, really *awful* song.

The golf-bag radio was not just a radio but a Sanyo radio-cassette, with auto stop. Thus it's possible that Czervik had the unit rigged to start playing the Journey song. Similar units are available on a certain well-known auction site for around $25.

The look on Tony D'Annunzio's face after he hears the music start and after he sees Czervik start dancing is one of the best "what on earth is happening here?" looks in a movie that's full of "what on earth is happening here?" looks. Tony D'Annunzio is the only one who is too cool to dance. The others get into the music, yet there was no music on the set. Harold Ramis simply told the actors to start dancing. The best dancer, by far, is Scott Powell, as Gatsby, who uses his Sha Na Na experience to spectacular effect. It's tempting to watch the main action in the foreground, with Judge Smails annoyed and Danny Noonan professing lifelong interest in noise statutes, but the real action is down the 12th fairway. Nobody dances, and nobody ever will dance, like Rodney Dangerfield. And the music all starts right in the middle of Judge Smails's too-short backswing.

Judge Smails tells them to "cut that off," but the music it too loud. Lovely. They keep dancing.

The music must have made the judge miss the green with his approach shot—Danny Noonan hands the judge a wedge instead of a putter.

The scene features one of those south Florida weather inconsistencies. It's sunny when Smails tees off, partly sunny when Dangerfield hits Smails in the nuts, then overcast during the fairway dance.

Just to the west of Davie, home of Rolling Hills, sits Weston, Florida, an enclave of relatively new, upper-middle-class neighborhoods in south Florida. Noise statutes are a big deal in Weston. The *Fort Lauderdale Sun-Sentinel* in 1998 reported that "city commissioners in Weston, Florida voted unanimously Monday to approve a noise ordinance that will give Broward County Sheriff's Office deputies the power to issue citations for people making 'loud or raucous noise.'"

Under the new ordinance, officers will be able to issue citations without a decibel meter. Using a decibel meter for citations is mandatory under Broward County law, which used to regulate Weston. John Flint, the Weston city manager, said, "Under the county ordinances, only a person trained with decibel meters could enforce the noise code. But to be realistic, most infractions occur in the evening, and we can't have someone with a decibel meter making sure it's a violation of the code."

When the wind is coming off the Atlantic in the Fort Lauderdale area, commercial jets flying into Fort Lauderdale–Hollywood International Airport must fly right over Grande Oaks, creating more noise than any golf bag could ever create. The good news, however, is that all the busses at the airport are now running on biodiesel.

Does the world need ditch diggers?

Those interested in a career in ditch digging and related disciplines might make as much as, or more than, judges. In fact, there is decent money in ditch digging, and as with so many jobs, technology has taken hold and completely changed the ditch digging industry to the point where there's not much ditch digging in ditch digging.

The epicenter of American ditch digging is in Perry, Oklahoma, world headquarters of the Ditch Witch company.

Ted Swanson—Production Manager

One the best decisions that the producers made was to hire Ted Swanson as their production manager. Swanson appears briefly on screen as the professional in the golf shop. In the 1970s, when Hollywood started to make more movies in south Florida, Swanson was, to use a term from the London freelance music scene, the "fixer," the man (or woman) who could get the producer from point A to point B, point A being the screenplay and Point B being hours and hours of film ready

for editing. Swanson uses a building analogy: "I'm the general contractor," he says. "The producer representing the studio agreed to 'green light' the script. The writers created the story. The studio has the financing. The producer and the director have agreed on the major actors. He's ready to build his building, the movie, but he must find a production manager to break down, budget, and run the construction company that's going to 'build' the building for the studio. As production manager, it's my job to put everything together."

The process for filming *Caddyshack* began when Jon Peters and his associates contracted Swanson to be the production manager. One of Swanson's first moves was to budget the movie and then persuade Peters and Brian Doyle-Murray to film the movie in south Florida.

Interviewing Ted Swanson about *Caddyshack* dispels the myth that the film's production and filming was chaotic. Throughout the shooting, Swanson provided the backbone, making sure that people were in the right places at the right time and ensuring that exactly the opposite of chaos took place—at least when it came to make the movie. The on-screen chaos could not have taken place without Swanson and his team ensuring that everything was ready. Ted worked with Stan Jolley, the production designer. Today, Swanson lives near Tampa, Florida.

BOOK OF CADDYSHACK: You were the production manager, is that the correct title?
TED SWANSON: Yes, I was also a line producer. I really covered everything, which I've been doing for years.

BOC: What is a line producer?
TS: Let's equate this to building a building. You have a designer, who has an idea for a building. He takes it to an architect, who finishes plans and concepts and that sort of thing. You have a general contractor that budgets and builds the building. That's what a production manager does. He builds the film. He hires the subcontractors, or his personnel. I organized casting and organized all the preproduction elements. A line producer breaks down the script so that then I can do a budget. And when I say breaking down the

script, I mean to the last word; I break every page of a script into eights and go from there. Then you create the cast list and come up with a time frame—all before anything has happened. You organize the budget down to the last penny: preproduction, production, and postproduction.

BOC: So you're the guy who really got the whole thing done.
TS: That's it. That's my responsibility, get it done and manage any conflicts that may come up between the studio and the director. I represent the studio.

BOC: So you were technically employed by Orion?
TS: That's right.

BOC: So Orion contacted you?
TS: They asked me if I'd be interested in doing the project. I happened to be finishing another film at the time. I had just returned from Singapore filming a two-hour movie version of *Hawaii Five-O*, nothing to do with golf. I met with Jon

Peters and a couple of other people at Orion; we seemed to get along.

BOC: Didn't they want to film in the Chicago area?

TS: Orion didn't. But those guys [Bill Murray and Brian Doyle-Murray] wanted to do it. That's where they grew up. They didn't realize there was a lot of weather you would be confronted with. I said we have to pick Florida so we don't have snow when we don't need snow. Orion said if that's where you want to make it, fine.

BOC: Did you start out in the film industry in south Florida?

TS: Oh no. In 1960, I went to work at the CBS TV station in Los Angeles. I went into the business hoping to be an actor and stunt man. I started out with the CBS affiliate KNXT-CBS TV starting as a page on the front desk. Then the mail room, the prop shop, and then cue cards. Then into the news department. Then all the commercials. Next was stage manager for two years. Then the station promoted me to producer of fifteen programs a week for public affairs. In the six years with KNXT, I went from walking off the street as a page to walking out as head of production. When I left CBS, I went to work at Universal Pictures as an assistant director. In those two years, I worked on quite a few of the major films they released during that time. Those first two years, when we moved from TV to film, is when I met Marian Polan [casting director for *Caddyshack*]. We did a couple of films in Miami, and Marian did all the extras casting for us.

BOC: Were you living in Los Angeles during *Caddyshack*?

TS: No. I was living in Fort Lauderdale.

BOC: You started in late fall. Why did you pick Rolling Hills?

TS: Because it had no palm trees. And they were very willing to do what we wanted to do. And they'd get a lot of exposure. They did pretty well, plus we paid them a location fee.

BOC: It was a nine-hole course?

TS: No, it was eighteen. The green we blew up, we built between two fairways. That was a phony green.

All those trees that were blown up, we planted. Those were all special effects explosions. We never saw hide nor hair nor had anything to do with the groundhog. That all came out of postproduction.

BOC: How much did the stars earn?
TS: I dealt with those numbers every day. I don't remember the fees at this stage of the game. Obviously, nobody made a lot of money. No negotiating millions for actors then. They were all comedians or television actors. Nobody made a ton of dough. I did *Rocky*; I made it for $1 million. We gave Stallone $17,000. But he made his money in the percentage points. Prior to *Rocky*, he was a bit part guy—but a terrific writer.

BOC: The figure that's around for *Caddyshack* production is $6 million.
TS: That seems right—for that period.

BOC: Rolling Hills was the main location. There were off-site locations as well. . . .
TS: Smails's house was in Lauderdale, at another golf course. It was somebody's home we used for the day.

BOC: You shot those scenes inside that house?
TS: Right.

BOC: What about Rolling Lakes, the yacht club?
TS: That was in Miami, on the way out to Key Biscayne. That was before you even get to the Virginia Key. It was not a yacht club; it was the Rusty Pelican restaurant. At the dock that collapsed, we used a piece of the marina adjacent to the restaurant, and we built that collapsing dock. We shot that stuff in just a few days.

BOC: Are you a golfer?
TS: Yes.

BOC: Do you still play a lot?
TS: Not right now. I have had a bad back for a couple of years now. I have my sticks in my car's trunk. You never have enough time to play golf.

BOC: Does it surprise you that this movie about golfers has become this *thing*?
TS: No, it doesn't surprise me. Because you think about the baby boomers turning sixty. They all were the people who saw this thing over and

over and over again. First of all, it's comedy. With the chemistry and that bunch of characters . . . that's big humor. And Brian Doyle-Murray was a wonderful writer. He did a neat job of translating their growing up and being in a golf world. I'll walk into a golf shop someplace and somebody will recognize me . . . from being in the golf shop. "Yeah—you were in *Caddyshack*!" and then they lapse right into the dialogue.

BOC: You were the guy behind the counter. . . .
TS: Right! It was Ted Knight who I was behind the counter with, plus his nephew. Ted was trying to get the kid to buy pink golf balls. And the nephew said these are for ladies. It was just a little bit. I did lots of little bits in lots of movies, because the crew loved it. They got to make up and dress the boss. They all took the shot.

BOC: Was it hard not to laugh when Rodney Dangerfield was around?
TS: No, it wasn't hard at all. It was work. Been there, done that. Rodney was a great conundrum. Rodney had many bad habits. We just kind of avoided his actions and you did your own thing

with Rodney. Rodney asked me to produce a movie later on called *Back to School*; I accepted the job and then I quit before we started shooting. I couldn't put up with Rodney or the director: they were just too weird. The *Caddyshack* cast—they were all funny people, all had their idiosyncrasies. Rodney never fit in anywhere in anything he did. Whether working on stage in Vegas or working nightclub routines or whatever. He was just a little off the wall. Ted Knight was a peach. Just a neat guy. I lived in the Palisades for a while, and he was my neighbor. We'd bump into each other all the time. My wife and I would be sitting in the deli eating lunch and I'd get this feeling that somebody was looking at me. I'd look up and I'd see Ted Knight looking at me. Ted was a great actor; he had been acting for a long, long time. He used to hang out with Adam West. Ted and Rodney didn't pal around. The secondary roles, the younger actors, they were all ready to go.

BOC: Did you get to go to the premiere of the movie?
TS: No, I was working on another movie.

BOC: When you first saw *Caddyshack*, what did you think?

TS: We had a screening, and I liked it. But you never realize how good something is when you film it. Just like *Rocky*. It was a nice little movie that they only gave me a million bucks to make. And in those days, a little movie was $3 million. Not quite the same with *Caddyshack*. I wasn't lacking for anything there. The contractual fees—producing fees, directing fees—were all above-the-line costs. Below the line are the guts of making the film—the crew!

BOC: There are plenty of bits that made it in the movie that aren't in the script. . . .

TS: Not really. We never approached any day without following the script—the script we had at that time. We shot the script.

BOC: *Caddyshack* had very young actors and young people, and it wasn't exactly a choir boy atmosphere around the set. Did that annoy you or get in the way?

TS: I had a reputation of having an iron fist. That's why Orion hired me. Harold Ramis wanted to add something; Orion didn't have the money in the budget, so he'd have to give something up in the budget. When push came to shove . . . there comes a point when you have to go to the financier, which is the studio, and have to make your case there. We didn't have any major problems with any of the young cast. Scott was fine, Mike was fine, Cindy was fine. She was a very pleasant girl—all very professional.

BOC: Harold Ramis, this was his first directing job. . . .

TS: Harold had directed theater and directed comedy, but not one frame of film.

BOC: Was it difficult working with him?

TS: No, Harold was OK. He had his own thoughts. Basically, we didn't have any real problems. I can't remember any horrific moments or problems—except for having to get rid of certain people who got in the way. There were a couple of kids like that. I'd have a member of the crew come up to me and ask: "Are we supposed to be doing what they ask us to." I'd say: "No! no!" Then I'd tell the guy who thought he was the boss to get off the set. Those young geniuses didn't have a clue about filmmaking, and we had a movie to make!

BOC: I look at the cast and crew list. . . .
TS: It was pretty much my crew. We got Ricou Browning to do all the water work. Ricou was the creature from the black lagoon in *The Creature from the Black Lagoon*. He created *Flipper* and directed *Flipper*. He directed untold work on Bond films, all the underwater stuff. Ricou's still a very dear friend.

BOC: How did you get the golf stuff?
TS: I called every manufacturer that was in the business at the time; I said: "Listen, I'm doing a movie in Florida with Ted Knight and Chevy Chase and Bill Murray and would you like your products on camera? We'll use them." And every company but one sent their stuff.

BOC: Which company?
TS: It was a California company, I can't remember. They were big then, but they disappeared.

BOC: If you look at the credits, there are lots of producers and executive producers and assistants, etc. How much did all those people actually do?
TS: For the most part, they just got in the way. Jon Peters had other projects on his plate and very little to do with making our film. Those guys were suits. There was one guy who really got in the way while we were shooting the pool scene. He went up to the best boy grip and said maybe you should get some bricks to put in the pool. I think I only saw him for two hours before I got rid of him.

BOC: Didn't you have to tie down the imaginary Bushwood set that Stan Jolley created?
TS: We did. It was during a hurricane threat. We got one-inch line, spools of it, and we literally looped it over the set. In the end, the real eye of the storm came nowhere near us.

BOC: Who was the costume guy?
TS: We called him little André.

BOC: Did you have a double for Chevy Chase for the golf?
TS: We didn't have any doubles.

BOC: It must have been a lot of work during shooting. . . .
TS: Jan, my wife, lives through the making of my movies. It's leave early and come home late at night. Jan's sister, Mimi Stacy, was my production coordinator.

BOC: Can you remember what you paid certain people?
TS: I think I paid the cameraman four or five grand a week—close to that.

BOC: Where did you get all the cars?
TS: From around the Fort Lauderdale area. There were dealers who had cars that were worth a quarter to half a million dollars.

BOC: How did the Al Czervik golf bag happen?
TS: Props built it.

BOC: Who has it now?
TS: It may have been a trophy for somebody—probably one of the producers.

BOC: That was Hank Scelza's granddaughter who played the caddy who initially tries to haul the bag. . . .
TS: She did a great job for a kid that never acted a day in her life. Hank was a close friend of mine. I miss him.

BOC: Did Ted Knight get along with Rodney Dangerfield?
TS: Rodney? Did you ever see anybody eat mash potatoes and drink milk all at the same time? That was Rodney.

BOC: What was your schedule like?
TS: I think the schedule for *Caddyshack* was usually between two to four pages a day. We go by pages. If something is really intricate, one-eighth of a page could take a day to shoot.

BOC: What was Doug Kenney like on the set?
TS: Doug had very little to do. He had an idea here or there. He was there, but didn't have much impact on anything.

BOC: What about all the improvisation?
TS: We had a script and we had a schedule, but there's almost no script that's shot as written. It goes through meetings and readings. That's just the way it works.

BOC: The golf is very authentic in *Caddyshack*. How do you think that happened?
TS: Bill Murray is a golfer and so is Brian Doyle-Murray. So there was no need to have someone there just to make sure that it worked. Lots of us on the set played golf. A friend of mine was the golf editor for the *Miami Herald*, so we played all over the place. Jan played too.

BOC: How long did you have to shut Rolling Hills down for?
TS: We didn't really shut them down all the way. Close to a month—probably more. I think we took over nine holes at a time so that they could still function.

BOC: The one who didn't seem stressed out during this whole thing was Chevy.

TS: In his own way. Before we make a movie, we have to get some of the cast examined for insurance purposes. So I sent them to Fort Lauderdale to my doctor. The doctor's assistant, her name was Marty, she was an ex-marine, tough as nails, and the doctor was a very nice guy. In his waiting room, Bill Murray was waiting to get examined. I heard this whole thing. Here's a waiting room with pretty much all blue hairs, and here's Bill Murray who comes in and lies down on the floor in the waiting room. Marty comes in and says, in her marine voice: "Get your butt off the floor!"

BOC: What about all the alleged partying? Did it get in the way?
TS: No. I didn't let things get in the way. In our business there are some rules: you're never late, you never ask, you show up for work, and you never let the team down. That's just the way it has to be. When I do a movie for TV, I shoot the whole thing in twenty-five days and a feature film in eight weeks. By the time they give me the script, I have about twelve weeks of preproduction.

BOC: What about the yacht club scene?

TS: We got the plane—it was a plane that took off near there every day, so we just got permission to shoot it. We got the stunt water skiers from Winter Gardens and the yacht fisherman from the manufacturer.

BOC: The club manager was actually the club manager?

TS: That's right. He loved it, and he was so excited to get the part—he was tickled pink.

BOC: Did you shoot the finale at the end of shooting?

TS: No. The scheduling is very intricate. You have to consider all sort of factors, like who is available when, and where you can shoot, and all that sort of thing. You always shoot exteriors when you have good weather. Always shoot interiors as bad weather cover. In forty-six years of doing this stuff, I've lost a day and a half to weather: I'm always planning ahead. It's my responsibility to make sure that everything was ready for shooting. A day lost costs a lot of money.

BOC: How long did you live in the Fort Lauderdale area?

TS: After *Caddyshack* we stayed a couple of years doing more films. I got to the point where, about a year after *Caddyshack*, we moved away—there was pressure to keep work coming in to keep these guys employed. They didn't work for me but with me; they were union members, but they were my team, my friends. I felt a terrific responsibility. When there was a dry spot, they don't make a living. I went up to Martha's Vineyard and bought an old whaling captain's house and built a B&B.

Judge Smails smacks the ball into the woods.

Gatsby and Scott have to work extremely hard not to burst out laughing after Judge Smails thumps the ball into the trees.

As Lacey Underall passes Danny Noonan, offering mild platitudes for the effort, she is still wearing her golf glove.

Thermonuclear gopher extraction. An airplane pilot flying into Fort Lauderdale International thought that a plane had crashed.
(Warner/Orion/The Kobal Collection)

Now comes the first skirmish in the gopher wars: Carl Spackler armed with a twelve-inch hose. In the script, attempting to rid the course of gophers with a hose and all that water was the job of Sandy McFiddish.

With Carl about to give the gophers a glass or two of fresh water, the scene switches from south Florida to southern California and back again. When the Gopher is about ten feet away from Carl, that's a simple hand puppet gopher. It's extremely unlikely that a gopher would bite a human, as they are generally terrified of anything else that moves, being that they are hard-core peace-loving vegans.

Budweiser is the beverage of choice for the Czervik golf bag. As the beer tap emerges, it's a good time to notice Tony's thin belt plus the leather piping on the pocket. It's also a good time to notice that the beer tap is remote controlled and that Franklin is the manufacturer of these boxing-glove head covers—so they were likely real boxing gloves, since there's no record of Franklin having produced boxing-glove head covers. Head covers come in all shapes and sizes today, from the basic wool/bobble combination to the animal themed. Those wishing to imitate Czervik can choose from a variety of boxing-glove head covers. PGA Tour player Pat Perez has a model, the Pat Perez Boxing Glove Headcover, that's available for around $25. The head covers helped boost Perez to $1,258,087 in official earnings in 2005, good enough for sixty-second on the money list. Pat's hobbies, according to the PGA Tour's media guide, include racing, boating, basketball, and watching TV, and, as he's a golfer and watches TV enough to list it as an "interest," that means that he watches *Caddyshack* and perhaps derived the boxing glove idea from Al Czervik.

Those people who are looking for different boxing glove head covers can find them on eBay; a quick search turned up the EVERGOLF boxing-glove head cover (available in black and red) and the Knock Out model, which is only available via eBay. There's nothing rope-a-dopish about the inventor's marketing here. Underneath his product, he states: "Hey Tiger, animal head covers are for little girls!!!!!" The inventor has patented his head cover, which he sells for $9.99, claiming that it provides him with an extra edge:

"THIS GLOVE TURNS HEADS EVERY WHERE I GO . . . . AND ALSO GIVES ME "A LITTLE ATTITUDE" EVERY TIME I BRING IT OUT OF THE BAG. IT REMINDS ME TO "FIGHT TO THE END" AND TO NOT LET UP ON MY PLAYING PARTNERS ON THE BACK NINE. I KNOW IT SOUNDS CRAZY BUT IT HELPS TO KEEP MY HEAD IN THE GAME OFF THE TEE."

So, perhaps this copy provides some insight into why Al Czervik employs boxing-glove head covers as an integral part of the megabag.

Pumping the word *Caddyshack* into eBay produces almost one thousand items, searching just titles. Search titles and descriptions, and the number balloons to around 2,600. Most movie critics cite *Citizen Kane* as the greatest movie ever made, but enter *Citizen Kane* into the search engine and only 776 items appear, and that's with a title and description search. And there are absolutely *no* Citizen Kane head covers available. Thus a simple eBay search proves that *Caddyshack* is better than *Citizen Kane* and thoroughly deserves the tag "The Greatest Movie Ever Made." However, movies that have a more populist appeal and numerous sequels tend to nudge ahead of *Caddyshack*. Type *Star Wars* into the eBay search engine and you get almost half a million entries (442,453, to be precise). *Caddyshack* actually wins here because nobody could ever sift through that many entries. For the hard-core *Caddyshack* fan, the number of items on eBay is manageable.

Of the approximately 2,600 *Caddyshack* items on eBay, a good chunk (1,700) are used videos, DVDs, and laser disks. And many of these items are movies with *Caddyshack* ties (*Grounhog Day*, *Bedazzled*). Narrowing the search to headlines produces significantly better results. Some interesting items typically show up under memorabilia. There are posters, lobby cards, dancing gophers, and autographed photos—the typical movie memorabilia fare. It's never outrageously priced. In the past few years, with the movie continuing to be so successful, a cottage industry has emerged producing and selling Bushwood hats, t-shirts, and golf shirts. The listings include a variety of interesting claims, but I like this piece of copy: "No free bowl of soup with this hat unless Judge Smails places a bid."

There are any number of sellers claiming to have exclusive rights and trademarks and other legal permission.

While a professional Web site designer might turn his or her head away in mild shock, caddyshack25.com offers a broad portfolio of *Caddyshack* merchandise—anything from hats to signed posters. For the extremely serious *Caddyshack* fan, an absolute must is a copy of one of the drafts of the script. These are readily available on eBay and through caddyshack25.com. The draft that's easiest to find on eBay is the third, dated May 18, 1979.

Al serves the beer in Dixie cups. After Al has taken a swig, he hands the used cup to Tony,

who hands it to Angie. "Boys Town" (What time you due back in Boys Town?) is a general term for an institution that helps "troubled" youths. In the western suburbs of Omaha, Nebraska, there's a town called Boys Town. In 1917, a young priest named Edward Flanagan founded an institution there to help young boys who were at risk of falling into a life of crime. The organization that Father Flanagan founded is now the Girls and Boys Town of America.

The USGA would deem the "Einstein" putter that Czervik produces as nonconforming, but it works for Czervik. Music, not golf, was Albert Einstein's bag away from physics. Einstein was certainly financially comfortable throughout his life, but it's not clear that he necessarily made a fortune. He could have: in 1944, he wrote out by hand his 1905 relativity paper, put it up for auction, and raised $6 million for the war effort. The Library of Congress houses the manuscript. Did he make tons of cash in physics for himself?

Einstein died in 1957, which means that the putter was at least twenty-seven years old. The head looks like it's an early Ping model—the B60. Wang takes a picture of the putt. Just after the putt, Tony D'Annunzio is helping himself to a beer. The interplay between Tony D'Annunzio and Al Czervik is one of the highlights of the early part of the movie.

On those furry greens, it's amazing that anyone made anything. The greens are considerably better today. The special effects team went above and beyond with the putter sight, making the numbers change as Czervik aims the putter. The numbers are N3, 34, two dots, 71 percent.

Nick Price, the famous golfer, counts *Caddyshack* among his favorite movies. The proof, perhaps, is his boat: a sixty-five-foot sport fisherman that he named, get this, *Caddyshack*. Price estimates that he has seen *Caddyshack* fifty times either on VHS, cable, or DVD.

"The more you watch it, the more you understand how cleverly it was written and filmed," he says. "The great thing is that Bushwood Country Club could be any country club in the world. At the club where I grew up, we had all the characters that are in the movie. So it's easy to relate to *Caddyshack*."

Price got to play in a tournament alongside Bill Murray in Chicago. Price persuaded Murray to act out the Augusta/Flower scene for the gallery. Murray obliged as soon as he saw a row of obliging flowers.

"Everyone was rolling on the floor," says Price. "He didn't miss a word."

At the 2002 Open Championship at Muirfield, on the Saturday in the gale when Tiger Woods shot 82, Price was in the middle of the tempest, playing a hole on the front nine—right into the teeth of the wind. Price was huddled under an umbrella on the 5th hole when caddy Jimmy Johnson turned to Price and said, "I don't think the heavy stuff is coming down for quite a while."

"I cracked up," Price remembers. "It made it a little easier."

Price's favorite scene is the pool scene—especially the caddy synchronized swimming. To Price, *Caddyshack* is about life at a golf club.

"Ted Knight was the best character in that movie. Epitome of a member who wants to be a snob but doesn't have the credentials. Here's a guy who has sentenced people to long prison terms and even death, and there he is shaking over a ten-foot putt."

Former caddy Jeff Medlin was a huge fan—just like all PGA Tour caddies.

"He grew up at a course that was very similar to Bushwood."

Price is also fond of Porterhouse—the locker room attendant.

"I've met at least a hundred Porterhouses in my travels," Price adds. "Guys with a great sense of humor who absolutely despise a few of the senior members."

After Czervik makes the putt, the action moves to what is now the 8th fairway at the far northwest corner of the golf course. The road behind

Bishop Pickering is SW 30th Street. The buildings in the background that are under construction are condominiums today. Note the hurricane-resistant breeze-block construction. In late winter 2006, none of the units were for sale. However, a condominium directly across from Bushwood CC was on the market for $234,500 (two beds, two baths); this condominium is on the seventh floor with "golf views," and the building looks relatively attractive and quiet, even though it's right underneath the flight path to Fort Lauderdale International. The condominiums that are under construction in the movie are not as attractive as the ones that are immediately across the road from the clubhouse. In the script, Judge Smails complains about the new construction.

THE FOURTH TEE
[Smails gazes at a row of new ranch homes across from the course, visible from the elevation of the tee.]

SMAILS
You know, Reverend, when we started Bushwood, you couldn't see a single house from here.

We called it a "country club" because it was in the *country*. Now look! They're almost on top of us.

To Smails and the Bishop, the large Czervik sign must be either awful or intimidating or both. "The very latest Czervik Condominiums . . . a Dazzling Way . . . Playgrounds for your kiddies . . . bingo . . . tennis and racquetball . . . parking galore."

Note that when Motormouth gives Danny a hard time after the admonition from the Bishop, Motormouth has put a pair of glasses on one of the head covers.

In 1979, Rachel Igel was breaking into Hollywood as a film editor. She had recently returned to the United States after seven years in London, where she had received a master's degree from the Royal College of Art and had subsequently worked for BBC Television. *Caddyshack* was an opportunity for Igel. She became an assistant film editor working with lead editor Bill Carruth and fellow assistant Robert Barrere. Igel remembers an apprentice editor also being part of the team. The *Caddyshack* gig lasted ten months and helped Igel reach her goal of becoming a full editor on later films. Today, she is treasurer of the Motion Picture Editors Guild, IATSE Local 700, in Hollywood, and she continues her editing work. In addition to *Caddyshack*, Igel has worked on many films and TV shows, including *Senses*, *Love Matters*, *Seize the Day*, *Fatal Instinct*, *The Letters from Moab*, *The Revolt of Mother*, *Pigeon Feathers*, *The Blue Hotel*, *Breathless*, and *All Night Long*.

When she meets people at social gatherings who are not in the movie business, they often ask about her credits. *Caddyshack* frequently gets more of a reaction than any other film.

Editing took place on the Warner Brothers lot in Burbank, California. The editing began as soon as shooting began in Fort Lauderdale, in November 1979. After each day's work on the set, a member of the crew shipped the raw film back to Los Angeles, where the team would get to work producing a first cut, or editor's cut, for the director to see when filming was finished. Igel's responsibilities included organizing the film and preparing the film for Carruth. In 1979, computer editing did not exist, and films were edited by hand, using tape splicers. Raw film arrived with notes from the script supervisor. The editing team worked with the script, which was vital, as *Caddyshack*, like almost every movie, was filmed out of sequence.

Even though Igel had been living in the United Kingdom, she was well aware of the fame of actors such as Chevy Chase, Bill Murray, and Ted Knight from their appearances on *Saturday Night Live* and other television shows. The unedited footage, called "dailies," was exciting to watch, was extremely funny, and presented a challenge to Carruth as he sought to capture in the editing the wackiness of the material. *Caddyshack* wasn't a big budget film by the standards of the day. There was a lot of talent around, but this was Harold Ramis's first full-length movie directing job. And Jon Peters's production company was relatively new as well.

"*Animal House* had been extremely successful, and that surprised the film community, because it was a completely new type of comedy. There hadn't been anything like it to that point. And so they weren't sure that it was going to work. This type of thing had worked on TV, but the big screen was a different format." Michael Medavoy was the Orion executive most involved in the production. Igel says that whether or not comedy is working is tough to judge after repeated viewings. The jokes cease to be funny after seeing them so many times.

Ramis, Doug Kenney, Peters, and others who had been in south Florida returned to Los Angeles and soon began working with the editor to produce the final cut. Bill Carruth left the project toward the end, and David Bretherton took over as supervising editor. Carruth's pre-*Caddyshack* work included *Jaws*, *Baby Blue Marine*, *The Island of Dr. Moreau*, and *FM*. He would go on to *The Karate Kid, Part III*, *Tequila Sunrise*, *8 Million Ways to Die*, *Die Hard*, *Alien 3*, and *Lethal Weapon 4*. Bretherton was a heavyweight whose first movie had been *The Living Swamp* in 1955. He left the mire to edit some of the finest and most commercially successful movies of the '60's and '70's, including *Peyton*

Place, The Diary of Anne Frank, Cabaret, Silver Streak, and *Coma.* After seeing the first cut, Ramis and Kenney realized that the few gopher scenes they had shot in south Florida worked well, so they persuaded Orion to pony up and hire John Dykstra and his team to film additional gopher scenes.

Hollywood editing rooms can, at times, be extremely tense. But everyone got along very well on *Caddyshack,* according to Igel.

"David and Bill were nice guys," she says. "And everyone who was around was very pleasant for the most part."

Once the picture editing process is over, the sound editors begin work on the film, adding sound effects, dialogue, and music, which is then mixed together in a mixing studio. To get a sense of whether the film is working, the studio screens an unfinished version in front of a live audience in what's called a "preview." The first one took place on the Warner Brothers lot in Burbank. There was no specific effort to cart in a busload of golfers, so it's likely that there were very few golfers in the audience. Yet the packed house loved the movie, and the editors and producers made very few changes.

"I've been to a lot of previews since *Caddyshack,* and I'm hard-pressed to remember one that went so well," says Igel. "So that made everyone pretty happy."

To Igel, *Caddyshack* is primarily about a "snooty golf club" that Rodney Dangerfield rocks to its core.

"Al Czervik is being honest about just how snobby Bushwood is, and that really appeals to an audience," she says. "It was Rodney's first movie, and he was great."

For much of the editing process, Dangerfield, Ted Knight, Bill Murray, and the cast treated Igel and the editing team to a series of wonderful performances. In an effort to secure a broad rating, some of the best (yet coarsest) Bill Murray scenes unfortunately had to hit the cutting room floor.

After the film premiered in theaters, Igel spent several additional months working on the TV version. So, for a new arrival to Hollywood, *Caddyshack* was a great gig.

Igel, a tennis player, still marvels at how *Caddyshack* keeps going and even continues to pick up steam.

"In the editing room, you never know how things are going to turn out," she says. "I think it turned out really well, but it amazes me that the film is still so popular. Nobody could have predicted that."

Czervik wanted a wealth of condos, shopping centers, and plenty of parking, but the area around Bushwood remains totally residential.

Rather charmingly, the caddies sit down and eat sandwiches while watching the in-bag television. It sounds like they're watching a shoot-'em-up Western.

The Smails party arrives at the halfway hut—a structure that no longer exists in real life. The unidentified caddy wheels Smails's trolley to the side. We meet Maggie O'Hooligan, the Irish girl. For the time, the prices seem a little steep:

Hamburger	$1.50
Cheeseburger	$1.75
Hot Dog	$0.75
Soup	$0.65
Potato Chips	$0.40
Milkshake	$0.90

Thus if Spaulding had had everything he requested, it would have set the judge back $5.30.

In the hut, notice the Budweiser/Clydesdale display to the right of Maggie.

The highlight of the scene behind the halfway hut is that it reveals that a portion of Danny Noonan's hair is coming out of the gap between the back of the hat and the strap.

The Noonan–O'Hooligan affair is much stronger and more involved in the early script and is one of the many parts in the movie that the performances of Knight, Dangerfield, Murray, and others push aside. Perhaps the reason that the Noonan–O'Hooligan affair seems so extracurricular is that most of it ended up on the floor of the editing room. Fleshed out, Maggie O'Hooligan could have been a much better, or at least deeper, player in the movie. There's also some tension between Danny Noonan and Tony D'Annunzio over Maggie, as both caddies are in hot pursuit throughout the movie. The tension comes to the fore just after Danny wins the caddy tournament and also at the swimming pool.

Sarah Holcomb has the distinction of having appeared in *Animal House* and *Caddyshack*. In *Animal House*, she played Clorette DePasto, the mayor's randy young daughter—the one who loves football, fraternities, and chewing chewing gum. Between *Animal House* and *Caddyshack*, Holcomb had a starring role in *Walk Proud* and a semistarring role as Judith Hastings in *Happy Birthday, Gemini*. After *Caddyshack*, Holcomb left acting altogether, never to surface again. Like Doug Kenney, the only other actor to have appeared in *Animal House* and *Caddyshack*, two of the top comedies that Hollywood has ever produced, Holcomb had a problem with substance abuse. Holcomb addressed her problem and is apparently alive today, but Kenney failed to deal with his. The Acme *Animal House* pages (acmewebpages.com) say that she's "living a quiet, obscure life in the middle of nowhere under a different name and does not wish to be found." One can only hope that Sarah Holcomb understands that she's a huge part of American movie lore and that she's enjoying her life without the aid of the same "cool" substances that have devastated and killed so many talents.

The day's golf ends close to the current 9th green. The Bishop holes out and tells the caddies to put him down for a five. In the script, the caddies believe that it's a nine; Motormouth actually signals a nine with his fingers, and Danny Noonan nods knowingly. Bishop Pickering, however, wins the award for best golf shoes. The judge's putt can't be more than eighteen inches; the tricky part is that his shadow is in the way, but it's just outside tap-in range. However, the putt gets a little longer as the scene progresses—and the gallery gets a little longer. From the angle with Al Czervik striding up to the green to organize the wager, it's also a downhill putt—not a slider necessarily, but a downhill putt, nonetheless. The judge uses what looks to be a classic Wilson 8802, one of the most beautiful putters ever made. Wilson 8802s from the 1960s are somewhat valuable and can fetch anywhere from $250 to $750, depending on condition. Wilson manufactured the forged version of the club into the 1990s and subsequently produced a cast version under the Robert Mandrella logo: Mandrella is a Wilson club designer. Wilson no longer produces the 8802 model; however, several name putter designers, such as Robert Bettinardi and

Scotty Cameron, have produced 8802-like models. Bettinardi's is the BB-2 and Cameron's is the American Classic III. These clubs, in both right-handed and left-handed models, fetch between $400 and $1,400. The Wilson 8802 is not a golf club for the faint of heart; it requires confidence to use plus a technically strong stroke. However, it provides superb feedback. When the judge misses the putt, he knows it—he *feels* it.

Julie Cole spent seventeen years on the LPGA Tour and was known as one of the better putters on the tour. Today, she is the director of instruction at the Dana Rader Golf School at Ballantyne Resort in Charlotte, North Carolina. She assesses Judge Smails's missed two-footer.

"Basically, everything that could pretty much go wrong goes wrong. His posture is awful. The knees are too flexed. The club is in the palm. He takes the putter head back with his wrists, and his eyes follow the putter blade. He pulls it because he decelerates. The left arm and shoulder are not working and, at impact, he has flipped

The apartments/condos behind the eighth tee were under construction during filming. They are at the corner of South Pine Island Road and SW 30th Street in Davie, near Fort Lauderdale.

(Courtesy of the author)

the wrist at the ball. That's the technical and me-chanical side of it all, but there are mental issues as well. The preshot routine is poor and/or non-existent, and he's too distracted—no surprise there. He also never looks at the target and simply tries to guide the ball. Basically, Ted Knight perfectly plays a really poor putter."

Just after the judge misses the putt, note that Lacey Underall is still wearing her golf glove and that Spaulding is sacked out on the ground next to his trolley. Tony D'Annunzio is lying up against the bag, shagged out after carrying that around. After the judge helicopters the putter, look down the fairway: Drew Scott helicopters his club and Gatsby is, once again, laughing his ass off.

00:27:19—The Judge Helicopters His Putter.

Good putters know that you never throw or helicopter your putter. It's more a spiritual thing than a physical thing. Good putters know that the putter is the most important club in the bag, and once a good putter has found the right putter, the good putter sticks with it. Know that if the putts aren't falling, it's the puttee, not the putter.

On the clubhouse deck, there are fifteen people. The sixteenth is Richard Richards, the club manager. This was Scott Sudden, who was the actual manager of Rolling Hills at the time. It was Sudden's only movie. Fred Buch played the "angry husband" and played the role perfectly. Buch appeared in several movies, including *The Pilot*, *Spring Break*, *Porky's II*, *Porky's III*, *Deadly Rivals*, and *Radio Inside*; he also appeared in the TV movie *The Wild and the Free* and the TV miniseries *Till We Meet Again*.

Note that the putter managed to hit the angry husband's wife and shatter the glass table. It also put a decent hole in the umbrella. So, all in all, it's been an expensive day for the judge: $100 on the first tee, lunch for Spaulding ($5.30), $1,000 on the final green, the angry husband's lunch, the umbrella, and probably the table. Perhaps it should be no surprise that the judge surprises Noonan with that whopping 25 cent tip.

6

Gopher Destruction Preparation.
Fourth of July Dance. How to
Improve a Porsche. The Zen Priest.
The Big Tournament.

Smails the third vomits
The doctor's seat smooth as a
Puke polished pebble
—poet/philosopher Basho (son of)

The Bushwood Bash. Mega-Flatulence, Czervik Style. Ty, Meet
Lacey. Lacey, Meet Ty. Earth, Wind, and Fire, but No Doorknobs.
A Flute with No Holes. Caddy Tournament. A Ten Footer for
All the Marbles and a Trip to the Yacht Club.

AFTER seeing Carl Spackler on the golf
course, the audience now gets to see
the increasingly demented assistant
greenskeeper in what can only be described
as a hovel that's perfect for the increasingly
demented assistant greenskeeper. One can only
imagine what the toilet in a toilet like that
would look like; thankfully, the director saved
us that revelation. The props people superbly
crammed Carl's work environment with the requisite kit. The action leaves Carl for the more upmarket (it's not that hard) environment of the
Bushwood Country Club Fourth of July dinner

dance. Al Czervik and Judge Smails have started their miniwar, but the snobs versus slobs battle intensifies and gets new ammunition during the dance. Ty Webb then putts with his feet and demonstrates the perfect way to deal with the old-fashioned stymie issue. The lessons from Webb eventually propel Danny Noonan toward a Zen priesthood and victory in the caddy tournament—plus an invitation to mow the judge's lawn and attend the christening of the *Flying Wasp.*

Scene time line: 00:23:15–00:42:53.

Carl begins the scene, where he is organizing his rifle (and sight) with an attempted rendition of some type of song. The rendition is so awful that there's no way to discern the tune. The bags are full of Milogranite, a fertilizer that's also popular for "material spillage." Carl has organized the bags bunker style. Carl mentions "superior intelligence" as one of his assets, but the "varmint cong" line is the best line in a scene that lasts only forty seconds.

With its lights and requisite Fourth of July adornments, Bushwood looks very attractive—for a dump. The producers chose the epic Boca Raton Resort and Club to film the scene. The early script describes the Fourth of July gig simply as a "dinner dance."

After the shot of the exterior, there's a general shot of the interior, with thirteen couples dancing. One of the couples is Chuck Schick and Noble Noyes; they are the youngest couple by about eighty years and thus are relatively easy to spot. Making the spotting easier is the fact that Chuck is wearing a white dinner jacket; he inelegantly drops Noble's right dress strap, and she quickly puts it back where it should be. Later in the early draft of the script, Chuck and Noble get married, in a major scene in the movie.

Here's how the third draft describes the scene at the dinner dance:

LACEY UNDERALL
She's sitting at a table with Judge Smails, his wife, MRS. SMAILS, a Wagnerian dowager, Spaulding Smails, the Judge's loathsome grandson, Dr. Beeper and his wife, CONNIE BEEPER, who is obviously much too charming and attractive to be married to a creep like Dr. Beeper.
Lacey looks great in an off-the-shoulder white cotton dress. Judge Smails is handling the introductions when Danny and Maggie arrive with the bread and butter.

In the movie, Dr. Beeper's wife is not a wife but a girlfriend. In the script, Judge Smails calls Connie Beeper Constance. The credits list Judy Arman as "Beeper's Girlfriend." Arman appeared in just one other movie, *A Night in Heaven*, about a married woman who falls for a male stripper.

With virtually the entire cast present and in great form, there's a lot going on. After

Carl Spackler (Bill Murray) at work in his hovel. The props and scenery are the work (and genius) of Stan Jolley and his crew.
(Warner/Orion/The Kobal Collection)

that young devil Chuck Schick has tried to undress the red-headed vixen, Ms. Noyes, the attention turns to the Smails table. But in the background, the Czervik table is having a massive time. The table to the right of the Czervik table on the upper deck is already complaining, and it's Doug Kenney, in an uncredited role, who with a wave of his hand turns around and tells the complaining party to get lost. The complaining party then brings a waiter over so that he can complain some more. Note that the woman next to the complaining party is wearing sunglasses.

Danny Noonan, new to the bussing industry, is handing out the butter and using his vantage point to check out breasts. He starts with Dr. Beeper's girlfriend's/wife's chest, then moves onto Lacey Underall's chest.

The script describes the fun table with the Fun Couples thus:

ANOTHER TABLE

In contrast to the Smails' table, these guests are having a rollicking good time. It's the FUN COUPLES.

And they are certainly having a "rollicking" good time. *Rollicking* is an interesting word, as it has two completely different meanings. The *Caddyshack* meaning refers to exuberance, but there's another meaning, used primarily in the United Kingdom: serious reprimand as in "He really annoyed me when he was talking during my backswing, so I gave him a good rollicking."

Judge Smails is not particularly amused when Dr. Beeper tells Mrs. Smails that she's looking lovely this evening.

The Bishop has a glass of wine; Spaulding has water. That will soon change.

The music, perfect for a dinner dance at an uptight club, is original. The beauty of the music is that it perfectly matches the seven-piece band: only the makers of The Greatest Movie Ever Made would have gone to such lengths, although I'm not certain that I hear a guitarist with a huge 'fro in the soundtrack.

The red tails that the judge sports are a solid replica of the kit that members of the Royal and Ancient Golf Club of St. Andrews wear. The Royal and Ancient is the most prominent golf club in the United Kingdom and has a worldwide membership of 2,400; it's a private club. Their imposing stone clubhouse sits behind the first tee of the Old Course. The Royal and Ancient Golf Club of St. Andrews (not to be confused today with the R&A, which is a separate but related body that primarily organizes the Open Championship and other corporate entities) is not the governing body of the Old Course and the other courses at St. Andrews. That is the St. Andrews Links Trust, whose governing body includes three members of the Royal and Ancient Golf Club of St. Andrews. Since 1974, the St. Andrews Links Trust has been organizing and maintaining the

Links of St. Andrews. The Royal and Ancient Golf Club of St. Andrews has a captain each year, but the captain of the R&A is not the "Captain of the Links of St. Andrews, Scotland."

In St. Andrews, there is a St. Andrews Golf Club, comprising mostly local members; even the captain of this club is not the captain of the Links of St. Andrews. The captain of the Royal and Ancient would not have given away the jacket unless the judge was a member and, even then, the judge should not have worn it outside the club.

Either way, none of the St. Andrews stuff is of any interest whatsoever to Lacey Underall—and it shows! Throughout the movie, she shows absolutely no interest in golf whatsoever. Perfect.

What are they eating at the Smails table? It's potatoes and what looks to be some type of red meat—with a big bone sticking out. Lamb?

In the script, the writers were somewhat specific about the amount of butter that Danny Noonan should give Lacey Underall: "about a pound."

Perhaps the reason that Al Czervik is so rollicking is that his wife, Mona, died "last winter." The Blonde Bombshell (so labeled in the credits) is Anna Upstrom, Brian Doyle-Murray's girlfriend—at least at the beginning of shooting. During shooting, Doyle-Murray mostly hung out with Sarah Holcomb. Upstrom appeared in the 1986 movie *Club Paradise*, about an injured fireman who retires to an island in the Caribbean and opens a club. Harold Ramis and Brian Doyle-Murray wrote the movie; Robin Williams, Peter O'Toole, Twiggy, and Jimmy Cliff appeared alongside Upstrom. She also appeared in a *CHiPs* episode in 1978, but has not to date appeared in *Law and Order*. The brunette to the right of Al Czervik is Suki, played by Brian McConnachie's wife, Ann. However, Gatsby's date, Wally, played by Cordis Heard, is the woman who is smoking at the Czervik table; she *did* appear in *Law and Order*, in 1999 as Mandy Lewis in an episode titled "Ramparts," and is the only one at the table who went on to appear in *Law and Order*. Heard may have made the *Caddyshack* cast due to Chicago connections: in the '70s, she was a member of two theater companies, including Chicago's Organic Theater Company. She later appeared in several movies, including *Heavy, Hero, Rock 'n' Roll High School Forever*, and *I'm Dancing as Fast as I Can*. She also appeared in the TV movies *Cast the First Stone* and *The Royal Romance of Charles and Diana*, as Gwendolyn Carrington.

What's amazing about Maggie O'Hooligan is that she actually goes to the chef and tells him that Czervik has said that the steak is low-grade dog food. Not just dog food, but *low-grade* dog food. In the script, the fart comes before Czervik asks for "another round for our table" and complains about the jockey marks on the steak. When the cameras show the Czervik table, there's almost always someone in the background giving them the evil eye: pay particular attention to the guy with the black-rimmed glasses and the lady with the short-cropped hair immediately be-

hind Czervik. But there are others equally annoyed. It's difficult to focus on the irritated: Czervik is the center of attention—so much so that Danny Noonan passes behind Czervik and Maggie O'Hooligan and nobody notices.

The jockey marks on the steak gag must have been a peach: it has the Fun Couples rollicking like they've never rollicked before—so much so that they almost choke on their food. Doug Kenney jettisons something, then tries to cover it up with his napkin.

00:30:57—Rodney Breaks Wind.

The obligatory fart joke is a doozy: pedal to the metal and designed to irritate as many people as possible. Czervik even rolls to his left for maximum flatulence, his face scrimped up in mock agony. The fart lasts 2.012 seconds, probably not a cinematic record but impressive nonetheless, a pure show stopper. It must have been loud as well: its retort shocks and shakes several tables into total silence. It even shocks the Fun Couples until Czervik delivers the oldie but goodie: "Oh, somebody step on a duck?" It was a straightforward fart, even though most farts, according to P. Cook, go straight backwards. If it wasn't already clear, it is now: everyone at the Czervik table is hammered, especially Doug Kenney, Gatsby, Wally, and of course the real estate/condo magnate. It's a generally attractive group of ladies at the Czervik table: all they need is a little cleavage.

Postflatulence, Dangerfield ratchets up his performance a few notches. The stark contrast between Czervik's gear and the black tie is now at its most noticeable. James Hotchkiss plays the Old Crony who Czervik slaps on the back; this was, tragically, Hotchkiss's only movie—he is excellent as the hyperoffended old boy.

The chef scene, even though it's just six seconds long, is superb, and a great favorite of children who get to see (certain bits of) *Caddyshack*. Frank Schuller played the cook, whose name is Charlie and, in the script, is Hungarian.

From the early 1960s to the early 1990s, Schuller enjoyed a busy career in TV and movies, appearing in *Cheers, L.A. Law, Dynasty, Hill Street Blues, Falconcrest, Flipper, Who?, Hello Down There,* and *Ghost Warrior*. His scene in *Caddyshack* perfectly breaks up the dinner dance; the dead straight-on camera angle adds to the effect.

The last thing that the Czervik table needs is a bar, but they go in search of one anyway. And why not? With Czervik mistaking the judge for a waiter, Lacey Underall is having a good laugh. She gets the joke: the slob coming into Bushwood to expose the snobs, beginning with the Smails table. Czervik's assault on said gathering is one of the highlights of the movie and may have been somewhat improvised: in the script, Czervik simply looks at the judge and asks: "Hey, who's the mummy?"

The reaction to Al Czervik from the assorted assaulted at the Smails table is varied. Mrs. Smails gives her best "I'm totally horrified" look, while Lacey Underall moves her thumb in a quasi–middle finger move. Ted Knight's look is a cross between sheer anger, bemusement, and cosmic rage; just after having a go at Spaulding, the judge even puffs up his chest a little. Dr. Beeper and wife/girlfriend share similarly shocked looks. Meanwhile, Team Czervik is loving every second.

Just after Al gets to the dance floor, the action moves back to the kitchen, where Maggie jealously gives Danny Noonan career advice about Lacey Underall, the biggest whore on 5th Avenue. In the script, she's the biggest whore in Philadelphia. You'd know the difference. Maggie also says that Lacey has been "plucked more times than the Rose of Tralee," which is an odd, albeit obvious metaphor. Today, in Ireland, the Rose of Tralee is big business—an international beauty pageant of sorts that takes place each August.

The Rose of Tralee festival originated around three key components of Irish life: betting, drinking, and tourism. A group of businessmen met in a bar in Tralee to discuss ways to bring more visitors to the area during racing season. They came up with a competition whose aim was to find the young lady that most closely resembled the woman in the song, "The Rose of Tralee." The Rose of Tralee festival first took place in 1959, and today it is a huge deal in Ireland, complete with extensive television coverage. The 1980 Rose of Tralee was Sheila O'Hanrahan; victors need not necessarily be stunners as there's no swimsuit session. The winner, one must assume, is a young lady of high repute, so it seems odd that Maggie would imply that the shag-centric Lacey would be anything like a Rose of Tralee. Or perhaps Maggie O'Hooligan has some special insider knowledge.

With the trombone now playing the lead in the band, the gopher dances just like the Bushwood ancients in the dinner dance; this moment represents the top achievement for John Dykstra and his team of gopher builders.

As Bill Murray emerges through the bountiful and sylvan boughs of Bushwood, there's more Budweiser: two six packs. A dinner dance is going on and, like most dinner dances, it's taking place at night; yet behind Bill Murray, it's clearly the middle of the day. The film editing team must have been throwing things around the film editing room. *Caddyshack* has its vulgar moments, but perhaps the most vulgar word in the movie is "poontang," as in "I smell varmint poontang." Poontang refers to a woman's private area and how she uses it in terms of gratification. Yet it's not a well-known word: an acquaintance at university had a Ford Mustang, and he got a request for the license plate "POON-TANG" past the North Carolina Department of Motor Vehicles license plate censorship department.

As Ty Webb admires the heifers who saunter past, Al Czervik and the Fun Couples are bantering about what might be the best fishing holes.

As Suki Scott introduces Ty Webb to Al Czervik, three members of Bushwood's youth movement are watching the action: Spaulding Smails, Chuck Schick, and Lacey Underall. When the camera focuses solely on them (in order to focus solely on Lacey Underall and her reaction to seeing Ty Webb), Noble Noyes has magically joined the group. Then she magically disappears. Motormouth, the caddy, is in the background; he, too, is moonlighting as a bus boy. Nice work if you can get it. Gatsby's bird, Wally, has her only speaking moment here: "I think someone's giving you the big eye."

The Webb/Czervik introduction scene shows that Doug Kenney was not particularly tall.

Even though the band is still playing its soporific dinner dance music, the guitarist with the afro is going bonkers.

Al Czervik, desperate for more booze, heads for the bar and orders a bull shot, quite possibly one of the most vile drinks that a bartender could have to create:

- Vodka
- Beef bouillon (cold)
- Salt
- Pepper

Thankfully, there are variations, but none of them seem any more appetizing. Here's bull-shot #4:

- Vodka
- Beef bouillon (cold)
- Lemon juice
- Tabasco
- Worcestershire sauce
- Celery salt

The knowledgeable bartender will know to serve the drink in a white wine glass then run, as the drinker is sure to regurgitate.

The two young girls at the bar are simply "First Girl" and "Second Girl" in the script—two young pre-debs. They receive cast credits: Kim Bordeaux and Lori Lowe. *Caddyshack* was their only listed movie. In the script, they have speaking parts and are trying to scoff drinks off Tony D'Annunzio.

FIRST GIRL
I'd like a G&T, please.

SECOND GIRL
Make it two.

TONY
What? Two T&As? You want to give me two T&As—good. Let's have a drink first, okay? Then I'll show you where the shark bit me.

[The girls giggle as Tony mixes their drinks. One of them smiles coyly at Danny. He smiles back politely, but keeps watching Lacey.]

The girls in the movie look too young to be boozing it up, but youth fails to keep Spaulding from indulging—in his own way. A close look reveals that the girls may actually have been successful in getting a couple of gin and tonics.

The band, rolling through its medley of well-known tunes, becomes a full-blown orchestra playing "Feelings" when the camera focuses on Lacey Underall. Seconds later, the strings have gone on break and it's just the house band. As Lacey and Ty express their feelings on the balcony/deck, the band continues to play "Feelings." Strangely, pumping the key lyrics of the ballad ("Feelings, wo-o-o feelings, / Wo-o-o, feelings again in my arms") produces a gaggle of strange sights dealing with depression, astrology, and psychology. In the early script, there's some touching dialogue between Ty and Lacey before their touching scene out on the balcony/deck.

TY
[He watches Lacey as she comes up to meet him.]

LACEY
Hello. My name is Lacey Underall. I'm seventeen and I'm trouble.

[Ty is amused and intrigued by her boldness.]

TY
Ty Webb. I bet you're not as bad as your reputation.

LACEY
[provocative]
Better. Will you dance with me?

The dialogue on the balcony/deck originally took place on the dance floor. The dialogue that made it into the movie is very close to the early script. The brief scene reveals Underall as part of the Czervik team—not exactly a slob, but certainly part of the group that's willing to take frequent shots at the snobs.

Richard M. Nixon played golf, only taking up the game in his forties. Nixon developed a decent short game but always struggled with the long game. With plenty of time on his hands after his stint in the White House, Nixon made time to practice and play.

Lacey's list of hobbies starts with skinny skiing, which, today, would likely have the moniker "extreme skinny skiing." The epicenter of nude skiing was Crested Butte, Colorado, where for twenty-five years a fairly significant group of people would happily take off their clothes and ski in the nude on the last official day of the season. The problem was not necessarily the nude skiers but the thousands of people who came out to *watch* the nude skiers. Toward the end of the run, a group of spectators who had had too much refreshment started throwing bottles at the police, and the experiment ended. Several Colorado resorts offer "lightly clothed" events, such as Telluride's "Ski a Thong," but finding a spot to ski with just boots on in the United States is tough. There's a naked cross-country skiing race in Austria; hard-core naturists, however, tend to gather in certain areas in Europe for their skiing holidays, typically confining their nudity to fondue parties and related events.

"Going to bullfights on acid" is less popular than skinny skiing; there's no record of anyone having achieved this status, although Ernest Hemmingway attended bullfights after having enjoyed a few beverages. An Ithaca rock band called Hubcap plays a song titled "Bullfights on Acid" that's available on the Halogen Sons album. Hubcap is sort of a 1980s mock REM version of ZZ Top. The song has absolutely nothing to do with bullfights on acid, but the lead singer used the line for the title.

Numerous individuals, when listing hobbies on Web sites where individuals list hobbies, list "going to bullfights on acid."

Using such a lame "pre-kiss" line as "let's pretend we're real human beings," Webb deserves to get the rejection, the quick final turn. Still, you have to hand it to Ty: the ball will not go in the basket unless the player shoots it. Sometimes the ball goes in the basket and sometimes it doesn't.

In the early script, Spaulding, clearly under age, tries to procure a drink from Tony D'Annunzio at the bar during the dinner dance. In another scene, Spaulding tries to get weed from Porter-house, who promises some fine "bongolese" for $75. That's the "stuff" that the youngsters smoke a little later at the yacht club.

Before taking care of the leftovers, Spaulding must have found some booze. He only drinks three beverages (while the band's guitarist pounds away), but he still manages to hurl after staggering around the Porsche. There's no mention of the couple who watches the event, although the man looks like the club manager—but the club manager surely would have done something instead of simply running away. You have to hand it to Spaulding; he puts his heart and soul into his vomiting.

After the puking in the Porsche scene, the action returns to the dance floor. Mrs. Smails provides one of just two mentions of the judge's first name.

MRS. SMAILS
Elihu, who is that disgusting man over there?

The tempo is more upbeat, but not upbeat enough for Al Czervik, who gets the band to cover the Earth, Wind, and Fire classic "Boogie Wonderland"—much to the delight of the guitarist, who bounces and bobbles with renewed vim. "Boogie Wonderland" had reached #7 in the U.S. charts in July 1979; the #1 record that month was Anita Ward's "Ring My Bell." "Chuck E.'s in Love" was also top ten and, mercifully, the sound crew chose "Boogie Wonderland" and not the Rickie Lee Jones classic. Earth, Wind, and Fire teamed with the Emotions on "Boogie Wonderland," a song with some of the more cryptic lyrics of the disco era.

> Midnight creeps so slowly into hearts,
> of men who need more than they get
> daylight deals a bad hand,
> to a woman that has laid too many bets.

The best disco dancer on the floor (apart from Al Czervik) is Noble Noyes, who is dancing with Chuck Schick. What goes around comes around. Chuck Schick is no longer around. Earth,

Wind, and Fire are still recording and touring; their twenty-third album, *Illumination*, hit record stores in late 2005. The name "Elihu" appears in the Phish song "Sample in a Jar."

The brief dawn golf course shot that immediately follows Dr. Beeper's argument with Spaulding's vomit is possibly the current 14th hole, which has a long water hazard down the left side of the fairway.

The three lady golfers are golf buddies of Marian Polan, the casting agent who hired all the extras. Note that the woman in blue is left-handed, and there aren't many left-handed lady golfers in the world. This left-handed lady golfer has a good putting grip and a good stroke—even if it's a little hasty. The shot only shows a threesome; however, it's clear that there's some type of game going on: the red-headed lady with the brown skirt, green top, and crazy hat (craziest in the movie) is watching the putt from right behind the line, a huge golf etiquette no-no unless the person is on the same side as the person who is putting. The left-handed lady must have made the putt: the threesome walks to the hole and left-handed lady picks the ball out of the hole, proving that left-handers are great putters. The ladies, while handsome in a lady golfer-ish type of way, are not stunners, yet they grab the attention of Uncle Carl, proving that Uncle Carl is obviously a little starved for attention. Tragically, after the assistant greenskeeper asks the ladies to bark like dogs for him, we don't see the threesome again. We also don't see Sandy McFiddish again.

The Ty Webb mentoring scene takes one minute and fifty seconds. The scene keeps the Noonan scholarship plot moving along and continues to feed the image of Ty Webb as the club's most talented and ethereal golfer. In the scene where Al Czervik manages to hit Judge Smails in the testicles, the judge is asking Danny about Ty Webb—definitely a member of Bushwood but a golfing loner, nonetheless. To the judge and others at Bushwood, Webb's golf is a mystery.

There may have been some improvisation here, but the final result is similar to the scene in the early script. Before the golf discussion, there's a touch of conflict over Lacey Underall: Danny is annoyed that Webb might be "getting" Lacey and almost hits Webb with the bunker rake. Webb's antics on the green are in the early version of the script.

Ty drops some balls on the green. He turns to Danny and backhand putts perfectly, into the hole. . . . Ty casually taps two balls at once into the hole. . . . Ty casually kicks a ball right to the edge of the hole. . . . Ty lines up another ball between his legs. . . . Ty taps the ball, and it hops over the kicked ball and into the cup.

The flute line and the Danish line are just a few of the lines from the early script that make it into the final version, indicating that Chevy Chase and Michael O'Keefe likely improvised much of the dialogue. The final advice in the early script from Webb to Noonan reads, "If you want to get what you want, you have to stop wanting it first."

There's no record of a Mitchell Cumstein existing or ever having existed; he's become a popular "user" name on several golf and nongolf message boards where several clever users have changed the *C* in Cumstein to a *K* in order to hide their identities—perhaps.

The Japanese poet and Zen philosopher Matsuo Basho (1644–1694) is one of the more famous practitioners of the haiku form—primarily because he *started* the form. Some Basho haikus:

> Waking in the night;
> the lamp is low,
> the oil freezing.

> It has rained enough
> to turn the stubble on the field
> black.

> Winter rain
> falls on the cow-shed;
> a cock crows.

> The leeks
> newly washed white,
> how cold it is!

The sea darkens;
the voices of the wild ducks
are faintly white.

Some Japanese haiku experts have said that the form pretty much begins and ends with Basho. Perhaps said experts failed to consider this haiku, from Japanese poet Buson (1716–1784).

Nobly, the great priest
deposits his daily stool
in bleak winter fields

Did the master haiku poet Basho know about flutes and Danishes with holes? A scan of approximately one hundred of Basho's poems reveals no direct references. Basho was an interesting character, born into nobility—a Samurai family. He became a drifter of sorts, a sort of Japanese Dead Head living off cash from his student poets and other admirers. In 1667, Basho moved to Tokyo, then named Edo, and started the haiku snowball. Basho was actually a nom de plume that came from his affinity for the soli-

tude that his *basho-an* hut provided. The poet believed that poetry, specifically haiku, could provide enlightenment and thus the Zen connection. The haiku form was somewhat nonsensical and even silly before Basho made it much more serious. However, haiku, from a literary perspective, was a sideline. His best work was travel writing, especially *Oku-no-hosomichi* (The Narrow Road to the Far North).

Kitaro Nishida (1870–1945), perhaps inspired by Basho, founded a philosophy called Basho. Kitaro based his ideas on the theory and practical application of what the English would describe as "bugger all."

"Man stands alone completely independent in the mysticism of an absolute nothingness," wrote Nishida.

The only member of the *Caddyshack* cast and crew who became a Zen priest is Michael O'Keefe, who played Danny Noonan. O'Keefe, only twenty-five in the year of *Caddyshack*, was an industry veteran, having appeared in two movies, *Gray Lady Down* and *The Great Santini*; he received a best supporting actor Oscar nomination for playing Ben Meechum in the latter. However, the bulk of O'Keefe's work pre-*Caddyshack* was in television, where he appeared in several series, movies, and miniseries, including *The Blue Knight*, *The Waltons*, *The Lindbergh Kidnapping Case*, *M*A*S*H*, and *The Dark Secret of Harvest Home*. Post-*Caddyshack*, O'Keefe has been busy with ample TV, movie, and theater work. Projects have included:

- *The Glass House*
- *Taking a Chance on Love*
- *The Pledge*
- *Just One Night*
- *Raising the Ashes*
- *Ghosts of Mississippi*
- *Nina Takes a Lover*
- *Ironweed*
- *The Slugger's Wife*
- *Finders Keepers*
- *Split Image*
- *House, M.D.*

- *Law & Order: Special Victims Unit*
- *CSI: Crime Scene Investigation*
- *The West Wing*
- *Law & Order: Criminal Intent*
- *Law & Order*
- *Roseanne* (36 appearances)
- *Fear*
- *Disaster at Silo Z*
- *Alfred Hitchcock Presents*

While at Mamaroneck High School just north of New York City, O'Keefe studied at the American Academy of Dramatic Arts. After graduation, he cofounded the Colonnade Theatre Lab. In addition to acting, O'Keefe has been a lyricist, most notably contributing to the Bonnie Raitt songs "One Part Be My Lover" and "Longing in Their Hearts." He has also written lyrics for signer/songwriter Paul Brady and is currently a candidate for an MFA in poetry at Bennington College.

O'Keefe became an ordained Zen priest in 1996; his Zen Bhuddist journey began in earnest in 1986, when musician John Miller took O'Keefe to an introduction to Zen practice meeting at the Zen Community of New York (ZCNY) on O'Keefe's thirty-first birthday. A significant part of O'Keefe's Zen practice is community oriented and revolves around peace making. To this end, O'Keefe has traveled to Vietnam and Northern Ireland. This article appeared in the *North Belfast News* in November 2002; despite the lead, which stereotypes actors as complete losers, the piece provides useful insight into O'Keefe's dedication to peace. It is reprinted with permission.

> Some film stars snort cocaine, wreck hotel rooms and suffer alcohol dependencies. Others are just far too healthy, indulging in fad diets and working out all hours, it's no surprise they cry hysterically at Oscar ceremonies. But one very special American film actor is involved in the art of meditation—a gift he says that can help societies like ours to make the often painful and difficult transition to peace.
>
> Michael O'Keefe is a Zen Priest. But he uses a broad range of meditations—many used in the Buddhist religion—in a plethora of situations and with people from all religious and political backgrounds. And he operates on a global scale. He also happens to be a Hollywood star, acting in scores of movies the latest of which—*The Hot Chick*—is due for release at Christmas in the States.
>
> The movie is the typical bubble gum wacky teen comedy romp. But more seriously he starred alongside Jack Nicholson in the 1991 film *The Pledge*. He was also nominated for an Oscar for his role beside Robert Duvall in the 1979 classic flick, *The Great Santini*. He has also appeared on TV playing the part of hit comedian Roseanne's brother-in-law and most recently in the slick smash series, *The West Wing*. A great friend of Hollywood heartthrob Aidan Quinn, the actor has also written songs with Irish songster Paul Brady. The two artists collaborated on the Irishman's *Spirits Colliding* album, writing the song entitled "Marriage Made In Hollywood."
>
> The O'Keefe name forever associates him with the Emerald Isle and the third genera-

tion Irishman has relatives living in Wicklow, Limerick and Cork. But it was an American human rights activist Tom Hayden that inspired his social consciousness and began a life journey in helping people from traumatised nations.

"Tom is a big role model for me. He was actually an international observer at the talks at Stormont in 1997. He advocates that there has to be social change as well as political out of any conflict."

The Irish roots have instilled in Michael O'Keefe a deep desire to help people of the world caught in the grip of hatred and conflict, the same way his ancestors fled poverty and hardship in the 19th century.

He is a member of the Peacemaker Circle, which is involved across the world in building a "global, effective force for social change." It integrates social action with spiritual practice, taking in the medium of mediation.

Michael O'Keefe has just completed a week of visiting various groups all over Belfast. One brought him to Woodvale in North Belfast to host a meditation session with women who were displaced during the loyalist feud. The group Families of the Displaced, Dispersed and Distressed were shown the great power of mediation, and Michael did sessions with loyalist ex-prisoners.

"You get a sense with these women that they have been kicked out by their own people and they feel a sense of hurt and that's understandable. If meditation can help them to look for something that can help them come to terms with their loss, they might be able to move on," he said.

The Peacemaker Circle has been instrumental in bringing together the most opposing peoples in the world.

"I spent three years traveling between the US and Poland and did reconciliation work in Auschwitz concentration camp. In 1996 we set up a meditation retreat there and about 150 people came from around the world," he said.

"Our cross community work was to get— not just children of the survivors of the

Holocaust—but also the children of the perpetrators coming along as well."

He explains the work of reconciliators like him and his community is to take no political or religious stance.

"We are not pro-Israel or pro any group. At the moment we have been creating cross community dialogue between the two communities in Palestine and Israel. For a number of years we have supported a commune led by a Muslim Sheik and a Jewish Rabbi in the region.

"I'm sure North Belfast has had its share of do-gooders but that's not what we're about. I came into the situation here as an outsider and I want to hear what the people are going through whatever their affiliation. We are honest brokers because we have nothing at stake in the (peace) process."

The actor has been a Zen practitioner for 16 years and became a priest in 1994. It complements both his reconciliation work and his acting.

"There's no particular form of meditation in anything we have done in the north of Ire-land. We come together and empower people so they can go back into their own communities. We try all different forms." The latest visit is not Michael O'Keefe's first to Belfast and nor will it be his last. He will return around February to do more work with various groups, including victims' groups in North Belfast. He is involved with local Zen practitioners hoping to found a Zen Centre in Belfast apart from his work with the Peacemaker Circle.

And he has also been dealing with former hunger striker Lawrence McKeown in gaining contacts in the American film industry for the Belfast Film Festival early next year.

He realises that his public image can do much to heighten the profile of the Peacemaker community. The community brochure states that it is signed up to "a culture of nonviolence and reverence for life, solidarity and a just economic order, tolerance and a life based on truthfulness and equal rights and partnership between men and women."

The core tenets are letting go of fixed ideas about ourselves and the universe and bearing witness to the joy and suffering of the world. In the dog-eat-dog world of multi-million pound movie deals and the tinsel town image of rich actors and actresses, it's a refreshing change to find an actor with a social consciousness and a spirituality that complements those values. Michael O'Keefe, his religion and his peace organization are such a thing and you could get away with affectionately calling him Red Zen O'Keefe.

The interview for *The Book of Caddyshack* took place in early 2006.

BOOK OF CADDYSHACK: There is so much information out there about the movie, I'd like to focus on what it was like for you to make the movie.
MICHAEL O'KEEFE: I pretty much credit Harold (Ramis) as the person who made the film work. Clearly everybody had their own role to play and did it well. For some reason, Harold had never directed before and I think has since proven himself to be a really interesting director. I think *Groundhog Day* is probably one of my favorite

movies, actually. He had a very easy hand, a very light touch, and a very real confidence in his own tastes. He was able to bring together a group of actors from a wide variety of backgrounds. Billy (Murray) and Chevy came from one school of comedy. Rodney was coming from a completely other place—namely the Catskill comedian phenomenon. Then there was Ted, of course, who was coming from years of experience in TV and a whole other approach. Harold was the guy who brought it all together.

BOC: How did you find out about the part?
MO'K: I had to go in and meet with the producers two or three times. *Caddyshack* was an Orion production, and Orion was a division of Warner Brothers. I had just done *The Great Santini* for them, so everybody at Orion was kind of digging on me at the time. Then I met with Harold and Doug and, if I remember correctly, Brian Doyle-Murray.

BOC: You had just acted in a great movie, a serious movie, and you were nominated for an

Academy Award. *Caddyshack* couldn't have been more different.

MO'K: Yeah, which is what really appealed to me about it on the surface. Also, I was a big fan of *Saturday Night Live* and knew of Bill and Chevy, and had seen Chevy in a show that National Lampoon had produced in New York called *Lemmings*. I was also a big fan of *National Lampoon* magazine and knew who Doug Kenney was; Doug was the guy who was probably the best writer on the team of Harold, Doug, and Brian. Which is not to say anything bad about Harold and Brian. It was just that Doug was one of these terribly smart, terribly funny guys who had come out of Harvard, was one of the people behind the Harvard Lampoon when he was in college, and was one of the creators of *National Lampoon*, the magazine. He was the one who, for instance, was responsible for all that Zen stuff that got into the movie.

BOC: Was he into Zen?
MO'K: Yeah, he was into it as much as anybody was into it back then. We knew what it was; we had probably all read one or two books about it, which of course because we were in show business probably made us experts on Zen! I have a really special place in my heart for him because he died right after they finished the film. He'll be forever young.

BOC: Who taught you how to swing the club?
MO'K: I got really lucky. When I was young, I caddied at Winged Foot in New York and grew up there. The teaching professional at Winged Foot set me up with his assistant professional at the time. I worked with the teaching staff at Winged Foot for about six weeks before I went down to shoot the movie in Fort Lauderdale. I had never really played before we made the film. I went out and hit every once in a while when I was a caddy and hit a little bit as a kid. But I never really chased the dream, as it were. So I got the part—of course I lied to them and told them that I played because, you know, I wanted the part. Then I got the part and thought, now I'm in trouble!

BOC: How long had you been a caddy?
MO'K: A couple of summers.

BOC: Enough to get a sense of what being a caddy is all about.

MO'K: Well, that I knew. I knew how to swing a bag, how to club people once I knew their game. I could talk people through shots and tell them what I thought. I was not a star caddy at Winged Foot. Nobody is going to have fond recollections of me clubbing them on number 10 at Winged Foot and getting them close to the pin. But I worked pretty hard on my swing. At the time, I tried to model my swing after Jack Nicklaus.

BOC: I noticed your head is cocked just to the right, just like him.

MO'K: Interestingly enough, it was a thrill of a lifetime. Three years ago, I got invited to play at the Nationwide Tour event in Greenville, South Carolina, and Nicklaus was there. We got to meet, and he was incredibly open and generous with himself and his time. He knew who I was and let me gush all over him in a rather, I thought, great way. I'm not given to falling apart around celebrities. But he was somebody who I definitely turned into a fan. I had read his book. The next day after meeting him, I went to warm up and I had read that he warms up before and after his rounds. He'll go back and work on things he didn't like that he was doing when he was out there. So I go down to warm up and there were like seventy-five spots on the range and seventy-four are taken, and the only one that is open is in front of Nicklaus, which I of course attribute to the fact that "Who the hell wants to stand in front of Nicklaus and have him look at your cut?"

So I go and stand in front of him and he says "Hey, Mike, how are you?" As I'm chatting with him, I'm like "I can't believe it." I hit my balls and I leave and then I come back after my round to do the same thing. Even though my game isn't the greatest thing in the world, I was trying to take it seriously and trying to play well. So I go back to hit and there he was again, the same thing—seventy-five spots on the range, the only one open in front of him. So after all those years later to connect with him, that was definitely a thrill of a lifetime.

BOC: When you run across other well-known golfers, do they get gushy over you?

MO'KK: ESPN called me two years ago; I was in New York doing a play and they asked me to go out to Westchester Country Club because the tour was in town and they wanted to do a piece they were going to show at the Western Open—the Evans Scholarship that they based the scholarship in *Caddyshack* on is associated with the Western Open.

We did this whole phony bit of me being Danny Noonan trying to get on the tour. And all of the sudden Lee Janzen, Mike Weir, Jerry Kelly, David Toms, it was unbelievable, and they all wanted to be in the bit. Next thing I knew, I was hitting balls with Lee Janzen and watching him hit drivers and saying, "Hey, not bad, Lee."

BOC: So many of them must love the movie that they get wobbly-kneed in front of you.

MO'K: They really are into it. Who knew it when we were all doing it. We were just giving it our best whack.

BOC: What was it like being around all the chaos of making the movie on and off the set? From what I understand, it was disorganized, and then the partying began.

MO'K: The partying. That was a big part of making the movie. Most of those guys like Doug and Harold and Billy really came of age in the '60s. So they started college in '69. Back then if you weren't partying, if you weren't getting high, people thought you were weird. The counterculture then was so pervasive.

Certainly everybody was not into it. I wouldn't want you to get that impression, but certainly I was and we had all bought into the ride on the '60s experience at that point. Believe me when I tell you it caused a lot of us a lot of problems. Doug Kenney ended up committing suicide.

BOC: So did Sarah Holcomb completely disappear off the radar?

MO'K: I think Sarah got her head and her heart all messed behind all that. Everybody had to go through their own changes. Making *Caddyshack* is like what David Crosby says about the '60s, which is that if somebody tells you they remember the '60s, then they weren't there. So it was just part of it. None of us thought it was anything but normal, so we just did it. Having said that, nobody stretched the boundaries so far that we couldn't do what we needed to do, or didn't show up to get the job done. There may have been one or two occasions of people straggling in late, but we're talking about an hour or two.

And generally speaking, these guys were really, really smart and really, really funny, and they weren't there to take advantage of the situation. They were there to make the best movie they could make. And I'm really referring to Harold and Doug and certainly Mark Canton—a Warner executive at the time; Jon Peters was there a lot and Peter Guber was John's partner. I don't remember Peter being around terribly much, but I do remember seeing Jon a lot. There was like $7 million on the line, and that was a lot of money. In 1979, that was a ton of money. So people were serious. People partied hard and people got high, but when it came down to it, they had a job to do, they did it, and they did it well.

In the set, there was a lot of looseness in the sense that there was improvisation, especially from Bill. Bill getting into the movie, if I remember this correctly, was all very last minute. He'd only done one other feature at the time, which I think was *Meatballs*. He was still doing *Saturday Night Live*, and was in the middle of the season. They made a deal with him probably the week before we started shooting, and there was no character written except there was this guy vaguely mentioned called Carl. In the original script, they say "Carl cleans out poop from the pool" or "Carl passes Danny and waves." Nothing there.

So they would get on the set, and when Billy was there, Harold would say to Bill, when he did the Augusta Masters commentary, Billy just wrote that based on Harold saying to him, "I think what this could be is like when you're on your own, you're just going around and doing your sports commentary on your U.S. Open appearance." And Billy says "Yeah, say no more, just let me do it." And they just turn on the camera and Billy does it, and that's the thing everybody still quotes. So Bill's genius was as a writer knowing exactly what to offer and how much to offer, and Harold's genius was to be able to select it.

So there was this kind of looseness in the sense that nobody was necessarily showing up knowing exactly what they were going to do. But once I saw them do that, you begin to get the faith that they knew what they were doing and that they can pull that off. In the situation, it's very high pressure. If you blow it, that was $150,000, $200,000 a day back then. If you blow it, what you're basically saying is, "We're going to have to eat $80,000 here before lunch because this isn't working." And those guys knew that. And the film speaks for itself. It's not necessarily high art, but it sure is funny.

BOC: How much did you improvise, or did you stick to the script.
MO'K: A fair amount. My job was not necessarily to bring the funny, as they say, although I think I did at times. My improv was limited to—if somebody improvved around me, I would improv back. Bill and Chevy were really leading on that

sort of thing, Ted occasionally, certainly Rodney. Rodney would throw things in there. So I did a fair amount. That exchange between Chevy and me about taking drugs everyday and all that, that was all improv.

BOC: How hard was it to avoid laughing when Ted Knight made all those funny faces?
MO'K: We call that corpsing. I'm not much of a corpser. Although, once you get me going, I can be a problem. I tend to be more the steady type. I'm the one who you can lean on if you think everyone around you is going to start laughing. Look at me and take me in. So I wasn't necessarily given to losing it on camera. Although a couple of times I did it because Harold would start to laugh off camera; if he liked what you were doing, he would start to crack up. Then I would crack up and then I would come over and mock choke him and say "What are you doing? You're killing me!"

But it wasn't so hard to keep it together around those guys. The thing is, for me it was a bonanza of working with people I thought were really funny in many different ways. I was a huge fan of the *Mary Tyler Moore Show*, which was on when I was in high school. I really watched all of those and thought it was great TV. So for me, working with Ted Knight was like being in heaven.

BOC: I'm sure you watched *SNL*
MO'K: Yeah, Billy was just starting out, just getting famous from the show. Chevy I knew from *Lemmings*, the Lampoon show they sent up to the Woodstock festival.

BOC: Sarah Holcomb from *Animal House*.
MO'K: Right, Sarah from *Animal House*. And Doug had written *Animal House*.

BOC: Any idea what Sarah Holcomb is doing right now?
MO'K: I really don't. I haven't seen her in years. I bumped into her at the Bottom Line folk club in New York fifteen or twenty years ago.

BOC: To many golfers, you're not Michael O'Keefe, you're Danny Noonan. I'm sure when you run into golfers, the lines come out. Do you like that, or do you run away from Danny Noonan?
MO'K: One of the reasons I didn't play golf after the film was because I really didn't want that. The pressure of showing up at a golf course and having everyone come out of the pro shop to watch me hit on the first tee was like, "Wow, I'm definitely not into this."

Frankly, I'm still a lefty, which is just shy of anarchism in a sense, and golf was not cool back then. If you played golf, there was no way any of the women I was interested in were going to go out with me. I have this vivid recollection of this documentary of Abbie Hoffman and the '60s, like in Chicago, and they had Abbie Hoffman on camera where he was saying, "Send us the arms, sends us the drugs, we're going to have a revolution." And those were the guys that I thought were really interesting.

In case you're wondering, misdirected is what I think of them now, having matured slightly since the making of *Caddyshack*. Back then, that's not what we thought. We thought it was a big party and it was fun to get on that train, and so I did without really much . . . I didn't have a thesis in progressive politics I could present back then, I just had an attitude.

When we were in high school and we were on the gymnastic team and they would sing the "Star Spangled Banner" before the meets, our team would refuse to stand. I just wasn't into it.

I stayed away from (golf) for twenty or twenty-five years and just got back into it three or four years ago. And the thing that really appeals to me about it now is I can show up at these events and play with guys who want to donate money to different causes. I show up and a fivesome will donate anything from $20,000 to $40,000 just to play golf with me. Who would have thought? Then the Elizabeth Glaser Pediatric Fund or the ALS Fund or people like that or foundations like that can get a bump, and all I have to do is show up and play golf. That's a no brainer. When I realized I had that opportunity and had the cachet of being Danny Noonan, I was like, "Let's get back into this, it's fun."

As soon as Alice Cooper started playing golf, everybody forgave the stigma of golf, if you know what I mean. So now it's not held in the same sort of contempt it was held in back then.

I tend to feel pretty much like William Shatner at a *Star Trek* convention, if you know what I mean. I actually saw him do a bit on *Saturday Night Live* once where he was making a speech at the *Star Trek* convention and being plagued by all these nerdy questions about dynamics of certain episodes and things like that, and he finally lost it and said, "you people, get a life; I did it for four years." For me, in the back of my mind, I'm like, "wow, man, you got to get some new material because that movie is about twenty-five years ago."

BOC: Nothing better has come along.

MO'K: Well, yeah, certainly not in terms of comedy. *Caddyshack* just captured people's heads for some reason. I don't think anybody can tell you why. It just did.

BOC: That first scene in the movie when everybody is waking up in the big bustling household there, where was that shot? The movie was shot partly in California.

MO'K: That sequence where you see me in front of all those great big mansions, that's Pasadena. The sequence in the house with the family was in Florida. I'm pretty sure, but if somebody tells me otherwise. . . .

BOC: Was that the first take-off-your-clothes moment when you were with Cindy Morgan?
MO'K: You mean for me on film? Let me think for a minute. Yeah, it was. Maybe I pecked the cheek of a girl or gave a girl a chaste teenage kiss earlier in my career. I had already been working for ten years at that point.

BOC: Your second movie, right?
MO'K: My second feature film, but I had been an actor for ten years. I started when I was fifteen. But that was the first one where the girl was topless. I may have been topless before, but I don't think that probably resounded in people's memories.

BOC: What was it like? Were you trying not to giggle?

MO'K: Actually, it was sort of difficult because Cindy was sort of shy and felt somewhat compromised, I think, because the producers wanted to have a photographer on the set and she wasn't into that. I think rightly so. I took her side. If I was her, I'd be shy, too. We were kids, we were young, and I don't think she had done much before and suddenly she was having to take off her shirt in front of a bunch of guys she didn't know and get it on with me, who was another guy she didn't know. So to make everybody comfortable, I suggested to Harold that everybody take their shirt off and then everybody on the crew took their shirt off—to get over the hump, as it were.

BOC: Getting back to that first scene—did you find it a bit bizarre to start a comedy with a crisis with all those kids running around?
MO'K: That came from Billy's family. The model for me and the model that is for Danny Noonan and the model for Danny's family is Bill's family, because I think from memory he is one of eight. And I'm the oldest of seven.

BOC: I was going to ask if you were from a big family. . . .

MO'K: That's an everyday thing. For me when I was a kid in high school to wake up and have six brothers and sisters fighting and jockeying for position in the kitchen to have breakfast and go to school was normal. So that didn't really strike me as anything unfamiliar.

BOC: Do you still keep in touch with cast/crew?

MO'K: I see Brian occasionally because we're on the celebrity golf circuit; he shows up for those things. He's probably the one I see more frequently. The rest of it I probably just bump into people on occasion. With films, it's kind of my analogy for filmmaking is like going to college. You bond, there's a really deep experience, then most of you go your own way. You stay in touch with maybe one or two people.

BOC: You're putting to win the caddy scholarship; how many takes did that take?

MO'K: That was the first one. I got lucky. It was a pretty easy putt. That golf course was not the most challenging golf course in the world that we shot on. If I remember correctly, it was a thirteen-footer with a little bend from left to right.

BOC: And you had people screaming at you as well. . . .

MO'K: Yeah, they couldn't believe it. I stuck it on the first take. There was actually one time with that sand shot that I make at the end. I was standing in the trap and Howard says we're going to rehearse, do you want to rehearse? And I say yeah, and he says we're going to roll just in case. And I said, yeah, whatever. I almost holed that thing. It was mind-blowing.

BOC: Mrs. Smails is a lovely character. What was she like?

MO'K: I loved her to death. That scene where she was in the shower and she asks, "could you loofer my stretch marks?" She was hysterical. That look that she gave me when she realized it was me in her bathroom. She cracked me up big time. She was great, a real pro.

BOC: Can you remember what clubs you used?

MO'K: I do, actually, because I just auctioned them recently. One of the things I got into is starting a Zen practice center in Belfast, Northern Ireland, with some friends of mine who are into Zen. I auctioned off the clubs and used the money so we could get things going in downtown Belfast.

BOC: So they did fetch quite a bit then?

MO'K: They did okay. I think we got $4,000 or $5,000. I was hitting Tommy Armour PGAs. They were blades, so they were a little tougher to hit.

BOC: Do you watch *Caddyshack* much today?

MO'K: No. All told, I've probably seen the movie twice.

BOC: When you first saw it, were you at all shocked? What were your first thoughts at the premiere?

MO'K: I don't think there was even a premiere, and if there was, I was probably working, because I was on a roll back then. First time I saw it I was actually in Dallas, Texas, and making a film called *Split Image* about religious cults, with Karen Allen, who was the star of *Raiders of the Lost Ark*. She and I were in this movie together. We went to see *Caddyshack* down there at the theater, and the only cogent thing I can remember, because when you watch yourself on camera, it's sort of like having a bee's nest in your head, because you're so focused on the minutiae of what you did and how you did it—Do I like this? Do I not like it? Generally speaking, most actors—and I would put myself at the top of this—aren't crazy about watching themselves. There's just a level of "Whoa, is that what I was doing?" I tend to be hypercritical, anyway.

I guess I liked it okay, and it was clear the audience liked it; they were loving it. It was a big house, and it was just about full. But the thing I remember, and I always regretted not saying anything, when I stood up there was a couple behind me like my age or younger, early twenties, the girl stood up and said, "Man that guy that got to play Danny Noonan was like the greatest golfer, wasn't he?" And her boyfriend turned to her and was like "Yeah, no, he wasn't so great." To this day, I regret not saying, "Well, actually, I didn't play golf that much before the film, but glad you guys thought it was interesting at least." I should have taken the opportunity to blow their minds, but of course I didn't.

BOC: I've read that Ted Knight didn't get along with Rodney Dangerfield all that well. You and Scott Colomby sort of have that tension as well. Did you guys get along?

MO'K: Oh yeah, Scott is great. I had worked with Scott before. He was the star of a TV show called *Sons and Daughters* back in the '70s. And actually Richard Donner was the director at the time of the show. We got along great.

There's a lot of brou-ha-ha about Rodney and Ted not getting along or Chevy and Bill not getting along, and frankly, I think that's all overrated. In a sense, my theory about movies, especially movies that people like, the more people like the movie, the more they want to know about the dynamic of it; that's probably one of the reasons you got a book deal. When you hear something like Chevy and Bill didn't get along, then you want to chase that, and understandably so. It's the chase of the press and from my point of view, they chase it to death because I get asked that a lot. I think all that's overblown.

I think actors in a sense come from different schools. Any kind of conflict that came up between Ted and Rodney or Chevy and Billy, and I think there was more between Chevy and Billy because they were naturally competitive, was more about coming from a different school than it was about having a problem with somebody. Ted had this kind of like, you know, summer stock, old pro, I've-been-up-on-the-boards type of approach.

Rodney didn't even know what "action" meant. The first day I saw Rodney in a scene, he comes in the first day of shooting, Rodney comes into the pro shop and wants to buy ten of this, twenty of this, and he's just sort of throwing money around and they're establishing that he's sort of nouveau riche, which is a nice way of putting it. He was standing sort of off camera in the corner of the store, where he couldn't be seen, and they roll and hit the clappers and Harold says "action" and nothing happens. And the other actors are out there and the crew is out there and Harold says "action" and nothing happens. Harold says, "Rodney." And Rodney goes, "Yeah?" And he says, "Action means you start." And Rodney says "Oh, you want me to do the bit?" And Harold says, "Yeah, do the bit." And then, boom! he comes barreling in and does the scene.

So there were bound to be issues. Because Rodney had to be kind of like schooled at the same time he was carrying a big load. Ted, God bless Ted Knight, he was terribly full of himself. So I'm sure he felt in a sense put upon in a way that a narcissist can only be when someone needs your help. Your first reaction is, "I beg your pardon? I'm sorry, did you say you needed my help? No, I'm sorry, I'm too busy acting over here to be any service to you. You figure it out."

So there may have been something like that that came up, but frankly I never saw it.

The one time I saw any kind of competition between Bill and Chevy, it was just sort of natural, sort of jockeying for position that two young

actors go through when they're stepping up to the plate and, also, extemporaneously writing a film as they're shooting it. That was, sort of, for my money, that sort of stuff has just been talked to death and really didn't have any more merit. When you're making a film, everybody's got opinions, everybody's got ideas, and they all come up. That stuff, I don't deal it a lot of credence.

BOC: Do you remember anything about how they came up with the props?
MO'K: That's all about the props guy. I don't remember the guy's name. All that stuff, like the hydraulics with the bags popping out, it was all the property department. There might have been one or two special effects guys.

BOC: Did they get locals for extras?
MO'K: Pretty much, although some of the extras were friends of the writers. A couple of the cute country club girls were aspiring actresses that were friends of the producers and writers who told them to come down to Florida—you get

$100 bucks a day. All you do is hang out, and we'll party. The thing that most people don't understand is that the people around the movie were very intelligent. A bunch of these guys went to Harvard. Brian McConnachie, who played one of the smaller parts, went to Harvard and is a writer and radio commentator in New York. Scott Powell went to Columbia. As soon as he finished chasing the dream as it were in Sha Na Na and chasing a little acting career like in *Caddyshack*, he went to medical school and got a degree practicing medicine in New York.

BOC: What's the weirdest *Caddyshack* thing that's happened to you?

MO'K: The weirdest thing is for people to have that image of me in their mind's eye. It's still Danny Noonan time and it's twenty-five years later. If anything, I look like Danny Noonan's dad. For anybody to put me together with the character . . . when people stop me on the street or stop me on the golf courses when I'm there to play, they say, "I just want to tell you that I really love *Caddyshack*." And I'm like, "How did you

even put that together." I'm surprised people can look at me and even say anything. I mean I weigh, I'm not exaggerating, I weigh fifty pounds more than I weighed back then.

During one of those interviews I did on NBC, I could stick out my tongue, turn sideways and look like a zipper back then. I probably weighed about 165 pounds. I weigh 210, 215, now. I had hair back then that rivaled the gods. Now, I've got thinning hair. In a sense, it goes by in the blink of an eye. My self-image is one thing, but when people approach me and say wow, *Caddyshack*. There must be some remnant, some gleam.

BOC: What is *Caddyshack* about?

MO'K: If I could tell you that, there would be a path beaten to my door and I'd be charging money for people to get the answer.

BOC: You were in *The Pledge* with Jack Nicholson. . . .

MO'K: I was in two with Jack actually, *The Pledge* and *Ironweed*.

BOC: He loves golf.

MO'K: Yeah, I just played with him two weeks ago.

BOC: So he must ask you about it.

MO'K: Not at all, he could care less. He's on his own planet. It's Planet Nicholson for sure. He did a benefit down at Trump National, you know, Trump just built a course down in San Pedro, which, by the way, is beautiful. I think the ladies, I think the LPGA tour, just played a tournament just before we got there. It's not really open, yet. Nicholson did a benefit for this camp for kids, Painted Turtle, which is the Paul Newman camp for kids with diseases. Gets them out to do something during the summer. We're all supposed to show up at eight, Jack shows up, gets out of a car, is kind of wandering into the place, and they're asking, as you can imagine, for press photos. I grab him and say "Jack, hey it's Michael O'Keefe," and he says "Michael, how are you?" I say "Great man, thanks for having me." And he goes "Yeah, we'll play a little golf." I say "How are you?" And he says "Mornings are not my favorite time." I was surprised to see him in the morning.

Those in Australia who love *Caddyshack* (and that's most of the population) may have been slightly confused when Danny Noonan, born on November 29, 1968, took the field for Clarence Football Club (Australian rules) in 1988. Noonan went on to enjoy a successful professional career in this most graceful of sports.

At the end of the Zen golf scene, Webb faces a classic old-fashioned stymie. Before 1952, when the rule changed, one person in match play could keep his ball between the opponent's ball and the cup. When this happened, then the golfer with the ball lying away from the hole would have to swerve it around the other ball or pop it over—just like Ty Webb. Ty Webb is barefoot and, like Judge Smails, is likely putting with a Wilson 8802.

The Zen golf scene took place near the current site of the 11th green—the highest point of the golf course.

If you really want to annoy an opponent in golf, run around the green after making a key putt, saying "na-na-na-na-na-na-na-na. . . ."

The caddies get together for the annual Caddy Day Tournament, the thirty-fifth at Bushwood Country Club. The prizes are not that exciting—a bag of tees for third, a pair of tube socks for second; I think I'd rather come in third! It looks as if there is a sleeve of balls available for first, plus the epic trophy, *plus* the Caddy scholarship.

As Noonan and D'Annunzio tee off, the small group of onlookers includes Danny's parents. Note also the professional-caliber Frisbee-throwing in the background. The caddies are teeing off on what today is the 1st tee at Grande Oaks. The 18th green is in the background. Note the two ladies to the far left—especially the one with the really silly hat. D'Annunzio is now wearing two black golf gloves and high-heeled disco boots. All the caddies are wearing the most awful golf attire known to man, with the exception of Danny Noonan. Joey D'Annunzio is caddying for his brother.

Scene time line: 00:39:48.

When Lou Loomis calls the caddies to the tee, he yells, "Noonan, D'Annunzio, Mitchell—you're on the tee." We know all about the first two, but it's the first and only time we hear Motormouth's name, only we get his last name—Mitchell, the actor's real last name.

Jim McLean, founder and president of the Jim McLean Golf School, analyzes Danny Noonan's swing: "Michael O'Keefe hadn't played much golf, yet his swing is really good. The guys he worked with at Winged Foot did a great job getting Michael ready. He's got a good waggle at the beginning. His feet are maybe a little far apart. He's got a great grip, good shoulder position, nice spine tilt, and his ball position is also very good. So it's a good set up—maybe the clubface is a little shut.

"He looks at the target and has a little bit of a forward press. On the backswing, he has a good motion, a solid one-piece takeaway. His head, turned a little bit to the right, looks like Jack Nicklaus. Noonan turns a little bit too much, with the club going past parallel. On the downswing, the club drops in really well. There's good lag and he gets off his right foot. His left wrist also looks great. He has what we call a "caddy dip," which means that he dips his head and shoulders down through the ball. The finish looks good—it's a Jack Nicklaus finish.

"For an actor who had not played much golf, it's a really great swing—a low handicapper's swing. He's obviously a good athlete."

Note Danny's parents in the background behind Danny as he's swinging.

The Dalai Lama isn't the big hitter; it's Danny Noonan. His ball has traveled all the way to southern California. The shot of the ball bounding down the fairway is a "fill-in" shot that the producers shot after they had left Fort Lauderdale.

As Tony D'Annunzio hits his cold top, notice that Danny Noonan is fiddling with his clubs and that Motormouth is there in the background on the left side of the fairway. Just after Tony D'Annunzio hits his shot, the weather becomes overcast. As the camera returns to Tony and his scatological comment, it's sunny again. Tony gives Noonan some grief on the first tee; Danny slings it right back. If you're going to give it out, you had better be able to take it, right?

Danny Noonan makes the putt to win the caddy tournament the first time, which explains:

- The look of shock on the faces of several of the actors
- Why the actors are yelling and screaming before the putt
- The slightly shocked look on Danny Noonan's face

The psychological warfare begins with some gentle razzing from Motormouth: "OK, Danny, this is for the gold." Then Tony D'Annunzio chimes in with, "You ain't got it today, Noonan."

All this before the massed cacophony of all the "Noonans" and then the final primal scream, just before the putt rolls toward the hole.

Note that Angie D'Annunzio has traded in his Night Riders t-shirt for one with an oriental motif that reads: "duck fou." Note also that Tony's brother is waving the flag just enough so that the shadow is waving in Danny's line.

Noonan's putter is likely a Ping classic, the A Blade 5 BZ, or a close relative or the Anser 5 BZ, perhaps the Cushin 5 BZ or Zing BZ5; in the world of Ping putters, any model that includes "5 BZ" has the same shaft/head configuration, with the shaft entering the head behind the face. Numerous putter manufacturers have used a similar design, so there's no certainty that it's a Ping. There is some certainty, however, that Danny has changed shoes.

There are twenty-eight people in the gallery, including the lady with the really silly hat, Danny's parents, plus the Smails. The lady with the really silly hat is just behind Danny Noonan's mother. Just after Danny's putter meets Danny's ball, there are a couple of shouts from the gallery of "Get in! Get in!" As the judge is congratulating Noonan, someone helicopters a putter behind the admiring throng, which includes the lady with the really silly hat.

Julie Cole assesses the winning putt: "Based on set up, stroke, and mental approach, it's no surprise that the putt rolls in the first time. Danny Noonan sights the target well, his eyes are over the target line, and before the putt he looks at the cup and sees the line well. He has really good posture and a well-paced stroke using mostly his shoulders. He is steady over the ball throughout the putt and has a good follow-through. Whoever taught him how to putt did a great job, and Michael O'Keefe did a great job getting his game ready for the movie."

⬤

How many of us have been caught totally off guard like this?

FRIEND: What'ya doin' this Sunday?
YOU: Nothing planned right now.
FRIEND: How would you like to mow my lawn?

⬤

Danny's mother takes the Polaroid. It's the last we see of her. It's also the last we see of Danny's father.

⬤

In the early script, there is no Caddy Day Tournament. Judge Smails invites Danny to the yacht club after the putter helicoptering scene as a thank you for helping the judge make up an ex-

cuse. In the early script, Noonan cuts Dr. Beeper's lawn—using the tractor-mower from the club.

DR. BEEPER'S LAWN
It's easily seven rolling acres of carefully land-scaped lawn, gardens, fountains, statuary, and topiary. The grass is a foot high. A very small, rusty push mower stands unattended in the middle of the vast, uncut expanse. A mechanical roar is heard approaching.

DR. BEEPER'S MAILBOX
It begins to vibrate as a monstrous machine passes.

THE GREENSKEEPER'S TRACTOR-MOWER
Danny sits atop the mechanical monster we saw on the golf course and steers it up Beeper's driveway. He manhandles the thing onto the spacious lawn and cuts the grass with incredible efficiency, doing the whole job in one sweeping circuit of the grounds.

DANNY
He turns around to admire the wonderful job he's done, when suddenly he's caught by the

neck by a line of laundry and pulled off the mower. A BLACK MAID runs out of the house, yelling at him.

Danny's mower chops up a hedge and runs through the yard of Dr. Beeper's neighbor, just as Dr. Beeper's neighbor is having a party. Danny runs off to a gas station to change into his yacht club kit, emerging from the bathroom looking like the "Prince of Whales."

If the Danny Noonan/Maggie O'Hooligan love scenes seem out of place and even superfluous, it's no surprise: in the early script, the affair figures much more prominently; it's playful, puppy-ish love. In the final version of the movie, the affair focuses more on the pregnancy issue: it's yet another hassle for the young caddy trying to avoid a life of terminal penury at the lumber yard. The tension between Tony D'Annunzio and Danny Noonan over Maggie pops up a couple of times in the movie but is, again, much more important in the early script. Sarah Holcomb, like many members of the cast, must have wondered where

her work went. Still, one of my favorite parts of the movie is watching Tony D'Annunzio bouncing up and down behind Maggie O'Hooligan's cottage.

Doug Kenney appears in the Fourth of July dinner dance almost as an extra; the credits cite him solely for his contributions as a writer and producer. In the scene with Rodney Dangerfield, Kenney fits right in with the Fun Couples, and it's a pity that he has only the small part. Kenney was just thirty-two in 1980; he was a big name in the comedy world as the founder and guiding force of *National Lampoon* magazine and its various incarnations and productions, including the magnificent *Animal House*.

In the early 1970s, *National Lampoon* was breaking all the rules, especially with its covers, one of which showed a cute puppy with a gun pointed at its head; the caption: "If you don't buy this magazine, we'll kill this dog." Volkswagen placed an ad in the magazine, touting the floatability of the Beetle. A few issues later, soon after Chappaquiddick, Kenney et al. created a mock advertisement, again with a Beetle; the copy: "If Ted Kennedy had driven a Volkswagen, he'd be President today."

One of the *National Lampoon* spin-offs was the weekly National Lampoon Radio Hour. There was also a New York City theater show. For the mother ship and the children ships, Kenney organized writing and acting talent that formed the foundation of American "sophomoric" comedy for decades. The head writer for the first season of *Saturday Night Live*, Michael O'Donoghue, came from the National Lampoon stable, which also included Gilda Radner, Harold Ramis, and John Belushi.

Hollywood pledged just $3 million for *Animal House*, and it returned a gross of over $140 million, numbers that made Kenney and fellow *Animal House* writer Harold Ramis extremely popular and sought-after.

Animal House was not *just Animal House*, it was *National Lampoon's Animal House* and, as such, was an extension of the magazine that Kenney fostered—the caustic, scatological, crazed, and extremely popular magazine. For *Animal House*, Kenney wedged a "snobs versus slobs" fraternity story into the National Lampoon template; the producers added gallons of Jet A-1 into the mix with a superb cast that featured John Belushi.

Even though the team that created *Animal House* split, with part of the team working on *Blues Brothers* and the other part working on *Caddyshack* pretty much at the same time, there's a clear *Animal House* influence in *Caddyshack*. It was a commercial as well as an artistic decision: studio bosses wanted another *Animal House*–style result. Without *Animal House*, there would not have been a *Caddyshack*, and without Doug Kenney and National Lampoon, there wouldn't have been an *Animal House*.

There's a salient comparison between American comedies and rock music. In the late 1970s, disco was popular, but it was always going to fade, while "hair" bands and "almost hair" bands such as Journey, Chicago, and Air Supply were supplying effete, well-crafted, and totally meaningless ballads to masses via the FM dial. Then came the Sex Pistols and other punk bands, and everything, thankfully, changed. Before *Animal House* and its inevitable but successful imitators, comedies that had resonated with critics and moviegoers alike included *Annie Hall* (1977), *The Graduate* (1967), *Harold and Maude* (1972), and *Shampoo* (1975). These were intelligent and well-made movies that appealed to film critics and the intelligentsia looking for a good date-night excuse to go out. Woody Allen was getting all intellectual as well, moving from the inventive quasi-slapstick of *Take the Money and Run* to the incessant navel-gazing of *Annie Hall* and *Manhattan*. At the box office, *Annie Hall* earned exactly the same as *Caddyshack* ($39 million); *Animal House* murdered *Annie Hall*, and it murdered *Manhattan*.

Mel Brooks was in great form in the decade before *Caddyshack* with *Blazing Saddles*, *Young Frankenstein*, and the excellent Hitchcock send-up *High Anxiety*, and these movies had their moments of blissful and elegiac scatology. Brooks was having box office success as well; however, *Animal House* set new levels of indecency, and the masses loved it. And those new levels of indecency originated with Doug Kenney, fellow *National Lampoon* editor Chris Miller, and Harold Ramis.

After *Animal House*, the *Animal House* team was red hot. Producer Jon Peters got to them first and organized a meeting with Orion executive Mike Medavoy. Kenney went to Medavoy saying that he and friend Brian Doyle-Murray had a concept for a movie about caddies. Medavoy gave the idea the green light and thus got the ball rolling for the production of The Greatest Movie Ever Made. Kenney, Ramis, and Doyle-Murray worked on the early scripts in New York City. Doyle-Murray could draw on any number of club types for inspiration, and so could Kenney, whose father had been a tennis professional. When it came time to cast the movie, the writing triumvirate started calling friends and got some additional help from casting agent Wallis Nicita—plus from Marian Polan in Fort Lauderdale.

During shooting in south Florida, Kenney had his role in the Fourth of July dinner dance scene; but with Ramis directing and Doyle-Murray tweaking the script and frequently popping up as Lou Loomis, Kenney worked hard to take care of details he wanted

Only Doug Kenney knows exactly how much Doug Kenney partied during the three-month shooting for *Caddyshack* in Fort Lauderdale. However, it seems likely that he wasn't going at it as hard as legend indicates; several cast and crew members remember Kenney making time for them to indulge in normal activities such as playing tennis or simply taking a walk on the beach—hardly the activities of the twenty-four-hour-a-day drug abuser. However, there was so much cocaine in and around the set that Kenney may have been on it a great deal.

After filming in south Florida, Kenney returned to Los Angeles and was present for much of the editing. However, with the premier nearing and the all-important promotional phase just about to happen, Kenney began acting like someone else. There are stories of shoving matches and Jon Peters in a Doug Kenney headlock. Kenney verbally abused film writers during a press conference. Completely understandable, but not very clever—said film writers slammed *Caddyshack*, proving

that journalists often base their work and opinions on how much they like the people about whom they are "reporting."

The writing world was, and is, chock-full of skilled writers. Doug Kenney, making the most of excellent connections and his well-above-average talent had, almost accidentally, turned his talent into megabucks. And he was on the brink of throwing it all away. He died in Hawaii in August 1980, just as *Caddyshack* was making millions of golfers and nongolfers laugh and the movie was beginning its incredible journey. The official conclusion was that Kenney fell from a crumbling cliff, breaking ribs and cracking his skull.

Just as there is nothing that's politically correct about *Caddyshack*, which is one of the reasons that it's The Greatest Movie Ever Made, there was nothing politically correct about Doug Kenney—and the hundreds of actors, comics, writers, and others who populated his solar system. If Kenney had lived and written more wonderful movies, the country would be in a much better spot: it seems extraordinarily likely that Kenney would have been the number one warrior in the battle against political correctness and that he would have called it what it is—censorship. Would today's "sensitive" and politically correct Hollywood have let *Animal House* and *Caddyshack* fly? Today's output provides the best answer to that question.

Author's note. Just moments before the galley proof arrived in my office, Josh Karp's biography of Doug Kenney, *A Futile and Stupid Gesture* (Chicago Review Press), hit the bookshelves. Anyone who enjoys *Caddyshack* should take a look at this entertaining and tremendously well-researched book: it details Kenney's life and thus a big part of the movie's DNA. The part of the book that details *Caddyshack* and Kenney's role in the movie begins on page 332 and ends with Kenney's death. The *Caddyshack* section of Karp's book goes deeper into the behind-the-scenes Hollywood smack-downs than this volume; it also discusses Kenney's hopes that *Caddyshack* would creatively supplant *Animal House*. Karp argues (successfully) that *Caddyshack* failed to live up to Kenney's expectations due to the creative interventions from the money men and that this sense of failure coupled with his substance issues help to fuel his demise. Perhaps if Doug Kenney could have seen sensed how popular and loved *Caddyshack* would become, then his fall would not have taken place.

7

Swimming

Niece of Smails promised
Swimmers find Plantation water
Smails three and false stool
—poet/philosopher Basho (son of)

The Caddies Invade the Pool. Lacey Takes a Dive. Synchronized Swimming. Baby Ruth Lost. Baby Ruth Found. Spaulding Retreats from the Brink. A Tasty Treat for the Associate Greenskeeper.

THE pool party is a *Caddyshack* favorite—and with good reason. In stark contrast to the formality of the Fourth of July scene, the pool scene is pure caddy-induced chaos purely for the sake of chaos. The scene slightly advances the D'Annunzio versus Noonan ego-battle plot and reinforces the snobs versus slobs theme, but that's about it: the scene is pure entertainment purely for the sake of pure entertainment. Any why not?

There's absolutely no golf in the swimming scene, although there's a golf course in the background—Plantation Golf Club. Ted Swanson and the location scouts found the pool, which was empty before shooting. They filled it up, shot the scene, and drained it.

Scene time line: 00:42:52–00:48:50.

00:42:52—Bushwood Swimming Pool Sign

The scene begins magnificently, with a brief shot of the Bushwood Swimming Pool sign with the smaller sign reading, "Caddy Day. Caddies Welcome 1:00 to 1:15."

Augmenting the scene is a nubile female with large mammary glands (no other way to describe them) who swans in front of the sign. It's the type of comedic touch that helps make *Caddyshack* The Greatest Movie Ever Made. Another wonderful touch is that we actually get to see the bared breasts toward the end of the scene when the young lady ends up on the shoulders of Glenn, the lifeguard.

The early script paints the picture of the serene country club pool. And the caddy invasion.

TWO KIDS are pulling the arms of a Spider-man stretchable doll. Other children are playing in the shallow end of the pool. It's hot and the sun is beating down. A portable radio is playing classical music. YOUNG MOTHERS and a few old retirees are sunning themselves on cushioned lounge chairs.

A few lines later, the caddies arrive.

TONY AND THE CADDIES
They march into the pool area with a triumphant Tony leading them, Joey beside him with the trophy, disco music pounding from a portable radio. The caddies race to the pool.

GOOFY
Let's get wet!

[He tries to vault over a lounge chair as he dives for the water, but catches his foot in it. The chair goes into the water with him.]

TONY
[He drops his rolled-up towel and his comb on a vacant chair and strips off his T-shirt, revealing lots of muscles and his caddy tan: his arms, neck, and face are very dark, but his chest and arms are very pale. The other caddies all have the same kind of tan.]

00:43:04—Lifeguard in the Lifeguard Chair.

A quick glance at Glenn, the lifeguard, might indicate that he has some type of problem with the sun and has lathered up his right leg in zinc oxide or a similar sun block. But he's shaving his leg—just as the script instructs him.

00:43:05—Beginning of the Caddy Invasion.

Most of the caddies arrive fully clothed but quickly lose their kit. Motormouth even brings his golf clubs, and he and his clothes and his golf clubs are the first in the pool; someone gets the "Let's get wet!" line and delivers it in the same fashion as a barbarian going into battle. One of the caddies performs a textbook rugby tackle on the waiter.

Marcus Breece played Glenn, the lifeguard. *Caddyshack* was his only movie. He has one of those 1980s lifeguard bathing suits that provides more information than is requested.

Pete Roseman worked on *Caddyshack* for ten weeks as an electrician, setting up lights and tackling key projects—and getting electrocuted from time to time.

BOOK OF *CADDYSHACK*: Does it surprise you that *Caddyshack* has endured?
PETE ROSEMAN: Some lines are just hilarious, and they work over and over again. I'm a big one for quotes.

BOC: Do you ever tell other golfers that you worked on *Caddyshack*?

PR: No, I don't do that. If I know them, or I get into the conversation more, maybe I will. The friends I hang around with are not in the film business.

BOC: It was Harold Ramis's first film directing job; was it clear it was his first job, or did he seem like a pro?

PR: He was doing well, although I really would not have noticed; the electricians really work for the cameramen. He seemed to handle it really well. I remember that we used this one actor for the Dalai Lama scene, and they fired him and brought on Bill Murray. It was the first scene we shot. I thought to myself: "What the hell is this guy talking about?" I had just come back from up north, doing commercials.

BOC: Did you know the ladies that Bill Murray was looking at when we first meet him?

PR: No. They played their part really well. With the actors, you fall into thinking that that's really the person. They looked like their part and sounded like their part. It was funny to see them away from the set as they walked to their cars—gosh, they're not really like that.

BOC: When did you first see the movie?

PR: As soon as it came out. I don't think there was a grand opening. I was immensely surprised how good the movie was. It was not shot in sequence, and if you don't read the script, you think, Gosh, this is really stupid. The script was unbelievable. It was a lot of fun.

BOC: Do you remember the general sequence of shooting?

PR: We did the Dalai Lama scene, and then we did more scenes around the clubhouse. We shot probably a week with the caddies. Then there's a house that the girl lived in, so we moved over to the house. Then there was a little restaurant that they stopped at for a hamburger. Funny because they did that scene, then we left and went on. And everybody thought that was the end.

There was a whole refrigerator of food that they had left there. Obviously, in the script they were coming back, but we didn't know that. So every day, when nobody was looking, we'd go over there and cook the hot dogs and hamburgers. When they said they're going back they saw that the refrigerator was empty, and so we had to sit there and wait while everybody went and bought more hamburgers and hotdogs. Then we moved to the back, the clubhouse, kept trying to be in sequence. Then we did the Bishop scene.

BOC: How did you do that with special effects?
PR: That was special effects. We used rain towers, special lights, flooded the whole area, and did it that way.

BOC: Who was your favorite character on set and in the movie?
PR: Bill Murray, obviously. I have a picture of Bill standing there when he was with the pitch-fork, and I'm on a big light standing behind him. It's me and him and the camera. It's an eight-by-ten picture. I can't remember the scene. I have photographs of the scene where they blew up the hill.

BOC: What is *Caddyshack* about?
PR: A crazy guy. It's really about him and the craziness around him.

BOC: You must have shot a lot of scenes that didn't make it into the movie?
PR: Happens all the time. And the worst part is, usually the ones you work the hardest on are the ones that don't make it in. It's night and rainy, you've gotten shocked, you're overtime.

BOC: A particular scene like that in *Caddyshack*?
PR: I remember one night we had a situation, they were in back of the clubhouse one night. It was all lit very pretty and they were outside. We had a huge generator that was around the side and back. I walked up to the gaffer. I said "We have good news and bad news. The good news, we don't have a problem because it will keep on

running. The bad news, we set the tree on fire. We have to call the fire department." We had just pulled so much electricity, it got that engine so red hot that we set the tree on fire.

BOC: They don't make them like *Caddyshack* anymore. . . .
PR: No, they don't. I go to the movies all the time. It's humor that's funny, it's witty humor. Every time you watch it, you get something out of it. I came home and told my wife that this twenty-three-year-old director is quoting *Caddyshack*. He wasn't even around when it was made.

Note, at 00:43:18, the fiftyish lady in the gray bathing suit who is sitting by the pool. She later returns as part of Mrs. Smails's entourage, along with the lady in the brown bathing suit and straw hat.

As Joey D'Annunzio takes off her shirt and hat, the audience learns that Joey is a girl and not a boy; it's the first time we see her mane.

00:43:25—Danny Noonan and Maggie O'Hooligan Arrive.

There's a high crane shot of the pool here; one of the waiters leaves his drinks and dives into the pool as well. Danny and Maggie are in the far right-hand corner of the shot.

The song that's playing during the initial part of the pool scene is "Mr. Night," by Kenny Loggins, off the album *Keep the Fire*. Here is first stanza:

I read your letter, it said between the lines
You're visitin' Mexico for an indefinite
    amount of time
Your love for burritos has now begun to cool
You need this drivin' fool to Detomaso the
    night away
Detomaso a ride away.

The song suits the scene well; it has an initially sparse and staccato atonality that leads to an all-out, brass-backed rock-out (without a prevalent guitar).

At 00:43:31, that's the tall, blonde caddy Grace diving into the pool, her hair enveloped in a cap. Fifteen seconds later, she has secured Angie D'Annunzio's bathing suit, and we get more information and more moon than we've requested. Thankfully, when Angie emerges from the pool, we discover that he has, like every male who goes swimming, decided to wear a jock strap.

00:43:31—Tony D'Annunzio Tries to Suffocate Spaulding Smails.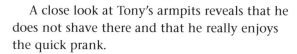

A close look at Tony's armpits reveals that he does not shave there and that he really enjoys the quick prank.

00:43:56—Joey D'Annunzio Jumps from the Diving Board.

Joey tells the lifeguard to "shave your ass!" perhaps in reference to the fact that he is shaving

his (right) leg. She jumps rather elegantly, crossing her legs.

00:44:00—Danny Noonan and Maggie O'Hooligan Arrive—For the Second Time.

Mayhem is now in full swing as Danny and Maggie, postcoitus, walk detachedly through the chaos, while the Bushwood members at the pool are aghast. Note the attractive lady to the left of the screen who has her hands on her head and her mouth wide open. In the background, the two Bushwood ladies are leaving the pool area to get Mrs. Smails. Just after Tony D'Annunzio arrives, the only use of the "F" word occurs; it's not in the early script. Tony's finest accoutrement is the pair of pure late '70s/early '80s large sunglasses with the mirror reflections. They are so gaudy and so unbearable that when Lacey Underall arrives, at 00:44:40, Tony has to pull them down slightly; he subsequently hands them to Danny, who tosses them over his shoulder.

After *Caddyshack*, Chevy Chase went on to *Fletch* and *Vacation*, while Cindy Morgan starred in *Tron*.
(Warner/Orion/The Kobal Collection)

00:45:07—Lacey Underall Mounts the Stairs to the Diving Board.

Cindy Morgan could not swim, and heights terrified her. However, she managed to climb the stairs; the producers found a stunt double for the dive and subsequent swim. Below is how it happened in the early script. Lacey is in a "tiny black bikini." Note that behind Lacey on that side of the pool, there are two Bushwood members asleep and oblivious to the mayhem.

THE HIGH DIVE
[Lacey steps out to the end of the board and prepares to dive. The pool area goes totally silent. She springs off the board and executes a beautiful swan dive. The caddies whistle and cheer as Lacey swings the whole length underwater and pops up at the shallow end between Tony D'Annunzio's legs. She pulls Tony into the water and they wrestle playfully.]

DANNY
[His face falls about a mile and a half.]

In the final version, Danny looks crestfallen as Tony makes his play for Lacey. Danny has also inserted a gun in his swimming trunks. As Lacey prepares to dive, that's Plantation Golf Club in the background.

00:45:42—The Caddies Begin Their Synchronized Swimming.

The scene is not in the early script—the sudden burst of "organization" and "choreography" only ratchets up the mayhem.

Synchronized swimming is an official Olympic event, and thus there are thousands of synchronized swimmers who take the "sport" extremely seriously. And there are hundreds of synchronized swimmers in the United States who attend university on synchronized swimming scholarships. It all started—surprise! surprise!—with an Australian, Annette Kellerman, who, swimming in a glass tank, attracted national attention at the New York Hippodrome as the first underwater ballerina. What sort of attention she received is not certain.

In 1980, the year of *Caddyshack*, the first American Cup took place in Concord, California;

obviously moved and motivated by *Caddyshack*, Team USA won all events.

The music for the synchronized swimming, Bushwood style, is "The Blue Danube Waltz"—what a contrast to the Kenny Loggins tune!

Whatever the music and whatever the inspiration, it looks as though that scene was a lot of fun for the extras who played the Bushwood caddies. It's their finest moment, and it has no connection to the plot and no connection to golf and certainly no connection to caddying.

When the movie leaves the swimmers and pans to the Bushwood members and to Danny, Lacey, Maggie, and Tony, they are nonchalant about the goings-on—even the attractive brunette in the turquoise bikini is simply casting a quick and inquisitive glance.

I would like to have seen the looks on the faces of the film editors when they got the pool party footage. I would like to have seen the looks on the faces of the Orion executives and money men when they saw the raw footage.

00:46:26—The Caddies Topple the Lifeguard Chair.

Note that Glenn has resumed his on-again, off-again relationship with his yellow baseball cap.

00:46:37—The Baby Ruth Candy Bar Appears.

Just after Joey nonchalantly lobs the chocolate bar into the water, the caddy mayhem reaches its zenith. It's useful to note that Motormouth Mitchell is still upside down, in full synchronization mode. The Jaws parody starts. A close look at the scene reveals how the girl who will soon be on the shoulders of the lifeguard manages to lose her bikini top; no surprise here, one of the caddies loosens the knot that's keeping it tied—a textbook piece of improvisation.

00:47:11—Mrs. Smails Arrives.

Mrs. Smails is there at the behest of the lady who was sitting by the pool earlier. Just after Mrs. Smails arrives, the director treats the audience to an all-too-brief close-up of the large mammaries (no other way to describe them) of the girl who has lost her bikini top. A closer look reveals that Glenn, the lifeguard, now has the girl on his shoulders, and he seems to have regained his sense of humor. However, the girl has also managed to change the color of her bikini bottoms. In the rush to leave the pool after the discovery of the doody (actually, the candy bar), the cameraman's focus turns from the bare breasts to the surfeit of fat on the young caddies. Note that Spaulding has the full kit—flippers, goggles, snorkel, and nose plugs.

00:48:03—Judge Smails Arrives at the Pool to Direct the Decontamination Efforts.

The early script has a DECONTAMINATOR organizing the decontamination work; the audience has no idea it's Bill Murray. Note that Motormouth's golf clubs are in the pool—a useful touch from the script supervisor. There's also a great line from the club manager that's a little hard to pick up: "Well, if you do find anything that looks like a fecal remnant. . . ."

Mrs. Smails has changed out of her clothes into some type of leisure outfit. Or perhaps it's her fainting kit. Before she faints, she looks rather sanctimonious as the judge barks out his orders.

8

Webb's Lair

Fast girl Mercedes
Enters grim playboy life den
Tuna colada please

—**poet/philosopher Basho (son of)**

The Young Underall and Mr. Webb. Born to Lick Your Face. Acupuncture. Can't Skinny Ski, So Why Not Skinny Dip?

THE "liaison" scene between Ty Webb and Lacey Underall came after the early script. However, Webb and Underall are a love theme, and so it seems more than logical that they should hook up; it seems logical that Lacey should hook up with *everyone*, seeing as she has such a "zest for living." After the swimming pool scene, there has to be letdown; or perhaps, to be fair, there has to be a bridge between the swimming pool scene and the sloop christening, and if there was going to be a "we've paid Chevy all this money to be in the movie and the audience expects him to be around so we had better get him in" scene, then this might be the perfect place.

Scene time line: 00:48:42–00:52:58.

The proof that Lacey is a fast girl comes at the very beginning of the scene, when she rockets up to the front door in her Mercedes and slams on the brakes. It's a Mercedes 450SL convertible with the hard top attached; the model has a V8. In good to great condition with low miles, the car today will fetch between $10,000 and $20,000. It's easy to tell that the car has a whopping engine: when Lacey stops suddenly, there's a lot of momentum shifted to the front brakes.

The design of the interior props up the image of Webb as this Zen type. The Benihana quip that Lacey makes is a clever one—she begins the process of knocking Webb down with this gag.

LACEY
Who's your decorator? Benihana?

Benihana is a Japanese Restaurant chain founded in 1964; today's Benihana tag line is "An Experience at Every Table." There are currently eighty-four Benihanas in the United States and one in Australia.

If this scene seems initially a touch contrived, Morgan and Chase had had a series of furious rows before shooting. There's no clear indication as to whether this scene followed a later draft of the script or was improvised; it seems like a combination of the two, although Morgan remembers the portion at the organ being unscripted; she also remembers going into shooting with a healthy buzz, a buzz that she augmented with real tequila during shooting.

In the Webb living room:

- Motorcycle helmet
- Old pizza
- Dying flowers

- Water ski
- His Wilson golf bag
- Hunting bow with hunting arrows
- Perrier bottles
- Tennis racquet
- Newspaper

For a vixen in search of her nightly shag, Lacey isn't exactly at her friendliest, bashing away at Ty's cash management, hobbies, and decorating skills. Perhaps it's the off-stage tension between the two.

00:50:37—Webb and Underall Move to Webb's Organ.

Webb sings "I Was Born to Love You" to Underall, a song that includes the extremely romantic line, "I was born to lick your face."

LL Cool J, Queen, the Temptations, and the Jackson Five all recorded songs titled "Born to Love You." The Chase version differs significantly from the Queen version.

Yes, Lacey was getting hammered on tequila during the shooting of this scene. They're about one-third of the way through the bottle: it's a good thing that there isn't a Porsche sunroof open nearby.

00:51:21—Lacey and Ty Get Into the Pool.

After Ty and Lacey have spent quality time at Ty's organ, Lacey is first down the water slide into the pool. It's just possible to spot her right breast as she rockets down the slide. Those who miss this important moment need not panic; she will soon reveal both in a more meaningful and longer-lasting fashion. Considering that she was not that keen on swimming, Lacey performs well in the pool.

00:51:31—Ty Starts Lacey's Massage.

The Webb-Underall scene is a bridge to the yacht club and, as such, is not the most memorable in *Caddyshack*. The one glaring failure in the scene comes when Webb tells Underall, "You have very small breasts."

There isn't a woman in the universe who would not run for the Mercedes 450SL (with the V8) after hearing that. Maybe it's the tequila or the script that keeps Lacey from bolting.

LACEY
You're crazy.

WEBB
That's what they said about Son of Sam.

A curious reference in a golf comedy. "Son of Sam" was David Falco Berkowitz, a New York–area serial killer who is serving 365 years in jail. Police arrested him in 1977.

Through the mock-acupuncture scene, Lacey looks genuinely surprised—she was certainly not expecting anything like this from Chase.

Caddyshack was Cindy Morgan's second movie. However, there's no evidence that her first, *Up Yours—A Rocking Comedy*, ever made it to movie theaters. Thus, *Caddyshack* was essentially her first movie; to that point, she had been an FM drive-time disk jockey. After *Caddyshack*, she appeared in *Tron* in 1982 and *Galaxis* in 1995. In 2006, she was working on a film in production: *Vendetta*.

Tron, which costarred Jeff Bridges, is a sort of *Caddyshack* for computer geeks. It's not a comedy, but among "gamers," or the men and women who spend huge chunks of time playing video and computer games in lieu of spending huge chunks of time on the golf course, *Tron* is vital viewing. Made in 1982, *Tron*'s plot centers around a hacker and arcade owner, Kevin Flynn, who finds himself split into molecules then injected into a computer. Once he's there, an application called Master Control starts to boss everyone around. To defeat the evil computer program, Flynn gets together with an accounting program and Cindy Morgan (Yori) to annihilate Master Control and replace him with Tron, the "white knight" operating system. *Tron* had a whopping budget of $17 million, and much of that must have gone to the special effects wizards, as it was one of the first movies to use computers for special effects. Its U.S. gross of $33 million was respectable, but far less that *Caddyshack*'s. *Tron* earned two Oscar nominations and generally favorable reviews. Here's what Roger Ebert wrote:

Tron "is an almost wholly technological movie. Although it's populated by actors who are engaging (Bridges, Cindy Morgan) or sinister (David Warner), it is not really a movie about human nature. Like *Star Wars* or *The Empire Strikes Back*, but much more so, this movie is a machine to dazzle and delight us. It is not a human-interest adventure in any generally accepted way. That's all right, of course. It's brilliant at what it does, and in a technical way maybe it's breaking ground for a generation of movies in which computer-generated universes will be the background for mind-generated stories about emotion-generated personalities. All things are possible."

There was much more commercially to *Tron*, a Disney production, than the movie: the video game was and is a whopping success, and Morgan and others in the movie continue to leverage their *Tron* appearances through trade shows, conventions, and related events. The same holds true for *Caddyshack*.

After *Caddyshack*, Morgan and her agents had a lot of Los Angeles lunches. *Tron* was a result and something totally different from *Caddyshack*, but Morgan has more TV credits, mostly as a character actress, in *The Love Boat*, *Vega$*, *ChiPs*, *Bring 'Em Back Alive*, *The Fall Guy*, *The Midnight Hour*, *Amazing Stories*, *Falcon Crest*, *Matlock*, *The Larry Sanders Show*, and *Out There*. She also continued her successful modeling career and has produced several projects.

Like everyone who was on the shoot, Morgan enjoyed filming *Caddyshack*. She was a movie star for the first time, and a female movie star to boot, with all the attention and occasional fuss that brought. There was a slight dustup with producer Jon Peters over the Jon Peters-organized arrival of a *Playboy* photographer who wanted to take shots of the nude scene in Judge Smails's bedroom. Morgan was shaky enough about appearing nude in the first place, so the last thing she wanted was to appear nude in the top nude magazine in the world. She won the battle.

In 2003, I invited Cindy to Charlotte, my adopted hometown, to attend a golf tournament and also discuss her possible participation in this book. The latter never panned out. However, her visit to Charlotte was tremendously memorable; Cindy was the first cast member I met, and she proved that most everyone around the movie was extremely pleasant. She was living in Brooklyn at the time and, despite a bad cold, arrived for a two-day visit. On the first day, I took her to the annual golf tournament at the Morrison Family YMCA at Ballantyne, where we parked on a tee box and happily took people's money for the privilege of having their photo taken with Cindy. In about three hours, she helped to raise over $700 for the charity. We had dinner that evening at a Charlotte restaurant, a dinner that well-known golf writer Ron Green Sr. attended. The next morning, we went to a radio station for an interview and to plug the golf shop that had helped to bring her to Charlotte. We then went to the golf shop for an autograph-signing session, where she was gracious and wonderful with everyone. Just before her flight back to New York, we had lunch in a local barbeque dive; a couple of *Caddyshack* fans who had missed us at the golf shop arrived at the restaurant, and one of them had dressed up like Judge Smails at the Yacht Club. That's the power of *Caddyshack* for you.

9

Sloop Christening

Yacht club snobs at play
Satisfaction in Smails drinks
Scratching the anchors

—poet/philosopher Basho (son of)

The Overdressed then Underdressed Danny Noonan. Dr. Beeper Gets Electrocuted. Good Seamanship Redefined. The Tea Party That Never Was.

CAST and crew trucked down I-95 from Fort Lauderdale to Key Biscayne or, to be more precise, Virginia Key. A restaurant called the Rusty Pelican sits near the site of the "yacht club" that's cleverly titled Rolling Lakes. There hasn't been any golf in the movie for a while, yet there's been plenty to entertain the moviegoers; this will continue for several more minutes as the mayhem continues in and around the yacht christening. Judge Smails breaks the golf drought with some nifty wedge practice in his bedroom after discovering Lacey and Danny naked in his four poster. The yacht club scene is the biggest production number in the movie, and the crew and cast pull it off even though the music is the cheesiest in the movie; thankfully, the action more than makes up for this minor flaw.

Scene time line (including the gratuitous sex): 00:52:55–01:00:52.

Note that the Rolling Lakes sign revolves— ever so slightly. The choice of name must have been a slight tip of the hat to Rolling Hills, where the cast and crew shot *Caddyshack*. Later in the scene, Judge Smails is wearing his Bushwood blazer, so perhaps there was some type of reciprocal relationship between Bushwood and Rolling Lakes. Perhaps Bushwood was really Bushwood Golf and Yacht Club. Why not? The water is chock-full of boats, as it's the Fourth of July weekend.

The yacht club scene follows the early script relatively closely. However, in the early script, Danny Noonan has had some work to complete before getting dressed up for the yacht club. He's been attempting to mow Dr. Beeper's lawn; he changes into his nautical outfit, then heads for the yacht club. Remember that Danny is driving the old family jalopy to the club. The early script sets up the scene thus:

GREAT LAKES YACHT CLUB
MEMBERS ONLY
YACHT CLUB PARKING LOT
Danny drives into the lot and looks around at the expensive Mercedes, Cadillacs, and shining sports cars parked in the lot. Danny starts to back out when a red-jacketed parking attendant jogs over, staring at the smoking heap. He tries to open the door for Danny, but the handle comes off in his hand.

DANNY
It's a classic. My father's having it restored for his collection.

INT. THE YACHT CLUB
Danny enters a large beamed room decorated with real ships' bells, models, and pennants. A

local rock band is playing "More" amidst a crowd of madras and cranberry pants types. Danny looks around uncomfortably.

LACEY
She and her friends are dancing, all dressed very casually in a variety of T-shirts, jeans, and cut-offs. Lacey is dancing with a long-haired sub-urban freak. They all turn and stare at Danny, standing stiffly at the entrance.

NOBLE
He looks like Dick Cavett.

They all giggle and smirk.

In the final version of the movie, Danny simply arrives (the Dick Cavett comment comes a little later), and that's all that's really required.

00:53:17—The Young People are Smoking at the Yacht Club Table.

Pretty permissive place that Rolling Lakes! Noble Noyes, the girl who complains about the weed, abuses poor Spaulding. Spaulding replies, "It's the best, man. I got it from a Negro."

The early script reveals that the "Negro" from whom Spaulding procured the marijuana is none other than our old friend Porterhouse (nee Smoke Westinghouse), who has promised Spaulding some great stuff for just $75. Here's how the deal goes down.

INT. THE LOCKER ROOM.
Smoke is vacuuming the rug when Spaulding approaches him. Smoke turns off the machine.

SPAULDING
(confidentially)
Uh—Westinghouse, do you know where I could get any—stuff?

SMOKE
(looking around)
Well, Master Spaulding, I might be able to get some fine Bongolese later to day (sic) for seventy-five.

SPAULDING
Seventy-five!

SMOKE
(shrugs)
It's the best.

Spaulding reluctantly hands Smoke the cash and splits.

The joke, of course, is on Spaulding, who believes that "Bongolese" is some type of extraspecial "stuff" and hands over the cashola.

A few pages later in the script, Westinghouse is hard at work.

EXT. CLUB MAINTENANCE GARAGE
The two-story converted stable has the feeling of an 18th Century English farm—grasscutting equipment, gardening tools and piles of mulch litter the courtyard. A potting shed is just opposite.

SMOKE
He's pulling dead, dry weeds out of the ground and stuffing them into a plastic baggie. He slips

away as Danny comes walking across the yard carrying a golf bag.

Thus young Ms. Noyes's complaints are fully justified.

Sitting at the table is a new character, Terry the Hippie, played by Mark Chiriboga. *Caddyshack* is Chiriboga's only movie. Note that the team of (mostly) teenagers has been able to secure not just "marijuana" but also some stiff drinks.

00:53:34—Danny Noonan Arrives.

Noble Noyes says that Danny Noonan looks like Dick Cavett, an odd reference because Dick Cavett has never been known for dressing up in yacht club kit; perhaps Noble thinks that there's a physical resemblance. Either way, it's an odd comparison, yet it resonates with the assembled and embarrasses Danny. Dick Cavett, however, was a caddy at Lincoln Country Club in Lincoln, Nebraska before becoming a talk show host.

00:53:40—Dr. Beeper Emerges from His Swim.

Not the funniest moment in *Caddyshack*, but it keeps the Dr. Beeper character going. In the early script, Dr. Beeper asks Danny about how the lawn mowing went. Danny says, "Uh—the lawn looks great." Dr. Beeper's bathing cap is a pleasant addition—especially as he's mostly bald. The fact that Dr. Beeper arrives at the table and asks the youngsters to save him a toke represents a clear indication from the medical community that smoking dope is absolutely acceptable.

Just after Dr. Beeper has electrocuted himself with his beeper, the one that he wears swimming in Biscayne Bay, Mrs. Smails gets the bullhorn out and summons everyone to the christening. Behind Mrs. Smails, Danny Noonan is getting some excellent rude faces from a four-year-old who is perched on some type of log and is wearing a nautical beret with red bobble. As the youngsters meander toward the sloop christening, they see Danny Noonan. Spaulding chimes in with, based on the early script: "Ahoy, polloi. Hey, Noonan. whadja just come from—a Scotch ad?"

There's some clever word play here from our friend Spaulding. The *hoi polloi* is a somewhat obscure and slang term for lower-class people, and Spaulding would certainly think that caddies are well below his station. Mrs. Smails points out that Danny Noonan is the young man who wants to be in the Senate, proving that Danny has big-time upwardly mobile aspirations—or he's just been talking trash to the judge and his wife in hopes of securing that caddy scholarship.

Note the man standing behind Mrs. Smails to her left. He's dressed in the nautical theme and also has a cravat, an old-fashioned fashion accessory that was popular at the time—in England. Note also that the extras/yacht club members/sloop christening invitees are in a huge rush to get to hear Judge Smails's poem.

Spaulding is wearing a multinational hat, proving that his boundaries stretch well beyond the country club life. The hat bears the title

"International Code" and sports various nautical flags.

The judge introduces Danny Noonan to Chuck Shick, although by this stage they have seen each other and probably met. It's the first time that the audience hears Chuck's name—and it's a perfect name for the aspiring ambulance chaser. As a clerk for Judge Smails, he's probably learning all the tricks.

Note that the judge has a Bushwood logo on his blazer and is also wearing a cravat. Perhaps the invitation read, "Cravats required," or maybe it was national American cravat day.

00:55:21—The Yacht Club Christening Begins.

Here's how the early script sets up the scene.

EXT. THE MARINA
Most of the boats are out on the lake, but a few beautiful yachts are still in their slips.

JUDGE SMAILS' SLOOP
The Judge is peevishly supervising two dock workers. They are finishing the slip-rails under the hull of Smails' new thirty-foot racing sloop, *The Bluebird*. Some members watch with mild interest.

Just as every *Caddyshack* fanatic should memorize the Dalai Lama speech, every fanatic should know the sloop speech as well. Ted Knight reaches back for his best sloop-christening poetry reading voice for this gem:

> It's easy to grin
> When your ship comes in
> And you've got the stock market beat.
> But the man worthwhile
> Is the man who can smile
> When his shorts aren't too tight in the seat.

The awkward, yet consistent meter (5-5-8-5-6-8) perfectly complements the rhyming pattern: aabccb. It's a superb little ditty that's not in the early script; the original speech lacked any punch:

The view across Biscayne Bay toward downtown Miami from the Rusty Pelican restaurant on Virginia Key. It was not so calm during the sloop christening.
(Courtesy of the author)

MRS. SMAILS
All right, everybody. It's time.
She takes a champagne bottle as the Judge prepares a little speech from the boat. Polite applause.

JUDGE SMAILS
Thank you, everyone—it's been many years and, frankly, many dollars to reach this point. (polite laughter)

Polite laughter from all but the judge, who firmly believes that his poem is one of the funniest of all time. He cackles for five seconds.

As Mrs. Smails christens the sloop, there's a bridge to her left; that's the bridge from Miami to Key Biscayne.

The part of the boat, sorry, sloop, that Pookie breaks off with the champagne bottle is the bowsprit. It's the first time that Judge Smails,

or anyone, has revealed Mrs. Smails's first name.

The *Flying Wasp* is a major improvement over the original name for the sloop: the *Bluebird*.

Meanwhile, back at the Underall/Noonan seduction, Lacey follows the early script, minus one exchange that failed to make the final cut.

DANNY AND LACEY
Lacey is rubbing the back of Danny's neck, touching his nose with hers lightly.

LACEY
Do you like me?

DANNY
(weak)
Oh, yes.

LACEY
More than being a Senator?

DANNY
Oh, yes.

LACEY
Then say it.

DANNY
I like you more than being in the Senate.

One has to imagine that there were certain senators in the year of *Caddyshack* who would have succumbed to Lacey's vixen charms. Maybe.

00:56:32—Al Czervik Spots His Buddy.

Because Al Czervik is always going to dominate any shot in which he appears, it's tough to look for extracurricular action; but in the bow deck some familiar faces are having a pleasant time. Gatsby is there, only without his wife; he's wearing the sun hat and he's chatting up the blonde who reappears in the men's bar scene later in the movie. The Scotts are also present, as is a woman with large mammaries (no other way to describe them). It's not crystal clear, but Ty Webb may be there as well.

The early script describes the Hell boat and its passengers with great clarity.

CZERNAK'S BOAT—LOW SHOT
The enormous hull roars by the camera. The whole boat has been "customized" with chromed horns, lamed life rings, futuristic radar and a snarling "flying tiger" face painted on the prow. We read the name, "Thunderball II" on the side as its entire length roars by, throwing up a huge wake.

CZERNAK
He's on the bridge in a loud Hawaiian shirt, now at the wheel of his 110-foot power pleasure cruiser. White-jacketed servants tend to the Fun Couples and other guests, including bikini-clad cuties. They drink and wave to the Yacht Club partiers.
Loud Music.

What Czervik's boat lacks in prescribed size, it makes up for in obnoxiousness and uproariousness. The yacht's full name in the final version of the movie is the *SS Seafood*.

The quick shot of the boat's captain, Swanson, surely named after production manager Ted Swanson, shows the bridge in the background once again; they are north of the bridge and thus in the vicinity of Virginia Key.

Just when it seems that Al Czervik could not be more rude and crass, he gets on his loudhailer to tell the judge, "Hey Smails! My dinghy is bigger than your whole boat!"

The chaos that ensues as Al steers his boat around the bay is superb, even though the music, with its early Moog vibe, fails to complement the action.

Being on one of the many and various sailing vessels in and around the *Seafood* could not have been very pleasant.

Just as the *Seafood* makes its first pass just feet from the *Flying Wasp*, Spaulding dives into the cabin. The next shot shows the Fun Couples et al. still partying in the back of the boat—oblivious to the huge wake.

Vessels in the sloop christening scene include:

- Sailboats (many and varied)
- Seaplane
- Miniyachts
- Megayachts
- Ocean-going cargo vessels
- Wave runners
- Speedboats
- Row boat

216 | *Chapter 9*

The best value in the entire yacht club scene comes at 00:57:36, when the *Seafood* runs through the johnboat with the black fisherman. Note the continuation of the Budweiser endorsement; he's about to crack open a can from his cooler when he notices the yacht heading his way. He swims extremely well to get out of the way of the huge boat, and hopefully he earned some danger money in addition to his regular honorarium.

00:57:51—The *SS Seafood* Crashes the Party.

One the foremost slapstick scenes occurs when Czervik's boat crashes into the party that someone has organized on the floating pontoon. The fourth guitar in the movie also appears—then sinks, along with the bongoiste (a bongo drummer who is also an *artiste* and vice versa). Imagine getting the call from extras casting agent Marian Polan: "Hello, this is Marion. I have a movie shoot coming up and I'm wondering if you're available. You are? Good. It's at Virginia Key and you'll be on a small pontoon dock. You'll be dancing to the music. This huge boat that Rodney Dangerfield will be driving—you know who Rodney is? Oh great!—will crash into the pontoon dock thing and you'll have to swim to the shore. Is that OK? Great. The fee is. . . ."

Those people must have been pretty desperate for cash or the opportunity to be in a movie. Or perhaps they knew that they were going to be part of The Greatest Movie Ever Made. Either way, it's a scene that would made the makers of *The Poseidon Adventure* very proud. Everyone takes a bath; to boot, there's even a brief shot of a woman's briefs.

As the *Seafood* approaches the *Flying Wasp*, there's quite a crowd watching from the yacht club. Spaulding is still on the boat, peering into the cabin, looking for glue.

"Hey! You scratched my anchor!"
The drop anchor sequence is in the early script; the excellent line above, one of the best

in the movie and very Al Czervik, is a welcome addition.

00:58:32—Lacey Has Sex with Danny Noonan.

There's a significant departure from the early script, which has Lacey driving Danny away from Rolling Lakes to a secluded spot in among some thick woods in the countryside. Remember how Lacey said that she enjoyed going to "bullfights on acid" as one of the activities that kept her from ennui? In the early script, in lieu of gratuitous nudity and whatever else follows, Lacey entices Danny to take his first trip on a powerful narcotic.

LACEY
Wanna do some real MDA?

DANNY
Pardon me?

LACEY
MDA—I got it from a guy I know in medical school. Go ahead.

DANNY
(taking a pill)
You sure this is okay?

LACEY
Oh, it's all bad for you.

Drug-induced tripping follows, followed by an outdoor semisex scene. However, in the early script, they still manage to end up naked in Judge Smails's house.

In the Webb/Underall massage scene, Ty Webb tells Lacey that she has *very* small breasts. He was wrong. They're just small.

00:59:24—The Smailses Enter Their Home.

When Judge Smails tries to kill Danny Noonan with his wedge, it's the first golf in *Caddyshack* since Danny's winning putt at 00:41:14. The audience has been without golf for almost twenty minutes. Note the forceful march that the Smailses take into their respective bedrooms;

Mrs. Smails has sustained some type of damage to her white sloop-christening outfit.

00:59:45—The Judge Walks in on Lacey and Danny.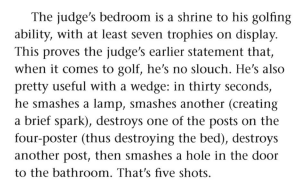

The judge's bedroom is a shrine to his golfing ability, with at least seven trophies on display. This proves the judge's earlier statement that, when it comes to golf, he's no slouch. He's also pretty useful with a wedge: in thirty seconds, he smashes a lamp, smashes another (creating a brief spark), destroys one of the posts on the four-poster (thus destroying the bed), destroys another post, then smashes a hole in the door to the bathroom. That's five shots.

01:00:22—The Judge Smashes a Hole in the Bathroom Door.

What *Caddyshack* fanatic cannot view the similar scene in *The Shining* and say: "Look at that! They're ripping off the famous Smails bathroom wedge scene from *Caddyshack*! How dare they!"

Ted Knight's brilliance shines particularly brightly in this scene: he says absolutely nothing and delivers some of the best visual gags of the movie. He has the turbocharged comic rage of a person for whom just about everything has gone wrong. First, Al Czervik wrecks his boat, then he gets home to find his niece shagging a caddy in his bed. For the uptight judge, it's the ultimate double whammy.

Note that as Danny hands the judge his robe, he's very excited to see his honor.

The *Caddyshack* shower scene is quietly just as epic as many of the more famous scenes in the movie—the shower scene is just a touch shorter. The scene is mostly unchanged from the early script.

INT. THE BATHROOM.
He [Danny] locks the door behind him, panting hard. As he bends to pull up his shorts he

suddenly becomes aware of something. The shower is running and a huge silhouette is splashing and scrubbing behind it. Suddenly, Mrs. Smails hand emerges from the shower holding a long, tubular abrasive sponge.

MRS. SMAILS
Elihu? Will you loofah my stretchmarks?

DANNY
(more coughing than talking)
Hrum, hrrump!
Smails starts beating down the door with his club.

MRS. SMAILS
In the shower, wearing goggles, funny shower cap and facial mud pie. She realizes something is wrong and slides open the shower door, revealing. . . .

DANNY'S FACE
The sight of Mrs. Smails naked is a memory he'll have to live with forever. He springs to the connecting door and flees through her bedroom as Smails finally breaks into the bathroom from the other side.

No surprise that the loofah has a phallic resemblance and that Mrs. Smails holds it as such.

01:00:40—Danny Races out of the Bathroom into the Hallway.

As Danny speeds past the butler, carrying a tray, he issues a quick "beep beep" like the Roadrunner.

⚬

Mel Pape played the butler. Ted Knight pushes him out of the way toward the banister.

⚬

As the contents of the tray (including the rose) clang to the floor, one story below, Mrs. Havercamp delivers my favorite line in the entire movie.
"That must be the tea."
The simple, yet classically ironic line has a million uses.

The airplane in which I'm traveling lands with a teeth-jarring thud that elicits gasps from the passengers. "That must be the tea."

I'm mountain biking, and I'm going too fast, and I hit a root or rock or both and end up over the handlebars and in a ditch. "That must be the tea."

I'm watching the men's downhill on television, and one of the Austrian skiers hits a patch of ice at sixty-five miles an hour, loses all control, hits a rock, almost hits the trees, loses his skis, skids down half the mountain on his left buttock, then stops in a tangle of fencing and lies there dazed for thirty seconds while the TV plays the slow-motion replay. "That must be the tea."

Lois Kibbee—Mrs. Smails

Caddyshack was likely Lois Kibbee's only motion picture. However, to those who spent most of their weekday afternoons parked in front of the television, Lois was probably an extremely familiar figure, having played in *One Life to Live*, *Search for Tomorrow*, *Somerset*, and *The Edge of Night*. She was also a writer for the latter. In *Caddyshack*, she is the perfect country club wife, and there's a part of me that would like to have learned what the body of an older country club wife looks like, even with the requisite stretch marks. Or maybe there isn't.

The cast and crew left the confines of dreary old Fort Lauderdale and drove well south, to Key Biscayne, for the yacht club scene. Even without an abundance of congestion, the drive takes forty-five minutes to an hour, plus there's a toll ($1.75) on the Rickenbacker Parkway over the stunning azure waters of the bay. My goal was to get to the very bottom part of Biscayne Bay to look for the "yacht club," but traffic and a tight schedule kept me from getting there. I'm not sure a visit was necessary, anyway: crossing the bridge to Virginia Key, it was clear that the first restaurant that comes into view coming across the causeway, the Rusty Pelican, is the place, with its faded wood exterior and views across the bay. I wandered around for a bit, looking for the tell-tale north-facing deck and found it, although it's now part of indoor dining—the rocks that Dr. Beeper mounts in search of weed provided the key clue. Ironically, that part of the restaurant is now very much the back end, with a stench of refuse and the typical restaurant sign: "no deliveries during lunch." I'll admit that there might be a restaurant further along, beyond Virginia Key, where they shot the yacht club scene, but if the Rusty Pelican isn't the one, I would be extremely surprised. But it's hard to know for sure—things change over the course of twenty-six years.

10

The Bishop and His Cinderella

Finest Bushwood round
Bishop coming too early
Toad in hole too long

—**poet/philosopher Basho (son of)**

Greenskeeper dreaming
Living and how to live it
Brusque bishop leaving

—**poet/philosopher Basho (son of)**

Reorganizing the Bushwood Flower Garden. The Emergency Nine. Another Emergency Nine. Ridding the Holes of Frogs. The Final Thunderbolt.

NOW comes Carl with his camo hat, shirt buttoned up, and oversize grip. In his very own day at the Augusta Masters, he lives the dream of every golfer with a modicum of raw ambition. Then the Bishop rudely interrupts Carl's reverie; miraculous golf follows until the Bishop makes the classic mistake of thinking that he might be on to a good round—the course record, in fact. When a golfer starts thinking about the final score and not the shot ahead, lightning appears from the heavens and smites the offending golfer. This happens every day in real golf at any level—just without the thunder and lightning and Bill Murray on the bag.

Scene time line: 01:00:54–01:04:24.

The most accomplished real-life golfer in the *Caddyshack* cast, Murray deliberately mimics a textbook really awful swing for the flower chopping-up scene.

Behind Carl, on the wall of Bushwood, is a version of the *Caddyshack* logo that Stan Jolley designed. Note also the fake leaded glass window—a great touch of authenticity.

Henry Wilcoxon—Bishop Pickering

Caddyshack was not Henry Wilcoxon's first movie. That occurred in 1931, when he appeared in *The Perfect Lady*. He subsequently appeared in more than forty motion pictures, including *The Doomsday Machine, Dragnet, The Corsican Brothers, The Ten Commandments, Sunset Boulevard, Tarzan Finds a Son!* and the 1931 version of *Cleopatra*,

in which he starred as Marc Antony. *Caddyshack* was his penultimate movie; he died in 1984. He was Cecil B. DeMille's son-in-law and became DeMille's associate producer. His autobiography, *Lionheart in Hollywood* (with Katherine Orrison) fully describes working with DeMille and Wilcoxon's related work.

It's excellent that one of the deeper and more varied Hollywood acting careers should conclude, or even climax, with a key, ironic role in The Greatest Movie Ever Made. Henry Wilcoxon pulls off the role of Bishop Pickering perfectly, reveling in the obvious ironies of the bigoted and eventually hammered man of God.

Bill Murray

Of all the *Caddyshack* cast, Bill Murray has been the most successful—at least from a financial standpoint. He pulls in a reported $9 million per picture and still finds time to play a lot of golf and appear in most of the requisite celebrity events. Movies since *Caddyshack* have included:

The Lost City
Garfield
Lost in Translation
Groundhog Day
The Royal Tenenbaums
Charlie's Angels
Hamlet
Larger Than Life
Ghostbusters
Scrooged
Tootsie
Stripes
Meatballs

Bill Murray was another superb addition to the *Caddyshack* cast, perfecting the iconic Carl Spackler and delivering two of the finest speeches in the movie: the Dalai Lama and the Day at the Masters. He even proves to be an adept caddy with the Bishop. A keen golfer to this day, Bill Murray is most easily spotted at a celebrity golf tournament or outing; the best way to learn about his golf and work is in his excellent book, *Cinderella Story*.

In the "19th Hole" documentary, which accompanies the DVD, Harold Ramis says that he wanted a scene that mirrored the fantasy world that every amateur sports fanatic enters from time to time. Bill Murray delivered. There's certainly nothing that even vaguely resembles the Masters moment in the script.

Tiger Woods hasn't yet hit a 350-yard five iron, like Carl, and Carl's 195-yard eight iron must have seemed crazed in 1980. Today, it's almost routine, even though today's eight iron is yesterday's seven. Still . . .

The most appealing aspect of Carl's session with the flowers is that he's destroying a golf course floral arrangement. It always seems odd that a golf course that prides itself on conditioning and attention to detail would spend its most valuable resource, cash, on flowers. Bushwood, and any golf course for that matter, would be better off handing the cashola over to the golf course superintendent. So, if you hate the flower arrangements at your golf course and decide, after a few libations, to imitate Carl Spackler, then have at it—all in the name of better pay and benefits for the men and women who look after your golf course.

Murray uses a weed cutter in the scene, but it could have been anything: golfers are famous for taking just about any implement that vaguely resembles a golf club and using it for practice purposes. In fact, several clever entrepreneurs have made money off this fact, taking an everyday item, painting it yellow, giving it a clever name, chartering an infomercial, and selling a bazillion of it with the promise of vastly better distance. If I were Bill Murray and his team, I would take that weed cutter, paint it yellow, charter an infomercial, and clean up. I'd name it the "Carl-Machine," or something like that.

Improv or not improv? Numerous cast members in numerous interviews for numerous *Caddyshack* interviews have said, or alleged, that much of the movie was simply made up or, to use the correct term among comedic cognoscenti, improvised. In the motion picture business, the screenplay is simply a starting point and the movie that precisely follows the script is an extreme rarity. Directors, producers, and others will change the script at the last moment, and even the most austere actors will miss a word here and there and, if the scene works in the editing room, then nobody is going to complain—except, perhaps, for the screenwriter, who if he or she understands Hollywood knows that the script is often just an initial suggestion.

Overall, *Caddyshack* was much more scripted and much more organized than legend has it. Some of the actors and some of the crew were partying like rock stars. Many had come from improvisational backgrounds, and stories abound about throwing out the script and simply making it up, but *Caddyshack* was much more organized—due primarily to the efforts of production manager Ted Swanson. There was a daily shooting schedule and a final draft of the script. Unless weather intervened, filming followed the schedule, and there are even chunks of scenes from the early draft of the script that made it all the way to the final version—even in scenes that were supposedly chock-full of improvisation. And the improvisation wasn't always successful—the most glaring example comes in the almost embarrassingly contrived scene toward the end of The Greatest Movie Ever Made, when Bill Murray and Chevy Chase pretty much just stare at each other in the Spackler manse. Improvisation wasn't necessarily to blame: Jon Peters, contributing to the creativity of the movie and also thinking about the money side of things, noticed that there wasn't a scene featuring Chase and Murray. So the writers created one out of thin air over lunch: the scene has its moments.

Any long discussion or debate about *Caddyshack* and the percentage of improvisation is essentially moot. It is what it is and it's The Greatest Movie Ever Made.

01:02:16—The Bishop Arrives for the Emergency Nine.

Bishop Pickering is wearing the same shoes that he wore during the round with the judge, Dr. Beeper, and Spaulding. He's sporting a different pair of trousers and a different top, and the top has one of those small crosses just above the left-hand pocket. A quick peek behind the Bishop shows a good shot of the bag stands from earlier in the movie.

It might be tempting to think that the Bishop going out while there's lightning and thunder around is a bit far-fetched. Yet plenty of golfers routinely and crazily go out in similar conditions. And die. Or at least lose their religion.

Talk of the course record comes up, yet the Bishop is teeing it up from the white tees. Still, there's no mistaking the pure joy that's on the face of the Bishop as he starts to play heavenly golf.

Just after Bishop Pickering holes the long putt and the club manager comes up to him, several caddies and members sprint right across the green.

01:03:20—The Bishop and Carl Discuss Whether to Play in the Weather.

Bill Murray delivers one of *Caddyshack*'s classic lines: "I'd keep playing. I don't think the heavy stuff's going to come down for quite a while."

With Noah-like rain tipping down all over the golf course and a few terminally optimistic souls waiting it out in the golf shop, this line will always bring some light to the gloom and a few knowing glances from the assembled. I've used the line from scum-bucket munis all the way to Pinehurst Resort, and it's always a winner.

The really sad part about Bishop Pickering's missed putt is that it hits the back of the cup and manages to hop up a little. Just a little bit less weight and *it's in the hole*.

Note that Carl has the flag for the 9th hole with him. So it would have been the course record for nine holes for the Bishop.

11

Fresca Redemption

Tardy Period
Youthful panic in lockers
Candy wrappers two

—poet/philosopher Basho (son of)

Going from Bad to Worse for Our Favorite Caddy. Danny's Up Early But Maggie's Late. Interview with His Honor. A Scholarship and a Fresca.

Scene time line: 01:04:24–01:09:09.

A mostly forgettable scene followed by one that is more memorable. The problem with the Noonan/O'Hooligan scene is that much of the Noonan/O'Hooligan affair never made it from the early script to the movie; the movie solidly develops Danny Noonan as a character, but Maggie, like most of the purely caddies in *Caddyshack*, simply lost out to the bigger and brasher names. Thus the caddy locker-room scene is much more about Noonan's pullulating problems than the relationship. The scene, however, is perhaps most useful for providing the audience with a peek inside the *Caddyshack* locker room, with its caddy graffiti and caddy posters. It's a truly awful place and a truly awful place to spend the night—who knows what must have crept into Danny's hair.

Ted Knight and Danny Noonan get the comedy and the plot back on track in the judge's makeshift office in the bowels of Bushwood Country Club. Danny, despite his activities the day before in, of all places, the judge's bedroom, manages to secure the scholarship he covets—all the while probably still stunned by the news that he may be a father and thus destined for a life in lumber. The offer of a Fresca, though, is an admirable touch from the judge. The scene brings together Michael O'Keefe, the great young acting talent, with Ted Knight, the seasoned industry veteran.

The graffiti in the locker room is gibberish and unreadable and probably scatological. However, there's a great poster that's clearly visible: it looks like some type of comparison between a fat girl and a thin girl and probably has something to do with the sexual attributes of the two. The posters have a *National Lampoon* look to them.

Just as Maggie thanks Danny for nothing, Lou Loomis shows up in the background, enjoying a breakfast of coffee and a cigarette. Just when it looks as if there's going to be a serious moment in *Caddyshack*, Lou asks Danny to pick up some trash.

01:06:50—Danny Enters the Judge's Office.

Danny Noonan rarely looks terrified in *Caddyshack*—except for the moment that he sits down and has to face the judge. The subtle mini-ironies generate the brilliance in this scene: the subject matter is serious, yet O'Keefe and Knight keep the audience, if not laughing, then certainly smiling and even giggling. The bite-size ironies and slapstick:

- Judge Smails asks Danny to sit down—
  Danny has already taken a seat.
- Judge Smails jettisons the lamp off the desk
  (it soon reappears).
- Judge Smails says that he has sentenced
  boys younger than Danny to the gas cham-
  ber—felt that he "owed it to them."
- Judge Smails says that he and Spaulding are
  "regular pals."
- Danny says that he is Judge Smails's pal—
  that will soon change.
- Judge Smails asks Danny if he'd like a
  Fresca. That's probably the last thing that
  Danny wants: he probably feels that he
  needs to take his daily dose of drugs and
  alcohol—now.

Top understatement of the movie:

JUDGE SMAILS
My niece is the kind of girl that has a certain
. . . *zest* for living.

The set is perfect: the office/bar of a golf
club anywhere in the world with all the requisite accoutrements and memorabilia. Comple-
menting the set, Ted Knight provides the audience with a wide range of his top facial
expressions.

With no clear translation in the French
for "How 'bout a Fresca?" the subtitles offer,
"Une rafraichissement?" Somehow, "How 'bout
a refreshment?" fails to provide the same
punch.

Today's Fresca, a Coca-Cola product, comes in
three flavors:

- Sparkling black cherry citrus
- Sparkling citrus
- Sparkling peach citrus

The official Fresca Web site describes Fresca as an "adult" soda. The first Fresca appeared in 1966, the year that England won the World Cup. In 1967, Fresca executives organized the Blizzard Girl as the advertising theme; 1980, the year of *Caddyshack*, was an important year for Fresca as, surely to complement its mention in *Caddyshack*, the drink got fresh packaging plus a sugar-free version.

What's tasty with a Fresca? Try a gin and Fresca. It's OK after about eight of them, and it's a lot tastier than a vodka and Tab.

12

Setting Up the Game at the Snobatorium

Discord unity
Around Bushwood pool table
Gatsby tit staring
—**poet/philosopher Basho (son of)**

Maggie Dances All Over the Green. The Bishop Wants Another Drink. The Al Czervik Invasion Continues. Judge Smails Demands Satisfaction.

Scene time line: 01:09:08–01:13:45.

Danny can breathe a huge sigh of relief as Maggie tells him that there's not going to be a new Noonan tyke. The sight of Maggie dancing across the 18th green in her nightie is not one that many of the audience would have found memorable. The Noonan/O'Hooligan affair plot channel ends. Before this, the usual Bushwood subjects have gathered for a quiet drink, only to have Al crash the heaving mob—complete with a bird in tow in the men's bar. After Maggie's own Riverdance, the judge delivers one of the better

lines in the movie: "I demand satisfaction!"
He quickly organizes a shot at getting some, setting up the climactic match.

To start the men's bar scene, Tony asks the burned-out Bishop if he'd like another Rob Roy. In the early script, the Bishop asks Tony for a Rob Roy while the Bishop props up the bar at the Fourth of July dinner dance. A Rob Roy is comprised of:

- 1½ oz. Scotch whisky
- ¾ oz. sweet (red) vermouth
- Dash of bitters (Angostura)
- Ice

It's sort of a martini, but with whisky replacing gin—pretty grim stuff. It looks as though the Bishop is having a single malt of some description when the Bishop tells Tony, "Never ask a navy man if he'll have another drink."

There's a sense that Tony has heard this one before from the Bishop. "There is no God," is the Bishop's last line in *Caddyshack*.

Before Al arrives, the crew in the men's bar includes the Bishop, Dr. Beeper, Judge Smails, Gatsby, Drew Scott, Ty Webb, and two old codgers who are sitting down reading the paper (at night). Porterhouse also pops up. It's good to see Scott and Gatsby, as they have been MIA for a while.

01:09:50—Al Czervik Enters.

The snobs versus slobs plot channel ratchets up a couple of notches here as Al Czervik starts to resemble the fool in King Lear with this great line, "Well who made you pope of this dump?"

The back and forth continues until fisticuffs almost break out. Earlier, the movie provides hints that Czervik is hanging around Bushwood because he wants to buy it, but now he reveals the truth, much to the appreciation of the blonde who's hanging on Czervik's every word. It's the thought of Czervik buying Bushwood that blows Judge Smails's gasket.

01:10:27—Judge Smails Attacks Al Czervik.

It's extremely easy to miss, but it's here that Rodney slips in his trademark "I get no respect."

Tony and the Bishop watch the proceedings from the bar, Tony with an ironic smile. But there's a lot going on elsewhere. Ty Webb gets Dr. Beeper in a full Nelson. But the prize in the scene goes to Gatsby, who completely ignores the semifracas and spends his time trying to look down the bosom of Al Czervik's bimbo. There is simply no way that, with this type of extracurricular action going on, any film critic worth his or her salt could not say that *Caddyshack* is The Greatest Movie Ever Made. Next time you watch this scene, watch Scott Powell as he tries to snake the blonde—the same one he was working on on Czervik's boat.

The boys who are working on the French subtitles must have given up by this stage: they don't even try to translate "snobatorium." One might think that the French would know a thing or two about the concept. Maybe.

Al Czervik's blonde smiles and laughs all the way through the argument. Lovely.

01:11:00—Maggie O'Hooligan Dances Across the 18th Green.

Immediately adjacent to where Judge Smails missed his putt, Maggie O'Hooligan dances across the green to celebrate her menstruation. The only good part about this scene is the brief look through her nightie at her legs.

The jacketed Danny Noonan just happens to be around the green. Enough said.

To solve their fracas, the assembled decide that drinking is the best avenue. Then they start talking about cash. Gambling is illegal at Bushwood! The good news is that they have sorted out their game well before arriving on the first tee. So they won't be holding up play.

Czervik's bimbo has departed. Gatsby is probably shagging her in the locker room, using protection that he's purchased at a shocking rate from Porterhouse.

13

Having to Think and Look Like an Animal. The Gopher Spies on the Proceedings.

WEDGED between the game setup scene and the game itself, this short scene gets lost. However, outside the Dalai Lama speech and his Augusta Masters moment, the plastic explosives scene is Carl's best moment. The gopher is also at his most expressive: earlier, he was dancing and burrowing, but here the special effects crew get the mechanical gopher to express fear, mild panic, espionage, and pure horror. Carl's first words in the scene:

"I have to laugh—because I've out-finessed myself!"

It goes downhill from here. Note that just after Carl says that he has to look like an animal and makes his best animal face, the gopher makes his best animal face, and it's an impression with the lower lip moving Carl Spackler style. Only people aiming to make The Greatest Movie Ever Made would have gone to such lengths and made such an effort—an effort that must have gratified Bill Murray, as imitation is the sincerest form of flattery. Note the subsequent line: "I've got to get inside this dude's mouth to crawl around for a couple of days."

A few seconds later, Murray provides the best "I'm Carl and I'm completely off my rocker" face.

14

Playing Through the Slum

Ty Webb Looks for His Ball in Carl's Domicile. Serious Grass. Serious Class.

D URING shooting, likely toward the end of the gig, Jon Peters, listed as executive producer, proclaimed that *Caddyshack* needed a scene featuring the two *SNL* stars Bill Murray and Chevy Chase. In the "19th Hole" documentary that accompanies the DVD, Harold Ramis says that the writer and assembled lunchers wrote the scene over lunch and shot it that afternoon. The "19th Hole" includes an outtake from shooting.

Scene time line: 01:14:55–01:19:34.

The scene that Peters demanded lasts more than four minutes (an eternity in a movie). The scene has its moments, but the animosity between Murray and Chase shines through, and the writing mostly fails. Obviously, the scene isn't in the early script. It would have been interesting to see what an early script would have scripted for these two. It's reasonable to think that the scene would have been shorter, funnier, less contrived, and less hairdresser motivated.

The Murray-Chase scene takes up more than four minutes of VCT (Valuable Caddy Time) and likely more than that in VDT (Valuable Drinking Time).

Note that Webb has bought some new clubs or is using his backup set: the Wilson bag is gone.

Proof that Murray was not a great Chevy Chase admirer: after the ball smashes through the window of Spackler's apartment, Spackler, with an implement in hand, says: "Show yourself, you little varmint."

It's all downhill from here. The scene provides the audience, many of whom were likely *SNL* fans, a look into the future of the *SNL* skit.

- Long-winded
- Not funny
- Poorly written
- Clichéd
- Packed with actors who hate each other

Still, there are some moments that salvage the scene. The grass that makes for a great green then can be smoked is a great concept. And making Chase hoover all that stuff is tremendous.

Carl talks about cutting Judge Smails's hamstring so that he blocks everything to the right. There's no need: the judge is already blocking everything to the right.

15

Gambling Is Illegal

The Rolls Royce Glides Across the Sylvan Fairways. The Explosive Climax. What Goes Around Comes Around. Helping the Judge Find His Checkbook with the Aid of Moose and Rocco.

*C*ADDYSHACK'S finale might confuse the golfer who is trying to count strokes and work out what is actually happening in the game and what role the rules of golf play in the event. Few in the audience would likely care: the finale works because all roads and all plot channels have led to this moment. The snob is playing the slob for real cash. The caddy looking for the scholarship is so confident in his character that he can't bring himself to brownnose the judge anymore—scholarship or no scholarship. And the assistant greenskeeper is about to try the ultimate gopher-eradication experiment. In the beginning, there was a gopher and in the end, there was still a gopher!

Scene time line: 01:19:34–01:33:56.

The finale is mostly inclusive. Just about everyone who has appeared in the movie appears in its final scenes.

On the first tee for the big match, Dr. Beeper is imitating Gary Player, Spaulding Smails has reappeared (as a caddy!), Judge Smails is sporting Sansabelt trousers, and Lou is looking his best. Note that Spaulding is wearing jeans—with really nerdy roll-ups in lieu of simple hemming. Motor-mouth has lost his glasses and Tony D'Annunzio is wearing his usual kit.

The sight of Rodney's Rolls rolling up the fairway of the dump that is Bushwood, golf bag protruding out the back, is one of *Caddyshack*'s seminal images.

The Rolls Royce with the steering wheel on the right perfectly illustrates Judge Smails's ignorant pomposity. He tells Ty to move the steering wheel back where it should be. Such an operation takes only around $1500 for a VW Golf but is slightly more for a Rolls Royce: if you have to ask, you can't afford it.

In the background (and at other times in the movie), it's possible to see some low condo-looking structures well behind the clubhouse. This is the hotel/dorm where many cast and crew members stayed and held prayer readings during shooting.

Ty Webb shuts his right hand in the car door, which, for a good golfer, should not be that much of a problem. Several excellent teachers believe that, in the right-hander's swing, the right hand is simply along for the ride.

Note that Al Czervik apologizes for being late. During his last round at Bushwood, he complained about having to wait for the judge and his group.

As the caddies wait for the golf to begin, a telephone rings—the caddies look around briefly in total bemusement.

One reason that *Caddyshack* is The Greatest Movie Ever Made is its prescience.

When Dr. Beeper's beeper goes off on the first tee and he wants to use Czervik's phone, Czervik asks if the call is long distance. Who said that multimillionaires throw money around?

As Lou Loomis asks that the assembled golfers not sue or sanction him, note that Spaulding is already rubbing his nose, clearly thinking of picking it.

In the end, the "keep it fair" incentive that Czervik dishes out to Lou Loomis is money well spent.

By the time that Ty Webb asks for his driver, Motormouth has found his glasses—and his smile.

01:21:39—Porterhouse Walks into the Golf Shop to Tell the Pro That It's Game On.

Porterhouse uses Ted Swanson's real first name. Swanson backs, with an easy smile, Team Czervik.

01:23:03—Ty Webb Sinks a Long Putt.

Note that Lou Loomis celebrates this—even though he's supposed to be impartial. You know that he has to have a book going on the game.

⊕

I love the way the caddies are watching the game by hiding in the bushes.

⊕

The judge is cheating, and it looks as if Dr. Beeper is cheating as well: when he hits the ball out of the bunker, it appears he has teed up the ball.

⊕

The quick look at the scorecard shows that Team Smails is up by five at the turn. At the turn, Maggie O'Hooligan is serving in the halfway hut.

⊕

One of the glories of *Caddyshack*'s final scene is the Smails nose-picking interlude. All the fun people from the movie are in on the bet.

01:25:18—The Gopher Sees the First of the Plastic Explosives.

Al Czervik tees off, hits a typically awful Al Czervik shot, and watches in mock horror as the ball comes back to hit him in the arm.

⊕

Just after the doctor examines Al Czervik's possible broken ulna, the doctor tells Al that he forfeits the match. Al argues and suddenly lets his arm flail in the air. Realizing his lapse, he brings his arm quickly back to its original position.

⊕

When thinking about the replacement player, Ty Webb says, "Sonja Henie is out."

Another odd statement and perhaps some type of in joke with the *SNL* buddies: Sonja Henie is perhaps the most famous Norwegian figure skater ever. She was also an actress; she died in 1969 on an airplane while recovering from cancer. In addition to being an excellent athlete, she also introduced the short skirt to her sport; she was not known as a golfer but was, at one time, one of the wealthiest women in the world.

01:27:04—Danny Noonan Officially Enters the Fray.

Note that Danny gets in the game wearing his Converse high tops. The best shot in the movie is Danny's bunker shot, where he's short-sided and the shot is downhill. He lands the ball in the fringe, and it ends up stone dead next to the hole.

01:27:26—Ty Webb Hits the Ball and It Ends Up in the Beak of a Blackbird.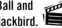

It's rare when a ball hits a bird, but it's happened—even in professional golf tournaments. Czervik tries to be encouraging by saying it's good luck, and Webb comes up with an excellent addendum: "In Haiti."

What would be good luck in Haiti? Not much, seeing as Haiti is one of the world's poorest and most run-down countries. However, residents can still hope for the best: on New Year's Day, Haitians don new togs and give each other gifts in the surely forlorn expectation that that this will lead to better things.

Word about the big match has spread around Bushwood and environs, and there's now a siz-able gallery that's no longer in the bushes or behind the trees. Everything's out in the open now.

In said gallery, there are plenty of familiar faces, mostly caddies. However, some unexpected yet welcome visitors have arrived, including the cook who wanted to place his meat cleaver in Al Czervik's cranium for saying that the meal was "low-grade" dog food.

01:28:50—Lou Loomis Declares That the Game Is All Even on the Final Green.

Thus Danny, without much help from Ty, has brought the game back from five down, which is quite a result. Things get a bit confusing here; ignore Dr. Beeper's and Ty Webb's putts because they offer no reaction at all save for mild disappointment. Judge Smails, however, gets all giddy when his putt falls and even giddier when Danny Noonan's fails to fall. There were no strokes on offer that we know about; when Danny's putt falls and Lou says "It's a birdie," then we know that Judge Smails's putt must have been for par. And if it was for par, then why is he so totally excited? Anyway, who cares?

It's The Greatest Movie Ever Made and the result is the *result*.

When Dr. Beeper putts, and there's a high shot of the green, there are sixty-two people in the scene, excluding Dr. Beeper and the people behind him who are not visible in the high shot. Even as the good doctor putts, Gatsby and his wife are organizing martinis; Gatsby is chugging them directly from the pitcher.

The Billy Baroo is likely a putter from around 1920. Later, Ray Cook, the golf manufacturing company, came out with a line of "Billy Baroo" putters that Amazon describes at "striking." The wristy putting stroke is actually perfect for that type of putter.

01:30:45—Carl Readies for the Explosions.

The song that he mumbles is about "The Green Berets." He sings the first two lines of the chorus.

Once again, right in the middle of someone's putter backswing, Czervik raises the stakes. Danny correctly and advisedly backs off and, eventually, with the help of some heavy earth-moving equipment, slots the putt. He actually makes the putt with Ty Webb's Wilson 8802, proving that it's one of the greatest putters ever made.

01:32:16—Danny Noonan Hits the Final Putt.

01:32:30—Carl Yells "Fore" and the Explosions Begin.

Most of the explosions took place at Rolling Hills, but there are some additional explosions likely shot in California. Stan Jolley, Ted Swanson, and the crew built the green that is just behind Carl—purely to blow it up. One of the better special effects in the movie occurs when the flag on that green rockets into the air. There are twenty explosions in all, but there were likely fewer during filming, as there were multiple cameras filming. However many explosions actually

The 12th, which plays slightly downhill (for Florida), is the hole where Judge Smails gets nailed in the testicles. Note the top-notch trash receptacle.
(Courtesy of the author)

took place, it must have been tremendous fun for the special-effects people at the scene.

Danny's ball hangs up on the lip of the hole at 01:32:22; it drops in at 01:33:13. The rules of golf allow ten seconds from the time the ball stops at the edge of the hole; if it has not gone in by then, it has officially come to rest and the golfer must play another shot. However, in this instance, the golfers let Lou Loomis be the judge and jury, and so it's up to him as the referee to rig the game.

01:33:33—Danny Noonan Runs Off with His Fans.

Maggie O'Hooligan and Tony D'Annunzio flank Danny as he runs to glory. Just to his right is an older lady with a floral dress and huge mammaries (no other way to describe them).

The scene with the bemused group of people looking at holes in the ground was shot in California.

When Czervik summons Moose and Rocco to help the judge find his checkbook, one of them has a golf ball that he's been playing with.

No other movie, in the history of movies, ends with a better line:
Hey everybody, we're all going to get laid!

The movie begins with a dancing gopher and ends with a dancing gopher. And as the credits rolled in the theater and the audience shuffled out into the summer sun and heat, what must they have been thinking? Or, more importantly, from a marketing perspective, what was the verdict? Obviously, the verdict must have been extremely positive, as the movie enjoyed a tremendous first run. Did the audience tell their friends or office mates or golfing buddies about the gopher or Ted Knight? Wang or the Bishop? D'Annunzio or Noonan? Beeper or Porterhouse? The quasisex scene? The yacht club scene? Bill Murray? Chevy Chase? The chaos at the swimming pool? There was, and is, a lot to like about *Caddyshack*. And surely one of those *Caddyshack*-goers said: "This movie is The Greatest Movie Ever Made and it's going to have serious legs and it's a ton better than *Ordinary People*."

Reasons We Love *Caddyshack*:

1. Even though several *Saturday Night Live* alumni appear in the movie, there's no overt political comedy in *Caddyshack*.
2. It's politically incorrect.
3. *Caddyshack* fans do not congregate at *Caddyshack* conventions in Las Vegas and dress up like *Caddyshack* characters.
4. It's not about two homosexual cowboys in Wyoming.
5. There's not much golf in the movie.
6. It's a common bond among 99 percent of golfers (and gophers) worldwide.
7. The actors have raised hundreds of thousands of dollars for charity—based on having been in *Caddyshack*.
8. Nongolfers like *Caddyshack*.
9. There are two scenes featuring full frontal nudity.
10. There really isn't a cogent or consistent plot, yet the movie works.
11. The actors made up much of the movie.
12. Really serious (too serious) golfers hate *Caddyshack*, and thus the movie provides the perfect litmus test when it comes to finding out whether someone's pants *are* too tight in the seat.
13. Bill Murray starred in it before he got into chick flicks.
14. It is, like Harold Ramis says, like a bottle of good wine.
15. A new generation, most of whom were not even close to being born when the movie came out, love the movie.

Appendix

Caddyshack Reviews

Perhaps the two most important *Caddyshack* reviews published at the time the movie first appeared were in the *New York Times* and the *Chicago Sun-Times*. The former, by Vincent Camby, wrote the film off as idiotic, saying that it was an *Animal House* spin-off. Key passages from the review:

"A pleasantly loose-limbed sort of movie with some comic moments. . . . Mr. Murray is funny mostly because he tries so hard. He reminds me of an usually clean-cut, buttoned-down type of suburban fellow who, after two or three stiff drinks, delights his pals with his uninhibited impressions of slobs and boors. You don't for a minute believe him—you are always aware of the distance between the performer and the performance, but you appreciate the effort and the intelligence behind it."

Roger Ebert was a little more optimistic:

"Caddyshack never finds a consistent comic note of its own, but it plays host to all sorts of approaches from its stars, who sometimes hardly seem to be occupying the same movie. . . . The movie never really develops a plot, but maybe it doesn't want to. . . . Dangerfield is funniest, though, when the movie just lets him talk. . . . *Caddyshack* feels more like a movie that was written rather loosely, so that when shooting began there was freedom—too much freedom—for it to wander off in all directions in search of comic inspiration."

A much better review appeared in the October 30, 2003, issue of the University of Tennessee student newspaper, the *Daily Beacon*. Under the headline "Classic Comedy *Caddyshack* Remains Humor Masterpiece," staff writer Brian Hubert writes:

"When historians look at the year 1980, they will see a couple of events that shaped the world: The 'Miracle on Ice,' the beginning of Ronald Reagan's presidency and the release of 'Caddyshack.'

"Well, the Cold War is over and the '80s are now being relived through shows on VH1. However, 'Caddyshack' is a timeless film that continues to be enjoyed by the masses.

"There are few things that are duller than watching yuppies play golf at a country club. Fortunately Bill Murray, Chevy Chase, Rodney Dangerfield and Ted Knight manage to make things at the Bushwood Country Club very interesting.

"'Caddyshack' spoofs the golfing community. Chevy Chase is Ty, a mysterious playboy golfer who never seems to be completely sane.

"Bill Murray is the idiot groundskeeper with a speech impediment. He is given the mission of killing a single pesky gopher (not golfer).

"Ted Knight plays the snobby Judge Smails.

"Rodney Dangerfield is the obnoxious rich guy who wants to buy the golf course and build condos on the land.

"The film was directed by comedy mastermind Harold Ramis. For those of you who are unfamiliar with this legend, he played Egon Spengler in 'Ghostbusters.'

"There really isn't a plot that would be worth printing besides the major theme of slobs vs. snobs. Do good comedies really need big elaborate plots? The witty humor of Chevy Chase alongside the crudeness of Bill Murray and Rodney Dangerfield is a comedy that nearly everyone can enjoy.

"After watching this masterpiece, it is perfectly normal for one to repeat many of the memorable lines in his or her sleep: 'Goonga goolunga,' 'Cinderella story . . . it's in the hole.' 'Caddyshack' is one of the greatest comedies of all time. This is a film that spans generations and countless people have come to cherish. (Note to reader: If you accidentally rent 'Caddyshack 2,' do not watch it. It will cause serious depression and nausea.)

Grade: A+"

Ted Knight Memorial Gof Invitational Contestants

Ablett, Steve
Anders, Rod

Appleby, Ross
Bond, Richard
Brown, Marie
Brown, Tony
Coffey, John
Cook, Brad
Ebert, Arnold
Eccles, James
Farrugia, Ben
Farrugia, Daniel
Farrugia, Karin
Farrugia, Manny
Farrugia, Michael
Feather, Craig
Gilchrist, Graham
Goncalves, Fernando
Griffin, Jeff
Hantzis, Pete
Jackson, Miles
Jackson, Rod
Kallaur, Andrew
Kavanagh, Bill
Kearney, Geoff
Kelly, Reg

Kukielka, Dianne
Kukielka, Kath
Kukielka, Mark
Lucas, Andrew
Lucato, Joe
McConachy, Rob
McDonald, Geoff
McDonald, Sue
McKenna, Dave
Merrett, Kevin
Mitchell, David
Mitchell, Rick
Nash, Ian
Pearson, Daryl
Podesta, Suzie
Pope, Eileen
Pope, James
Pope, Jane
Pope, Len
Pope, Pius XIII
Pope, Val
Pope, Val (T)
Pullen, Steve
Rowell, Julian

Sandford, Bob
Scroggie, Anthony
Scroggie, Clem
Scroggie, Steve
Smith, Wayne
Smith, Chopper
Spratt, Nigel
Tudor, Louie
Vienet, Barry
Wilson, Brett
Yodgee, Denis

Ted Knight Memorial Gof Invitational Champions

2004 B. Vienet
2003 V. Pope
2002 A. Scroggie
2001 G. Gilchrist
2000 A. Ebert
1999 R. Sandford
1998 R. Sandford
1997 A. Ebert
1996 M. Kukielka
1995 G. Gilchrist

1994 R. Bond
1993 R. Sandford
1992 D. Yodgee
1991 S. Pullen
1990 A. Ebert
1989 M. Kukielka
1988 R. Jackson
1987 R. Jackson
1986 W. Kavanagh

Caddyshack at the Box Office

Caddyshack's domestic gross to date is just under $40 million. On its first weekend, it opened in 656 theaters nationwide and collected an average of $4,790 per theater, for a total of $3,142,689. In today's numbers, this would be around $10 million—extremely respectable.

Credits

Executives in Charge of Production
Mark Canton
Rusty Lemorande

Associate Producer
Don MacDonald

Casting
Wally Nicita

Costarring
Albert Salmi
Scott Colomby
Dan Resin
Elaine Aiken
Henry Wilcoxon
Lois Kibbee

Featuring
Brian Doyle-Murray
Ann Ryerson
Thomas Carlin
John F. Barmon Jr.
Peter Berkrot
Hamilton Mitchell
Scott Powell
Ann Crilly
Cordis Heard
Brian McConnachie

Production Manager
Ted Swanson

First Assistant Director
David Whorf

Second Assistant Director
Charles Persons

Supervisor of Special Effects
John Dykstra

Supervising Editor
David Bretherton

Editor
Robert Barrére

Assistant Film Editor
Rachel Igel

Apprentice Editor
Mellissa Bretherton

Assistant to Harold Ramis
Trevor Albert

Additional Photography
Stanley Gilbert
James Pergola

Costume Supervisor
Eric Seelig

Men's Costumer
Andre Lavery

Women's Costumer
Vivian Cocheo

Second Unit Director
Ricou Browning

Production Sound
Michael Evje
D. G. Fischer

Sound Rerecording
Ray West
Robert Minkler
Richard Tyler

Sound Editor
Clive Smith

Music Editors
Jack Tillar
Roy M. Prendergast

Art Director
George Szeptycki

Set Decorators
Don Ivey
Tom Coll

Make-Up
Beth Lambert

Hair
Diane Johnson

Script Supervisor
Susana Preston

Assistant to Jon Peters
Hillary Ripps

Production Auditor
Sam Bernstein

Assistant Auditor
Susan Montgomery

Camera Operators
Michael McGowan
Oscar Barber

Assistant Camera
John Louis Winner
John McGowan
Donald Carlson

Gaffer
Calvin Maehl

Still Photography
Dan Williams
Steve Wever

Grip
Edward Knott Jr.
William Carr

Electrical
Bill Smalling
William Swan Jr.

Property Master
Jack Johnson

Assistant Property
Larry Goodwin

Special Animation
Jeffrey Burke
Grant McCune
Pat Brymer

Effects Production Supervisor
Robert Shepherd

Transportation Captain
Hank Scelza

Extras Casting
Marian Polan

Unit Publicist
Vic Heutschy

Production Secretaries
Mimi Stacey
Dee Dee Winner
Mary Lou Bird
Diane Morrison

"I'm Alright"
Lyrics and Music by Kenny Loggins

"Lead the Way"
Lyrics by Kenny Loggins and Eva Ein
Music by Kenny Loggins

"Mr. Night"
Lyrics by Kenny Loggins and Richard Stekol
Music by Kenny Loggins
Loggins courtesy of Columbia Records

"Something on Your Mind"
Written by Hilly Michaels and Morgan Walker
Performed by Hilly Michaels

"There She Goes"
Written by Paul Collins
Performed by the Beat

"Anyway You Want It"
Written by Steve Perry and Neil Schon
Performed by Journey

"Summertime Blues"
Recorded by Eddie Cochran

Music Coordinated by Michael Dilbeck and
    Kenny Loggins.
Music Production Supervised by Bruce Botnick.
Special Effects by Apogee Productions Inc.
Creative Sound by Neiman-Tillar.

Rerecording
Glen Glenn Sound

Title Design
Dan Perri

Matte Paintings
Rocco Gioffre

Production Assistants
Jonathan Fairbanks
Peter Tors
Matthew Cokee
John Murray

Special Acknowledgement to
Mel Howard
Janet Davidson
Herman Ripps
Ed Murray
Dick Wetzel
David Price

Manufacturers Thanked
Clossco-Adidas
Ram Golf Corporation
AMF-Ben Hogan Corporation
Wilson Sporting Goods
MacGregor Golf Company
Browning Sporting Goods
Ping Golf Clubs

Official Locations Thanked
Rolling Hills Golf and Tennis Club (Davie, Florida).
Boca Raton Hotel and Country Club (Boca Raton, Florida).
Governor's Office, State of Florida

Full Cast

Chevy Chase	Ty Webb
Rodney Dangerfield	Al Czervik
Ted Knight	Judge Smails
Michael O'Keefe	Danny Noonan
Bill Murray	Carl Spackler
Sarah Holcomb	Maggie O'Hooligan
Scott Colomby	Tony D'Annunzio
Cindy Morgan	Lacey Underall
Dan Resin	Dr. Beeper
Henry Wilcoxon	The Bishop
Elaine Aiken	Mrs. Noonan
Albert Salmi	Mr. Noonan
Ann Ryerson	Grace
Brian Doyle-Murray	Lou Loomis
Hamilton Mitchell	Motormouth
Peter Berkrot	Angie D'Annunzio
John F. Barmon Jr.	Spaulding Smails
Lois Kibbee	Mrs. Smails
Brian McConnachie	Scott
Scott Powell	Gatsby
Ann Crilley	Suki
Cordis Heard	Wally
Scott Sudden	Richard Richards
Jackie Davis	Smoke
Thomas Carlin	Sandy McFiddish
Minerva Scelza	Joey D'Annunzio
Chuck Rodent	Mr. Gopher
Kenneth Burritt	Mr. Havercamp
Rebecca Burritt	Mrs. Havercamp
Bobbie Kosstrin	Noble Noyes
Scott Jackson	Chuck Schick
Anna Upstrom	Blonde Bombshell
Ron Frank	Pat Noonan
Patricia Wilcox	Nancy Noonan
Debi Frank	Kathleen Noonan
Tony Gulliver	Ray-Old Caddy
Kim Bordeaux	Pre-Deb
Lori Lowe	Pre-Deb
Marcus Breece	Lifeguard
Mark Chiriboga	Terry the Hippy

Fred Buch . . . . Angry Husband

Frank Schuller . . . . Charlie the Cook

Mel Pape . . . . Butler

Marge McKenna . . . . Lady on Boat

Bruce McLaughlin . . . . Old Crony

Dennis McCormack . . . . Dennis Noonan

Violet Ramis . . . . Noonan Child

Judy Arman . . . . Beeper's Girlfriend

Dr. Dow . . . . Mr. Wang

Paige Coffman . . . . Little Girl at Pool

Donna M. Wiggin . . . . Woman at Pool

James Hotchkiss . . . . Old Crony

Bibliography/Webography

Internet Movie Database (imdb.com). Includes full
information about the cast and crew, plus links.

The Kuder Preference Test (kuder.com).

TV.com (tv.com). Useful information about the television appearances of several *Caddyshack* actors.

Space Age Pop Music (spaceagepop.com).

Ask Andy About Clothes (askandyaboutclothes.com)
and Alden (alden-of-carmel.com). Information
about wax buildup on fine leather.

Rose of Tralee International Festival (roseoftralee.ie).
Information about the Rose of Tralee.

WikipediA (wikipedia.org). General information
about everything.

Beau Productions Multimedia Downloads
(beauproductions.com). Nixon's golf swing.

International Institute for Asian Studies
(iias.nl/iias/show). Information about Basho.

About the Author

SCOTT MARTIN is the author of *The Insiders' Guide to Golf in the Carolinas* and collaborated with *GOLF Magazine* Top 100 teacher Dana Rader on her book *Rock Solid Golf*. He compiled Ron Green's *Shouting at Amen Corner* about The Masters and has contributed to numerous regional and national periodicals including *Golfweek* and *Executive Golfer*. He lives in Charlotte, North Carolina, and is a member of The Machrihanish Golf Club in Scotland.